LOOK AT THE INVISIBLE • STUDY THE UNKNOWABLE • DISCUSS THE UNSPEAKABLE

THAT'S NOT
RIGHT

For more information about Scott's novels, visit scottmeyer.rocks.
For more of Scott's comics, visit basicinstructions.net.

LOOK AT THE INVISIBLE • STUDY THE UNKNOWABLE • DISCUSS THE UNSPEAKABLE

THAT'S NOT RIGHT

SCOTT MEYER

THAT'S NOT RIGHT

Published by Rocket Hat Industries
Text copyright © 2024 by Scott Meyer
All rights reserved.
Cover & illustrations by Missy Meyer

ISBN: 978-1-950056-11-8

PROLOGUE

Amber Cardoza cursed under her breath as she looked at the in-dash GPS screen. It said the time was 9:13 p.m. and the satellites had gotten her as close to her destination as they could.

She scanned the darkness and groaned. "On top of everything else, I can't find the place."

She was creeping her rental car down a road just outside Yakima, Washington. This far out, the city provided no streetlights, so all illumination came from the car itself and occasional porch lights. None of the buildings looked like a radio station. Very few of the houses had obvious street numbers, or light shining on them if they did. This did not surprise Amber. She doubted people moved out here to make visiting convenient.

The houses sat just close enough together that the area qualified as a neighborhood. This was the opposite of a planned community: an assortment of low, wide, one-story dwellings. Some looked professionally built. Others did not. More than a few seemed to be double-wide trailers with wooden additions grafted on where a porch would usually be. Almost all of the homes sat next to pens holding several small animals or one or two large ones.

This was an area built out by people who probably didn't know what a homeowners' association was and might point a shotgun at anyone who tried to explain it to them.

Amber stopped the car, double-checked the address on her phone, and squinted at the door of a house. The porch light shone directly on the house number, displayed using the black-and-silver reflective number stickers one might use on the side of an old motorboat. Beside the house, she could make out a hulking box made of corrugated steel. That had to be the studio. It looked like a garage or some sort of barn except for the jumble of antennae and satellite dishes on its roof.

She pulled into the driveway, which she found blocked by a rolling gate. She rolled down the window and looked at the call box, trying to figure out how to buzz for assistance, but before she could reach out of her car window the gate clattered open. Amber drove forward and parked in front of the garage, next to a pickup with a license plate that read NOTRITE.

The front door opened before Amber stopped the car. A petite but tired-looking woman somewhere just north of her fiftieth birthday stepped out, smiled, and waved.

As Amber shut down the car and gathered her camera bag, she whispered a self-directed pep talk. "Okay. Stay cool. You're a professional . . . now. Don't think about how much is riding on this. Don't let him know that you've been a fan since you were a girl. In fact, don't think about that. Just stay cool and make a good impression."

Amber got out of the car and said, "Hello. I'm Amber Cardoza, Mr. Owens's new field producer."

"Yeah," the woman said, smiling. "I know."

"I'm sorry I'm late. I'm just, I'm so sorry. I'm usually never late. I hope Mr. Owens isn't angry. He's angry, isn't he?"

The woman laughed. "No. *Mister Owens* isn't angry. Your plane was delayed, right? That's not your fault. He gets that."

"Oh! Okay! Good. I'm sorry. It's just this is a big deal for me, and I'm kinda nervous."

"Really?"

"Yeah. But it sounds like Mr. Owens is reasonable?"

"Ish."

"Good," Amber said. "It's good to have a boss who's reasonable-ish."

The woman tilted her head and furrowed her eyebrows. "He isn't really your boss, I don't think."

"No. Not my boss, but you . . ." Amber trailed off.

The woman laughed hard. "He's not my boss. Not even close!"

"No?"

"No. He's my husband. I'm Renee Owens. Good to meet you in person. Come on in."

"Oh! I see. I'm sorry. When we were lining things up on the phone, I didn't realize I was talking to Mr. Owens's wife. I thought you were his assistant."

Renee laughed. "That happens a lot. People assume that if a man's even a little famous he must have a big staff. Good thing you didn't start bad-mouthing him, eh?"

"I wouldn't do that."

"Wait and see."

Inside, the house gave the instant impression of being clean and comfortable but also dark and cluttered. A huge leather recliner sat on a deep-pile carpet, next to a couch that seemed to be made from two more huge leather recliners grafted together. A very large TV sat on a cabinet made of strategically charred pine coated in a quarter inch of shellac. An oil painting of an orca swimming past what appeared to be the submerged wreckage of Seattle's Space Needle hung behind the TV. A long-haired cat so big it almost seemed like a medium-sized dog wearing a cat costume sat on the floor, surrounded by foam balls, toy mice, the plastic rings from milk jugs, and another slightly larger cat, which Amber had mistaken at first for a small footstool.

Renee walked through the living room to the kitchen, beckoning Amber to follow. "You want something to drink? We have water, pop, I think there's some SunnyD."

Amber said, "No, thank you," as she made eye contact with another hairy oversized cat sitting on the dinner table. She glanced to the side and saw another enormous mass of fluffy hair and bored-looking eyes draped over the kitchen counter.

"Beautiful cats," Amber said.

"Thank you. They're Maine coons."

"You breed them?"

"No, I just like them."

Amber followed, listening and nodding, but stopped short when she realized Renee had led her into her and Jack's bedroom. Her discomfort lessened slightly when she saw stacks of folded clothes and an open suitcase on the bed, along with another oversized cat.

Renee put the clothes into the suitcase. "Jack does the show and I concentrate on the business end of things. My mom always said, if there's one end of anything you want to keep an eye on, it's the business end. She was mostly talking about guns, but it goes for work too."

Amber said, "And you're packing for him, I see."

"Yeah, he'd usually do it himself, but we weren't sure he was going."

"What? I'm sorry. This trip has been all planned out. You and I discussed it. I flew out here so we could travel together and prep on the plane. We take off in the morning. What do you mean you weren't sure he was going?"

Renee rolled her eyes. "I was about ninety percent sure he would. He was adamant that he wouldn't. Now he agrees that he's in, and the packing needs to get done."

"So he changed his mind."

"He's accepted reality. You should probably talk to him. The tunnel to the studio is at the end of the hall. Make sure none of the cats get in."

Amber started down the hall, but stopped and looked back into the room at Renee. "I'm not walking into a fight here, am I?"

"What? No. He won't argue with you. He got it all out of his system on the phone with the suits. Just make sure you never make it sound like he has any option but to go. You know how they say if a sheep can get its head through a hole, it will eventually get its body through too? As sheep are to fences, Jack is to this trip. Don't give him a hole to stick his head in."

At the end of the hall, Amber found a thick metal door and a sign that read No Cats Beyond This Point! The door emitted a quiet squeak as it opened. She heard multiple sets of oversized paws stampeding toward her. She darted through the door, pulled it shut behind her, and stood there a moment, listening to the muffled cacophony of scratching and meowing from the other side.

The windowless hallway connecting the home to the studio building definitely resembled a tunnel, but it functioned more like an airlock, providing a buffer zone between the broadcasting booth and the house. She walked to the far end, where a glowing red sign that read On Air hung over another thick door, this one with a window. Inside, she saw the man himself, Jack Owens, wearing a large pair of headphones and sitting hunched over, staring down at his console with great intensity. As a caller spoke, all Amber heard through the glass was a low baritone mush.

Jack Owens looked like his promo pictures. Slightly portly, in his fifties, eyes a little too small and a little too far apart. Nostrils a little too large and a little too close together. Black and gray hair combed into an unimaginative side part and cut longer ago than was optimal. Instead of his customary tweed jacket, black button-down, and silver skull-shaped bolo tie, he wore a black T-shirt with an airbrushed wolf on the front.

She looked down at her smartwatch. The only notifications were four messages from Brian. She dismissed them, looked back up, and jumped when she saw Owens looking at her, beckoning her to enter, even as he was still speaking. His eyes darted to the bottom edge of the door as she pushed it open, but when she entered with no feline escort, he relaxed. The caller began speaking again. Jack stood up, leaned over the console, and shook Amber's hand. "You must be Amber Cardoza. I'm Jack. Good to meet you."

"It's my honor. I'm a big fan."

"Thanks for not letting the cats in."

"They must make it hard to do the show."

"Not really. Problem is they steal the parts from my models. Make yourself comfortable. I'll be with you in two minutes. Sorry you got dragged into this mess."

Amber started to ask what mess Jack meant but didn't want to interfere with his work. Instead, she looked around. On the ceiling was a chaotic jumble of model airplanes of every size, type, and historical period, hanging by fishing line. Shelves holding more completed models and the boxes of models waiting their turn covered most of the walls.

In the center of the room, there was a worn-down pool table with a sheet of smooth finished plywood covering most of the felt and partially assembled models covering most of the plywood. This seemed to be a staging area. Now that she stood in the room, Amber could see that the main assembly and crafting station of Jack's model-building enterprise was a foot-wide counter between him and his broadcasting console. A craft knife, a tube of glue, and a partially built WWII fighter lay on a mat, the plane upside down, its landing gear sticking up in the air. A light and a magnifier hung from the ceiling, held by the same kind of articulated arm that held the microphone.

Jack sat down and turned his focus back to the model, depositing a drop of glue onto a strut and using tweezers to hold a tiny wheel in place as it dried.

The caller said, "It's all based on an obscure physics principal called the Dzhanibekov Effect. A cosmonaut discovered it."

Jack flipped a switch with his free hand and leaned in closer to the microphone. "A cosmonaut named Dzhanibekov."

The caller said, "That's right! You've heard of it!"

Jack smiled at Amber and winked. "Yes, but please, talk the listeners through it."

The caller said, "He discovered that in zero gravity, a spinning object that's off balance in a specific way can just flip over, all on its own, one-hundred-and-eighty degrees, and stabilize again, still spinning."

Jack reactivated the microphone and said, "That's certainly a strange phenomenon."

"The cosmonaut thought so too," the caller said, "but that's not the weird part, Jack. The weird part is that when he reported it to his superiors, the Soviet Union classified it top secret as a matter of national security."

Jack smiled at Amber. "Here comes the crazy."

He activated the microphone. "Why, Professor? Why would the Soviets want to keep that secret?"

The caller said, "They claim they were concerned, and they wanted to avoid a panic."

Jack said nothing, but nodded and waved his right hand in a circular motion, silently encouraging the caller to go on.

The caller said, "They thought people would worry that the Earth might accidentally flip over."

Jack smiled broadly, held up a finger, and mouthed *wait*. He activated the microphone. "That's what the Soviets claimed, Professor. But the truth is—"

"There is reason to believe that they are trying to deliberately melt Antarctica and change the planet's center of gravity to flip the Earth on purpose."

Jack muted the microphone and said, "Ta-da!"

The caller continued, "We Americans always knew they wanted to take over our place in the world, but we thought they meant our economic and political position. Turns out they literally want to take over our physical location on the globe! Our placement gives our country an advantage. They want to trade hemispheres with us."

Jack told Amber, "The key is to sound as if I believe them while being noncommittal."

With the microphone live, he said, "The implications are mind-boggling. The very idea of it gives me chills."

As the caller continued, Jack told Amber, "The hard part is you've got to ask any obvious questions your audience will think of or else you lose credibility, but you want to do it in a way that keeps the nut on the phone talking. Of course, the great thing about radio is that I don't have to keep a straight face."

The caller finished his thought: "—and the sun will come up in the west and set in the east, which can't help but impact the tourist industry."

Jack let go of the tiny plastic tire on the model airplane and nodded with satisfaction when it stayed put. As he did this, he said into the microphone, "No doubt. I wonder what you would say to those who might point out that the United States and the former Soviet Union are both in the same hemisphere?"

"No, we're in the Western Hemisphere. They're in the Eastern."

"Yes, but dividing the globe the other way, the United States and Russia are both in the Northern Hemisphere. And given the way the earth rotates, we already trade places with them every day. You're saying they're trying to flip the world upside down."

"Yes, obviously."

Jack said, "Obviously. So, if they succeed, they'll trade places with Australia, not us."

"Huh," the caller said. "Why would they want to do that?"

Jack looked as if he might laugh, but his voice did not change. He glanced up at the clock and said, "We don't know, Professor, but history has taught us that the Russians don't do anything without a good reason. A disquieting thought for us all to ponder during these brief messages from our sponsors."

Jack pressed a button marked Reverb. He sounded like a giant singing in the shower as he said, "That's not right," then shut off the reverb to continue, "will be right back to look at the unseen, ponder the unknowable, and discuss the unspeakable."

Jack turned down the volume, flipped a few switches, and said into the mic, "Hey, Lou? Yeah, I need to deal with a little business on my end here. Please play a couple of the prerecorded filler spots next segment. Use the song about Leonard Nimoy having an affair with Bigfoot. That's a good one. We'll come back after the next break. Cool? Thanks."

He took off his headphones and smiled at her wearily, like a soldier in a war movie offering his comrade a cigarette in the calm moment before they rush into a suicide mission. "So, tell me, Amber, what did you do for a job before you got roped into this fiasco?"

"Before I landed this job I was the videographer, editor, and director for a YouTube channel called *The BGA Tour*."

"BGA?"

"It stands for Bros, Golf, and Alcohol. It was drunk country boys playing bad golf on a sort of improvised nine-hole golf course around their parents' farms—in the fields, around all the equipment, through the barns."

Jack snapped his fingers. "I think I've seen that. Maybe. I don't remember seeing lots of golf, just a lot of farm boys getting hit in the nuts by golf balls."

"Yeah. We put together a montage and threw it out there to draw fresh viewers. Part of the course is alongside a feedlot, you know, for cattle, so a lot of the rough is really rough. Like, you-need-hip-waders rough. If the ball stays on the surface, they add a stroke and play it as it lays, because seeing a drunk guy in shorts wading through manure is what the viewers subscribed for, but if the ball sinks in the . . . rough . . . the penalty is one of the other players throws a golf ball at his crotch as hard as they can while all the other guys chant 'Lose a ball; lose a ball' in couplets, like that. The first time describes the offense, the second time explains the penalty. 'Lose a ball? *Lose a ball!*'"

Jack said, "That's harsh."

"Most of the guys have developed pretty quickly into good golfers."

"And the channel's done well?"

"Two million subs."

Jack let out a long breath. "Sounds like you had a promising career. As I said, I'm sorry you got dragged into this. I tried like hell to get us out of it, but no dice. Still, maybe we'll get lucky, miss our connection in Seattle, and have to cancel the whole thing, eh?"

"Why would we want that?"

"You don't see what's going on, do you? They probably told you it was some great opportunity. Well, I'm sorry, but this is sabotage. This is your boss, Hal Drake, trying to torpedo my show."

"I don't answer to Mr. Drake, Mr. Owens. My boss is Ivy Atkins."

"Call me Jack, and I've never heard of her. She works at Live Air?"

"Yes."

"With Hal Drake. This has Drake's sticky little thumbprints smudged all over it. He can't stand the fact that I'm still on the air and he has to work for a living."

"You work for a living."

Jack pointed at the microphone. "This isn't work. Anybody who tries radio and finds that it feels like work quits. There's other work that pays a hell of a lot better. I got lucky. It doesn't feel like work for me. And then I got very lucky and found a niche. Hal never found a niche, and now he sits at his desk and tries to destroy mine every chance he gets."

"But, Mr. Owens—"

"Please, call me Jack."

"Jack. This isn't sabotage. This is an opportunity to let your viewers see the things they've been hearing about."

"That's the sabotage. I don't want the audience to see these things. If they do, they'll see that it's all a load of crap. Radio's the perfect medium for this garbage because when it's just people talking, you can't really prove anything, so nobody expects you to. Any nut can call in and swear that he saw . . . I don't know, the ghost of James Dean's mechanic, and that's the whole story: 'Jack's talking to a guy who says he saw a thing.' If someone wants to believe it, they can. If we get a camera involved, the story'll be that I'm talking to a crazy-looking guy who's pointing at an empty space, saying, 'It was right there. He told me not to skimp on brake-pad maintenance, and no, I didn't get a picture.'"

Amber said, "This is your show, you know. How can you talk about it this way?"

Jack sighed. "Look, my show's pretty good, for what it is: three hours of nightly garbage to distract the sleep-deprived and the dumb."

Amber said, "For your information, I'm a regular listener."

"And I'm grateful to you, as I am to all of my faithful listeners. I hope whatever sleep disorder you're suffering gets sorted out. What I'm saying here is that this stuff I talk about works fine on a listening audience of the distracted or the drowsy, but if we start showing it to people who are alert, they're going to realize that it's nonsense."

Amber shrugged. "I don't want to sound like I'm bragging, but they hired me for this job because I'm pretty good at it. I think I'll be able to make interesting content even if some of our subjects are a little lacking in credibility."

"*Some are a little lacking?* Try *all* are *totally* lacking." Jack stared at Amber for a moment. His eyes widened and his jaw dropped. "Oh no! *Oh no!* You actually believe in this crap!"

"You're telling me you don't believe in any of the things you cover on your show?"

"Yes! I'm telling you exactly that! You disagree? You believe in monsters and ghosts and the smallcano? You think the smallcano is real!"

"You've done, like, four or five shows about the smallcano."

"Yes," Jack said. "But I never believed it's real."

"I thought you were supposed to be a journalist."

"That's another thing you're wrong about. We can add it to the list, right after *the smallcano is real.*"

Amber shook her head. "I never said I firmly believe the smallcano is real."

"But you're open to it? A five-foot-tall active volcano in the middle of a cornfield in Iowa? It's bullshit. Hell, they're out in farm country. The smallcano might literally be a pile of actual bullshit."

"I definitely believe that volcanoes exist, and that they are different sizes, so some are smaller than others. I find the idea that one is only five feet tall far-fetched, but that's what makes it interesting. As for monsters, a bear would be a monster to a person who's never seen one before. So would a python, or a giraffe, for that matter. So the question isn't if I believe in monsters, it's if I believe there might be animals we haven't discovered yet, and to that I have to say yes."

"What about ghosts?" Jack asked.

"I don't believe there are ghosts, but I definitely believe there are people who believe there are ghosts, and there has to be a reason they believe. Look, I don't for an instant think we're going to find ghosts or monsters. I'm hoping we'll just find what is actually there, because that's going to be interesting."

"But there's going to be nothing there. We're going to find nothing. And nothing is less interesting than . . . *nothing.*" Jack bit his lip. "That was a difficult sentence, but you understand what I'm saying, right?"

Amber nodded. "Yes, I do. But I disagree. There's never nothing, Jack. Say, for the sake of argument, we went looking for a ghost. If we found proof of a ghost, that'd be a really interesting story. But more likely, we'll find some weird set of circumstances that fooled people into thinking there was a ghost. I gotta say, I think that's a really interesting story too! Or we could find some jerk who made up a story. Why would he do that? What drove him to it? How did he fake the evidence? No matter what we find, it'll be a story. We just have to be creative enough to make it interesting."

Jack said, "And I'm sure you're great, but just because somebody's an expert turd polisher doesn't mean I want to point them at my toilet and say, 'go nuts.' There are some things I'd rather people didn't see, no matter how shiny you make it."

"I'm surprised that you're so skeptical, Jack—of our project and of your show's guests. But I'm here because I honestly believe that together you and I can—you and I *will*—make great content."

Jack looked at Amber for a moment and sighed. "I can see they have you sold."

"They didn't sell me. You did. I'm a listener, Jack. I'm a fan. They didn't want me to work with you."

"What?"

"At first they assigned me to some morning show."

Jack stood up from his chair. "Really?"

"Really! When I told them I wanted to work with you instead, they were against it."

"Seriously?"

"They nearly fired me rather than assign me to your show. The only reason I'm here is that I fought for it."

Jack stared at her for a moment, then shouted, "Honey!" He bolted for the door. Amber watched him go, confused, then followed. By the time she reached the door, he was at the far end of the tunnel, entering his home. As the door opened, she heard a thundering stampede of paws.

"Back!" Jack shouted. "Back, you damned monsters! I said get back! Honey! Where are you?"

Renee's distant voice called out, "I'm in the living room."

Jack put a hand against the wall to catch himself as one of the huge cats leaned hard against his shin and knocked him off balance. Four Maine coons swirled in tight circles around his feet as he struggled his way to the end of the hall. "Dammit! Get out of the way, you furry little freaks! Renee, these cats are going to be the death of me!"

"They love you."

"Yeah, and sharks love seals!" Jack reached the living room and stood there, holding the back of a recliner for support as the cats continued to swarm over his feet and around his legs. "You won't be laughing when they kill me!"

"I might. It depends on how they do it. What's got you all worked up?"

"Her!" Jack jerked a thumb over his shoulder at Amber, who slunk behind him into the room. "The field producer! Get this: Drake didn't assign her to me! The suits didn't want me to go make videos in the first place! She talked him into it! Turns out she's a fan!"

Renee laughed as she placed Jack's fully packed suitcase and travel bag next to the front door.

"It's not funny!" Jack shouted as one of the cats head-butted him in the back of the knee, causing his leg to buckle; he clung to the recliner to avoid falling down.

Renee laughed harder. "No, but you are. You're funny when you're angry. You go all Donald Duck."

His voice rose an octave and grew hoarse. "I do not! Stop saying that! I do not go all Donald Duck when I'm angry!"

"Yes, you do. You get mad and you stop thinking. Then you make mistakes, so you get even more mad and think even less. It's a vicious circle."

He shook his fists and attempted to stamp his feet, but the cats crowded around the foot he kept planted and took up so much space that he couldn't put the other foot down without stepping on them, so he stood there on one foot with the other held high in the air, glaring down at the cats as he shook his fists and shouted, "I . . . argh! I just—wanna—*Dammit!* A man can't even stomp anymore!"

Renee said, "Honey, you're treading cats. You'd better sit down before you fall."

She laughed with obvious affection in her eyes, looked at Amber, and shook her head. Amber fought the urge to laugh herself. She knew that showing any amusement would only make him angrier, which only made it harder for her to keep herself from laughing.

Jack, still standing on one leg, started to say something, stopped, and let out a series of unintelligible grunting noises as he leaned over and pulled himself into the nearby recliner. The cats streamed up into the chair and settled in, three draping themselves over his lap and legs and the fourth sitting upright, facing Jack at almost eye level from a few inches away.

"There," Renee said. "Isn't that much better?"

"I'm so goddamn hot right now," Jack grumbled.

"Well, just sit there and calm down a second."

"No, I mean I'm hot physically. These cats are like little furry furnaces! And I can barely hear over the damned purring."

The cat facing Jack lifted a single paw and pressed it against Jack's lips, as if telling him to shut up.

Amber chuckled, but stopped when Jack glared at her.

Renee said, "So, Amber, you requested to work with Jack, is that it?"

Amber said, "Yes."

"Well, that's very flattering, isn't it, Jack?"

"Yes," Jack said through gritted teeth. "I just wish she could've thought of a way to compliment me without destroying my career."

"She hasn't destroyed your career yet. Jack, dear, there's no reason to panic or lose your temper. I know you think this is going to be a disaster, but you can't get out of it now. It's going to happen."

Jack said, "Those are both excellent reasons to panic and lose my temper."

"See, I think this might be good for you. It'll pull you out of your rut."

"I like my rut. I've worked hard to create this rut. We're damn lucky to have a rut this nice. A lot of people would love to have this rut."

"The rut will still be here when you get back. The kitties and I will take care of it for you. And these trips won't completely disrupt your life. They'll just fill up your weekends."

Jack grumbled, "I finally get my schedule down to a four-day workweek. Now I have to spend my three days off traveling around helping this kid show my listeners how untrustworthy my guests look." He reached his hand up to scritch the chin of the cat facing him. He managed three full scritches before the cat clamped its teeth down on the webbing between his thumb and index finger and did not let go. Jack winced in pain, tried to pull his hand away, and winced again as the cat bit down harder and brought up its paws to hug his wrist, with all of its claws extended. Jack just left his hand there, pinned in place by all of the cat's sharpest bits.

Renee said, "It's not all of your weekends, Jack; just the next four, isn't it?"

Amber said, "Five."

"See?" Jack said. "It's worse than you thought."

Amber asked, "If you're so convinced this is a mistake, why did you agree to it?"

Jack said, "There's a clause in my contract that I have to make myself available for promotional travel and appearances. It's for trade shows and that kind of thing. If I refuse, I breach my contract and they can fire me tonight. The lawyers figure spending a month and a half of my weekends traveling around the country with you counts. I have a bunch of them saved up because they've never once sent me anywhere to promote to *That's Not Right*. What does that tell you? The people who don't want to help my show want me to do this."

Renee said, "The point is, if you refuse to go it'll do more damage to your career than going might."

"It's not just my career at stake. What about our marriage? I'm a successful, famous man. She's an attractive young woman, and a fan."

Renee looked at Amber, then looked back at Jack. "Yeah, I think I can trust her to control herself."

"But she's not the only one involved here."

"I trust her to control you too. Jack, I know you better than anybody. You're a gentleman. You have plenty of flaws, but you're gentlemanly about them. I have no doubt that the two of you will get along fine as two coworkers. If you can get your attitude under control, this could be a great opportunity, and even if it doesn't work out, it's a chance for you to get out there and meet your fans."

"I talk to my fans every night when they call in, and I promise you, I don't want to meet them in person."

Amber said, "Jack, that's hurtful. I'm one of your fans."

"Yeah," he said. "You are, and this meeting is going so well."

"You can't judge them all based on the ones who call in," Renee said.

Jack sagged. "I suppose that's true. I only get calls from the ones who have a story, so they're either making up lies to get attention because they're crazy or they actually believe what they're saying because they're even crazier."

Amber said, "It's really disappointing to hear you say that."

"And it's disappointing to have you disagree with it. You still don't get it, do you? I'm not the only one who's screwed here. They're sabotaging you too."

By giving me what I asked for?"

"Yes. That's usually the best way."

The Polk County Eel-Man

1

Jack crouched in the grass next to a jogging path, reached into his duffel bag, and pulled out a folded piece of black cloth and a coiled black cord. He threaded his arms through elastic bands on the sides of the cloth, then draped it over his shoulders so that a pressed collar popped up around the back of his neck. The two parts flapping over the front framed the airbrushed coyote walking past a cactus printed on the front of his green T-shirt.

Amber glanced at him as she fiddled with her camera, then watched him for a moment before asking, "What is that, some kind of dress-shirt bib?"

"It's called a dickey," Jack said as he fastened the buttons down the front, shaping the cloth into the collar, shoulders, and upper front of a black shirt. "A dress-shirt dickey."

Amber snorted and looked back down at her camera. "'Dress-shirt Dickey.' Sounds like a terrible nickname."

Jack smiled as he threaded the black leather thong of his bolo tie through the collar. "Yeah. Dress-shirt Dickey: the least feared gunslinger in the Old West." He slid a silver skull-shaped clasp onto his bolo tie, checking the tiny black microphone Amber had taped to it.

"Can we come up with a different place for this mic?" he asked. "It looks like the skull is wearing a little Russian hat. It kinda ruins the vibe."

Amber looked at the LCD screen on the back of her rig. A motorized gimbal frame held a black sponge-covered microphone, a storage drive, and a large lens stuck to a small camera that shot professional-quality 4K footage at sixty frames a second. "The mic won't show against your black dickey, but if it bothers you, we can put it somewhere else in the next shot or try the camera-mounted mic. Hold on a second."

They both stood there and smiled as an elderly woman in shorts, a lavender T-shirt, and giant white sneakers walked between them. Amber knew this was the cost of setting up a shot with her and her subject standing on either side of a jogging path.

The woman looked at Jack.

Jack smiled and said, "Good evening."

The woman looked at Jack's T-shirt, his dickey, and the inexplicable power cord stretching around from his bolo tie to one of his rear pockets. She nodded, said nothing, and increased her pace as she walked away.

Jack scowled at her retreating form, then pulled a folded tweed jacket from the bag and put it on.

Amber clamped her headphones onto her head, covering her left ear but leaving the right one exposed. She peered at the screen of the wireless digital audio recorder she had attached with Velcro to the camera. "Okay, now say something so I can check your recording levels."

Jack said, "This is a terrible idea, and you owe me an apology for roping me into it."

"I heard you loud and clear."

"So, are you going to apologize?"

"No. You ready to shoot this?"

"Yeah," Jack said. "I guess. Make sure you've got all your settings and everything right, because you're only gonna get one take."

"That's not a very cooperative attitude."

"Hey, I don't want to do this at all. Even giving you one take is me meeting you more than halfway."

"Why are you bothering to do it, then?"

"Because when this thing fails, I need it to not be my fault. You've put me in a real terrible position here. If the videos fail because I sabotaged them, I look bad and get canned. If the videos succeed, I'll probably become a laughingstock and get canned. I need them to crater and disappear quickly while I look like I was trying to make them work. That'd still make me look bad, but not as bad. The sweet spot I'm shooting for is mediocre competence. I'll do my best, but I'll only do it once, and then I'll have to trust that the whole project is a terrible idea and is destined to fail."

"You know, Jack, this is for your benefit. If this channel's successful, it'll be a great thing for your show."

"Yeah. You, a young person with no show, are here in your benevolence to help me with my show, which is doing just fine. Man, I'll tell you, one of the best ways to know you're a real success is when other people start volunteering to help you."

"That makes no sense."

"It makes all the sense. I promise you, the first time a caveman managed to kill a musk ox, ten more cavemen appeared out of nowhere to help him drain the musk or whatever, and that's how tribes were invented. You say you're here to help me, by getting yourself paid to shoot videos I don't want to make based on the content of my successful show I already have."

"You're being really ungrateful right now, Jack."

"Yes! I am! I am not grateful!"

"Well, you've gotten that point across, so you can stop working at it. Nobody's coming down the path. Let's do this. I had an idea. What do you think about starting and ending each segment with you walking into the frame at the beginning and walking out at the end? I thought it might give things a cool *Twilight Zone* kinda vibe."

"Yeah, that could work. Whatever. Just shoot me from the waist up so they can't see that I'm wearing shorts instead of long pants."

Amber aimed her camera off to Jack's right. "Way ahead of you. Rolling. Go when you're ready."

Jack cleared his throat, stepped into the frame, turned as if studying the placid, greenish-brown pond and thick, soggy swamp foliage behind him, then looked into the camera lens. "Polk County, Florida: a peasant . . . pleasant . . . Damn! Okay, let's go again." He took two quick steps backward.

Amber said, "I thought I only got one take."

"You get one take I'm happy with, okay?"

"Fair enough. When you're ready."

"One second. People coming."

They stood still and said nothing as a middle-aged couple in shorts, T-shirts, and sun hats approached. The woman's shirt featured a cartoon drawing of a kitten drinking a margarita. The man's shirt had probably started out black, but had faded to a charcoal gray. It had *That's Not Right* and the frequency and call letters of an AM radio station written on its front in cracked white letters. Amber started to comment on this, but Jack shushed her and turned his back to the couple, acting as if he found the distant horizon fascinating.

As the couple passed, Jack rotated to keep his back to them, and only risked turning back around several seconds after they were gone.

Amber asked, "Why'd you do that? That guy was wearing one of your T-shirts."

"You just answered your own question."

"He was probably a fan."

"Exactly. And that wasn't one of my T-shirts. Mine stand up to repeated washings better than that. That was probably made by some local radio station's marketing stooge to give away at events."

"You should have introduced yourself. It probably would have made that guy's day."

"But what would it have done to mine? Wanna try again?"

"Yeah, when you're ready."

Again, Jack stepped into the frame, looked at the swamp behind him, then turned to the camera. "Polk County, Florida: a pleasant, if humid, mix of strip malls, suburbs, and unspoiled swamps. Just south of the theme parks of Orlando, events have transpired here in recent months that, though fantastical, are far from a dream come true. The local authorities have received reports of brutalized livestock, frightened townsfolk, and sightings of a strange creature that appears to be half man and half eel."

Amber said, "Okay. Good. I think that'll work."

Jack immediately sloughed off his jacket and lifted his arms, displaying dark pit stains. "This outfit's not meant for tropical climates. There's a reason you don't see goths and priests hanging out at the beach. So what do we do now?"

Amber put the camera in the open back of their rented SUV, which was only a few feet away, as the pond and jogging path they were filming ran along the edge of an apartment complex's parking lot. She started collapsing reflector stands. "After I pack up the stuff, I want to get a quick shot of that sign."

She pointed to a sign, sticking out of the pond's shore, that bore silhouettes of a snake and an alligator and read Caution: Every Body of Water in Florida is Home to Dangerous Animals. "It might make good B-roll. We interview an eyewitness next. He lives a couple of blocks away. Later, we have an appointment with a sheriff's deputy. Then we rest, get a shower at the hotel, have dinner, then tonight we come out back out and hunt the Eel-Man."

"Do you really need me for that last part?" Jack asked.

"Don't tell me you're afraid." Amber slid the collapsed stands into the SUV.

"Of course I'm afraid," Jack said. "Any reasonable person would be. Not of the Eel-Man. But we're going to be traipsing around after dark in a state where there are signs warning that something might eat you."

"That's only near bodies of water."

"It's Florida. The air is a body of water. But I'm more worried about the people we're interviewing than I am about the Eel-Man."

"Why?"

"Well, they exist, for one thing. Also, they're Floridians. Even if there were an Eel-Man, who do you think kills more people each year, Eel-Men or Floridians?"

Amber powered down the camera. As she stowed it in its case, she sneaked a peek at her smartwatch. Two messages from Brian. She dismissed them. "I don't think you have anything to worry about, especially at the sheriff's office."

"You think they're less dangerous because they're law officers, but I just see them as armed Floridians."

As she climbed into the driver's seat, Amber noticed a man in a gray suit at the far edge of the parking lot, looking at her. She would not have seen that if she had not been looking at him. For a moment, they looked at each other, and then he ducked around the corner of one of the apartment buildings.

She said, "Huh."

"What?" Jack asked.

"There was a guy over there. I think he was ogling me."

"Gray suit?"

"Yeah."

"He's been watching us most of the time we've been here. I figured it was just that they don't see a lot of documentaries made about parking near a swamp, but maybe you're right. He might have been ogling both of us."

Amber started the engine. "I don't know. There are guys who are into younger women, and guys who are into older men, but one guy into both of those things? I think that might be even more far-fetched than an Eel-Man."

* * *

The witness, a soft loaf of a man in his early twenties named Ben Riley, led them to the spot where he claimed to have seen the Eel-Man. Amber carried plenty of memory cards and batteries for the camera, so she kept rolling and captured the entire walk. The camera was heavy, but she could handle it, and its motorized gimbal smoothed out any jerkiness in her motion. This allowed Jack and the interviewee to converse naturally and not get nervous or freeze up when the camera was rolling. Not that either of them did much talking.

Neither man was in particularly great shape. Jack felt the need to wear his tweed jacket, black dickey, and bolo tie whenever the camera was rolling. He had brought black slacks to go with the ensemble but kept his cargo shorts on instead, after making Amber promise that she would try to keep his legs out of the frame. Even with bare calves, he lasted for only a few minutes in the Florida heat before he loosened the tie and undid the top button of his collar—which cracked Amber up, as the garment was not much more than a collar to begin with.

She didn't blame Jack for trying to make himself even slightly more comfortable, though. Amber was from California. She knew and understood summer heat, but even in early September Florida was muggy—almost insultingly so, as if the only explanation for this much humidity was nature just being a dick. The air was so wet that she could almost feel it flowing around her teeth when she inhaled.

After a brief stroll down the sidewalk, they took a right turn leading onto a municipally managed and maintained elevated boardwalk that went through, and three feet above, the thick swamp. Once the path turned a corner, the only sign that civilization had ever existed was the walkway under their feet. Amber had grown up in a farming community on the outskirts of a medium-sized city. She was used to either being in town or not being in town. The idea that this environment that resembled Yoda's backyard was less than a five-minute walk from an Arby's felt deeply strange to her.

Ben stopped at a corner where the walkway bent nearly ninety degrees. He pointed to a spot ahead of them where the path bent again in the opposite direction, forming a zigzag and disappearing into the trees.

"There," Ben said. "There's where I saw him."

Jack flapped the lapels of his jacket, trying to move some air around his torso. "You were there?"

"No, I saw him there."

"And where were you?"

Ben looked at Jack as if he were an idiot. "Here."

"Okay, I get the picture. What time of the day was it?"

"Night. Half-past ten or so."

"So it was dark."

"Yeah, but there are lights on the trail."

Amber looked along the railings and saw that every fourth post had built-in LED lights, but they were small, mounted at waist height, and pointed down at the walkway itself. With the dense foliage blocking the moon and stars, she doubted there would be enough light on the path to identify someone unless you already knew them or they wore particularly distinctive shoes.

Jack asked, "Why were you out here alone in the dark, Ben?"

"I was looking for my dog. He got loose and ran off. I really wanted to find him. Do you know what a beagle puppy costs? He was a good dog. I named him after my dad."

"What was the dog's name?"

"Dad. I walked all around the neighborhood yelling for him, so I figured I'd look in here, and I was tired, so I just spent some time listening. Thought he might bark or growl, or maybe I'd hear his collar rattle."

"Makes sense. So, you came around this corner, and what exactly did you see?"

"It was on the path right over there, like I said. The creature had two arms and two legs, like a person, but it was naked. It had scaly-looking skin and was covered in slime. It was this yellowish-white color, like Miracle Whip that's gone off."

Jack looked meaningfully into the camera. "It was the Eel-Man."

Ben said, "I don't know. I'm not sure."

Amber leaned out from around the camera. "On the phone you told me you thought it was the Eel-Man."

"*You* called him the Eel-Man. What I saw wasn't human, and even if it was, I'm not sure I'd call it a man. It was naked, like I said, and I didn't see any . . ." He trailed off, glancing at Amber as if he was uncomfortable saying what he had to say on camera, in front of a lady, or on camera in front of a lady.

He thought a second, leaned in closer to Jack, and in a quiet voice said, "Junk. I didn't see any junk. Man junk or woman junk. Just nothing. Like it was some third thing, or a combination of the two. What's the word for that?"

"Hermaphrodite," Jack said, arching an eyebrow at the camera. "The word is hermaphrodite. And it certainly adds a new twist to what was already a strange tale. So, what did the Eel . . . we'll continue to call it the Eel-Man, though we've noted your reluctance. What did the Eel-Man do?"

"It bared its teeth at me."

"What did they look like?"

"Nasty. Jagged. Jacked up. They were shiny; I think they had slime on them."

"That must have been terrifying. Then what happened?"

It cursed me and ran away."

"You say it cursed you; do you mean, like, it said, 'Those who behold me are doomed to die a—'"

"It shouted, 'Son of a bitch!'"

"I see. And it ran away. It didn't swim?"

"No, it didn't swim. It was up on the path. There's no water on the path. But it ran weird: kinda slidey." Ben mimed running with extra-wiggly arm movements to give the impression of sliding with each step.

"That sounds like an encounter you won't soon forget."

"No sir, I don't think I'll ever forget it."

"Did you find your dog?"

"No, I stopped looking after that."

"You must have been badly shaken."

"Eh, I figured if you go looking for a missing dog and you find a monster instead, it sort of gives you a good idea of what happened to the dog."

2

Jack sat in a hard metal chair in a cinderblock-walled interrogation room, across a table from Buck Dalrymple, the sheriff of Polk County.

Amber stood with her back to the large two-way mirror and fiddled with the cameras and lights. "I'll be ready in just a moment, sir. I want to make sure you're well lit."

The sheriff said, "If the goal is to make me look good, take all the time you need."

"We appreciate you talking to us," Jack said. I thought we were going to interview someone a little lower down on the totem pole."

"You were going to get our PR officer, but I elbowed in. If anyone in this department's doing an interview with Jack Owens, it's going to be me."

"So you can nip this nonsense in the bud, eh?"

"No, because I'm a fan."

"What?"

"Listening to you is one of the best ways to keep awake on the night shift. There's not a deputy here who hasn't listened to your show, Mr. Owens."

"Please, call me Jack. Nobody said anything when we came in."

"I ordered them not to. People get uncomfortable when law-enforcement officers want to talk to them, especially if the officer is smiling. I told the deputies to keep their distance, but they're all excited. Why do you think we're doing this in the interrogation room instead of my office?"

Jack shrugged. "I just figured your desk was a mess."

"Not hardly." Sheriff Dalrymple turned to the mirror behind Amber. "Hey, someone turn the light on in there."

The light behind the mirror came on. At least fifteen people in uniform appeared beyond the glass, all smiling.

Amber turned around and let out a startled yelp at the sight of the excited deputies.

Jack said, "Oh! Uh, hi!"

Most of the people waved. The one at the leftmost corner of the front row reached over to a button on the side of the mirror's frame. He spoke, and his voice came from a speaker in the ceiling. "It's a real thrill to have you here, Mr. Owens. We're all big fans."

"Thanks! Glad to hear it. I'm, uh, I'm surprised to hear that so many of you believe in the occult."

The sheriff laughed. "Oh, we don't believe hardly any of it, but you make it very entertaining."

The deputy pressing the intercom button said, "I especially enjoy the episodes about the smallcano."

Jack nodded. "Yes. The smallcano certainly is a strange story. The idea that nature could harbor such a bizarre and dangerous surprise gives me chills."

Amber remembered the night she first met Jack—which was easy, as it was only two days ago. He had told her then about his technique of sounding as if he agreed without ever making any definitive statements. Now here she was again, watching it at work.

"So the smallcano just erupted out of that lady's backyard?" The deputy asked.

"So she says, and I think we can all agree that would be a terrifying experience."

The deputies all nodded. Jack noticed the smile on Amber's face and winked at her.

Amber said, "Okay, we're ready to go. I've got cameras on both of you, and I'll be wandering around with a third, so just ignore me. Start whenever you like."

The lights in the viewing room switched off, transforming the window full of excited deputies back into a mirror.

Jack looked directly into his camera. "Eyewitness testimony, though compelling, is notoriously unreliable. When it comes to matters of proof, physical evidence interpreted by experts is the gold standard. I'm speaking with the sheriff of Polk County, Buck Dalrymple. Sheriff, please tell us about your department's involvement in the Eel-Man investigation."

"None, officially, Jack."

"So you're investigating the Eel-Man in an unofficial capacity?"

"We aren't investigating your Eel-Man at all. We only investigate things that are real. It's a better use of our time. We're looking into a few vague sightings and some unusual attacks on local livestock."

"But you can't rule out the Eel-Man as the attacker?"

"Technically, no, I suppose we can't, but it's far more likely to be one of the usual culprits for livestock attacks."

Jack looked at the camera and said, "Aliens?"

"No, Jack. Predators."

Jack smiled. "Perhaps you aren't aware, Sheriff, but the Predator was an alien."

Muffled laughs filtered through the one-way mirror.

The sheriff smiled. "I'm not talking about the Predator, and you know it."

"Yes. Sorry. Just a little paranormal humor. You're referring to other animals. Bobcats. Wolves."

"Those are possibilities, but this is alligator country. At first, animal control assumed that this was a gator attack."

"But now they've ruled that out?"

"No, but there's a discrepancy that prevents them from closing the case. See, the alligator is a very low-slung animal, so when one attacks a cow, you usually see wounds to the legs or belly or postmortem wounds to the back, made as the cow lay there after death. Most of these cows' wounds were on the flank, along the top of the prone carcass, suggesting that the bites came straight down, like the assailant was standing over them. That's not something alligators can do."

Amber cleared her throat. "I'm sorry to interrupt, sheriff, but do you have any visual aids to help our audience understand what you're describing? It's better to show than to tell."

The sheriff said, "I'd bet the Fish and Wildlife Service still has one or two of the carcasses in their freezer. Would you like to go take a look?"

Jack said, "I think pictures are good."

"Yes," Amber agreed. "And I will take many pictures, of you, looking at the carcasses in person."

The sheriff made phone calls while Jack posed for photos and left outgoing messages on deputies' voicemails saying they couldn't answer because they were busy exploring the mysteries of the unknown. Sheriff Dalrymple found that the officers of Fish and Wildlife still had one carcass and were also excited to meet Jack, because they, too, had a night shift. After a fifteen-minute drive and another twenty minutes of Jack shaking hands, posing for photos, and leaving outgoing voicemail messages for the Fish and Wildlife officers stating that they were busy tracking mysterious beasts with unknown origins, Jack, Amber, and the sheriff all donned parkas and accompanied wildlife officer Selena Tomkins into the freezer.

The freezer, in this case, was the size of a small conference room. Shelves lined the walls, each full of indistinct lumps wrapped in plastic sheeting and marked with tags. Larger specimens, more draped with plastic than wrapped, lay on rolling stainless-steel tables, all lined up against one wall except for one placed out in the center of the room for Amber and Jack's visit.

Amber recorded footage and watched as the good mood Jack had built up interacting with his fans dissipated before her eyes.

"So, this is the, uh, the victim?" he asked, as he looked at the immense lump.

Officer Tomkins said, "Yes, sir. One adult Holstein cow, attacked at night by an unidentified predatory animal. This attack took place four days ago, but it's part of a two-year-long pattern of cows, horses, and other large livestock that have either gone missing entirely or been found with these confusing wounds."

Jack nodded his head thoughtfully and pointed at the lump. "A cow, you say?"

"Yes, sir."

Jack looked around the freezer and smirked. "You, uh, ever tempted to sneak in here and cut a couple of steaks to take home?"

Officer Tomkins did not laugh. "No, sir. Working in this room makes you less hungry, not more." She pulled the plastic sheet off the cow and Amber immediately saw what she meant. Cows don't look particularly delicious, even when they're alive and healthy. But seeing one like this—curled on its side, glassy eyes staring into nothing, lips pulled back, tongue and teeth exposed, and chunks missing from its shoulders and hindquarters—put all thoughts of lunch out of her mind. She framed her shot to get both the cow and Jack's reaction. He looked disgusted, but to her surprise he was looking at her, not the cow.

"Why are you shooting this?" he asked. "We can't show this, can we?"

Amber said, "Not all of this. I'll blur the disgusting parts."

"The disgusting parts? It's *all* disgusting parts. You're going to have to blur everything."

"Just the cow. I won't have to blur you."

"Me? Doing what? Looking at the blur? I mean, come on. You can't show this to the audience, and if they don't have to look at it, I don't see why I do."

"You have to because they can't," Amber said. "They may only see you and a blur, but they'll see you being horrified by that blur. People empathize; they feel the emotions they see other people experience. The audience will feel your disgust and be disgusted."

"Well, that sounds like ratings gold."

Amber nodded emphatically. "It is! Now, Sheriff, you said that the bite marks don't suggest an alligator?"

"That's correct," the sheriff said. "The cow is laying here in roughly the position we found it in, so picture this in a field instead of a freezer and it's pretty much what it looked like. The wounds seem consistent with alligator bites: big, ragged wounds with lots of ripped flesh and crushed bones, and marks that suggest big sharp teeth. See what I mean?"

The sheriff looked at Amber for a response, but she tilted her head out from behind her camera and nodded at Jack, encouraging him to answer instead. Jack looked directly at the wound and croaked, "Yeah, I see."

"But," the sheriff said, "the wounds are placed weirdly. If this is how the cow was laying when attacked, then the bites had to come from above, but alligators can't do that."

Jack asked, "What if the cow somehow got . . . flipped after the alligator ate enough? Maybe the gator pushed it over before it left. That would bring the . . . uh . . . damaged area closer to the ground."

The sheriff stroked his chin. "Eh, perhaps, but there's no reason for an alligator to do that. Besides, then the wounds would be directly against the ground, and the only way the alligator could make them would be to burrow up, somehow, directly beneath it as it slept."

Officer Tomkins said, "Alligators can't do that either. And we would have found the hole when we were looking for tracks."

"Looking for tracks?" Jack asked.

The sheriff said, "We couldn't find any alligator tracks in the pasture. Alligators leave this really distinctive trail, a long S-shaped trough with footprints on either side. Even on spongy ground you usually can see signs of it. We couldn't find an S. Just indistinct footprints that might have been the rancher for all we know."

Jack said, "I can see why you don't believe it was an alligator."

The sheriff said, "Oh, no, Jack. I fully believe it was an alligator. The bite position is wrong, but the bite mark is consistent with an alligator. I can't think of anything else around here that has a mouth that does that kind of damage."

"We spoke to a young man this morning who says he saw the Eel-Man with his own eyes, and he described the creature's mouth as . . . how did he put it, Amber?"

Amber said, "Nasty. Jagged. Jacked up."

"Jack, earlier you said yourself that witness testimony is unreliable."

"And how do you know I said that? Because you witnessed me saying it—or is that testimony too suspect to pay attention to as well? I kid, but Sheriff, you can't rule out the Eel-Man."

"No, but I can't technically rule out any creature over four feet tall with lots of teeth, real or imagined. I can't rule out a bear or a werewolf, or an alligator with really long legs, for that matter. Something happened here that I can't explain, but it feels more likely to me that the normal signs of an alligator attack were obscured than that the attack was perpetrated by some creature we've never seen before. No, I'm convinced some kind of animal killed these cows."

"Certainly, but I remind you that like everyone else, the Eel-Man would be some kind of animal."

"The imaginary kind."

"I hope you're right."

"Then I've got good news for you, Jack. I am."

3

Amber pulled the straps on the back of Jack's chest harness tight. "Can you breathe?"

"Barely."

"Are you comfortable?"

"No," he said, bending and twisting his torso. "I'd like it a little looser."

"Good," Amber said. "That means it might be tight enough."

They stood in a pool of light under a streetlamp, next to their rented SUV. Nearby, a wall of foliage and darkness loomed where the swamp began. The lit elevated boardwalk cut through the darkness and receded into the distance.

"Do I have to wear this thing?" Jack winced as he pulled on his sport coat over the vest-like harness with a two-foot strut sprouting from the chest-piece.

"Yes. You don't have to wear the tweed jacket over it if you don't want to."

"The tweed jacket's an important part of my image. People see a man in a tweed jacket and they automatically think he's smart."

"Not if it's hot out and he's in a swamp. You should at least take off the hat. It doesn't really go with the tweed."

He reached up and removed the dark green trucker hat that read Polk County Sheriff's Office in gold letters. "Yeah, fair enough. Maybe I should put on some of the other swag they gave me. How about my honorary deputy badge?"

"It's plastic. You know they give those to kids, right?"

"Kids and me. Don't be jealous. I'm sure they'd have given you some stuff too if you had asked."

"I think they meant that pile of stuff they gave you to be for both of us."

"What makes you think that?"

"There were two of everything. But that's fine. You can keep it all. Just don't wear any of it on camera."

"It would be a nice way to thank the department for their cooperation."

"Another way is just to say that we thank them for their cooperation." Amber picked up a sports camera encased in a transparent plastic container and locked it into the mounting point on the pole sprouting from Jack's sternum, then squinted into the distance.

"Hey," she said. "I think that's that guy."

"Who's that guy? I mean, that's which guy? Which guy is that . . . guy?"

"The guy I'm looking at."

"I know you're referring to the guy you're looking at." Jack turned to follow Amber's gaze. "What guy do you think he is?"

A block away, a man in a gray suit stood on the sidewalk, lit by a passing car.

"The guy who was watching us earlier," Amber said.

The man in the suit saw that Jack and Amber were both looking at him. He leapt off the sidewalk, away from the streetlights and into the dark of someone's yard. Less than a second later, motion-activated flood lamps on the house blazed to life, bathing the yard with light. The man froze for a moment, then ran around the side of the house and out of sight. A second later, they heard a dog barking and trash cans falling over.

Jack and Amber shrugged at each other. Jack twisted one way and then the other, watching the camera swing out in front of him. He shook his head. "I can see why you didn't want me wearing my new hat. We can't have me looking silly."

"Yes, the chest mount looks ridiculous, but the viewers won't see it. They'll just get a closeup of your face. Remember what I said about the audience experiencing your emotions with you?"

"And you want them to share my embarrassment? Or maybe my lack of surprise when we find nothing."

"We'll find something, even if it's that the Eel-Man isn't there."

"See, Amber, that's why this whole thing is doomed. We're working at cross-purposes. You want to deliver the truth. I sell mystery. My show gives people permission to believe crazy things for three hours a night. Your videos will rescind that permission. Believing that there isn't a scary monster in the swamp isn't fun, and footage of a monster-free swamp won't be fun to watch."

Amber fiddled her own camera. "You getting scared in a dark, spooky swamp will be. And I don't think we're really going to find an Eel-Man, but I think Ben Riley saw something. Maybe we'll see that, whatever it was. If we're very lucky, maybe we'll find his dog."

"Yeah. That'll be heartwarming, the dog licking his face while he says 'Dad, I've missed you.'"

"And don't forget, something killed that cow. If we don't feel like the swamp is paying off, we could go to the pasture and see if we can find that. Maybe buy some steaks as bait."

"No way. We're definitely not going anywhere near any pasture. Whatever bit that cow—the Eel-Man, an alligator on stilts, or whatever it was—the last thing I want is to get anywhere near it. Besides, two defenseless humans carrying raw beef as bait would be redundant. We're all the bait we'd need. Although the idea that we're bait would be good for the intro. I might use that."

"I think you should." Amber took a quick peek at her smartwatch and dismissed some text notifications from Brian.

"The camera on your chest mount is rolling. Just look at it and do your intro when you're ready."

Jack stood with his eyes closed for a moment. When he opened them, he stared directly at the camera protruding from his chest. "Amber, I feel ridiculous."

"I know. Push through it."

Jack looked at the camera. "Cooperative though the hardworking and intelligent officers of the Polk County Sheriff's Office were, they left us with more questions than answers. It is now obvious that if we're to prove that the Eel-Man exists, we're going to have to go find him ourselves—or, more accurately, make ourselves available so he can find us."

"Wow," Amber said. "That was great."

"Thanks. I've been spouting that kind of gibberish from off the top of my head for years. That and interviewing people. It's all second nature at this point."

Amber gestured toward the wooden walkway. "Shall we?"

"If we must."

Jack took three steps, then stopped and turned back to look at Amber, who had not moved. She stayed standing still, filming him as he walked away. "Aren't you coming?"

"Yes. I'll be right behind you."

"Right behind me?"

"Yeah, a few paces behind you."

"Why? So if we find something dangerous, it'll attack me first and you can run?"

"No, so if we find something dangerous, it can attack you first and I can film it. The whole point of this is to get footage of you searching for the Eel-Man. I can't do that if I walk along beside you. I have to either walk behind you or go up ahead and walk backward."

"Then do that."

"No, it's no good. I can't frame the shot while walking backward. I'd trip and break my neck. Besides, this shot's more dramatic, and from back here I can't see your chest camera."

"Well, I'm in favor of that, I guess."

Amber gestured to the path ahead. "Then, after you."

The two of them began walking along the path, Amber following ten feet behind Jack. The lights mounted along the guardrails kept the path ahead easily visible and turned Jack into a dramatically lit silhouette but also kept their eyes adjusted to light, rendering the foliage above them a dark mass blotting out the stars.

Amber said, "Talk. Tell me what you see."

"Darkness. I see the path ahead of me, and I see darkness. Every now and then there's a branch to remind me that if it weren't for the impenetrable darkness, I'd see impenetrable swamp. I don't know, Amber. I feel like I'm babbling."

"No! That was good. I appreciate that you're making an effort here. I know you don't really want these videos to succeed."

"I wouldn't say that."

"No?"

"No. I'd say that I specifically want them to fail."

"That wouldn't do wonders for my career."

"And I'm not happy about that, but at the end of the day, it's not my problem. I have to look out for my career. You have to look out for yours. You didn't do me any favors when you started this."

"But I was trying to do you a favor. I thought these videos would help your career."

"And how has that worked out?"

"We don't know. It hasn't worked all the way out yet. But you have to admit, so far it's better than you expected."

"I would have been more inclined to agree with that before you cinched me into the BDSM harness and made me go on a nocturnal swamp march. The sheriff's office was cool, though. It's good to be reminded that there are sane people who listen to my show."

"You had to know I couldn't be the only one."

"Amber, I like you fine, but I'm not sure you're one at all. I've gotta ask, what's the deal with your messages?"

"What messages?"

"Your messages on your watch. The ones you check for every ten minutes but dismiss without reading."

"Nothing. It's nothing."

"I see."

"Really. It's nothing."

"I understand. It's nothing. You've told me it's nothing three times now. That sends a clear message as to how unimportant the nothing we're talking about is. Yes sir, the best way to highlight the non-importance of something is to state, repeatedly and with increasing stridency, that it is nothing."

"It's my ex," Amber snapped. "They're messages from my ex."

"Okay, so it's not nothing. It's something that's none of my business. Your ex calling, trying to get his stuff back, is not something I need to know about. I'm sorry I asked. I'll drop it."

"What makes you think I still have any of his stuff?"

"I don't, but isn't that the usual pretext ex-boyfriends use to stay in contact with attractive young ladies who dumped them?"

"It is, thank you. But that's not exactly the situation."

"He dumped you. Sorry. Let's drop it."

"Let's. But I dumped him." They walked in silence for a few steps, then Amber said, "His name's Brian. He was the host of the series I used to work on."

"Ah. You met working on the show."

"No. We were already dating when I created the show. He and his idiot buddies would get together, drink too much beer, and hit golf balls around. I started taking videos and edited some clips together, basically to prove to my girlfriends that the guys really did the stupid things I said they did. It'd start normal, but by the end of the day it always ended in nudity, a fistfight, or a nude fistfight."

"Sounds like they were a real brain trust."

"I showed it to Brian. I thought it would embarrass him and he'd knock it off."

"Let me guess: he was proud."

"He uploaded it to YouTube and insisted that I film them the next weekend. Over time, I started having more fun with the edits. I made comments in text. I added music and other video clips. I edited things to stress the stupidity. His account got more and more subscribers. He monetized his channel and got some sponsors. He and his friends became internet famous."

"Famous for being drunken idiots?"

"They didn't seem to mind."

"Yeah, in some ways, drunken idiocy is self-rewarding. And what did you get?"

"I got to use the cameras and computers he bought for his channel, as long as it was only for related projects, and I got a guilt trip any time I asked about partial ownership of the show, or even a salary. It seems shooting and editing the videos is the easy part. Drinking beer and getting hit in the head with a high-speed Titleist took real skill."

"That's the problem with making your job look easy. People think it's easy. So you gave him the finger and set off on your own."

"No, I told him I was going to, unless things changed."

"And?"

"He proposed."

"Really?"

"Yup."

"And you said?"

"Yes."

"But congratulations are not in order?"

"The next time I brought up a salary, he told me that if we were getting married, the work I did was for the good of our family, and that by taking a salary for myself I'd be stealing money from *us*."

"Interesting angle."

"A week later he asked me to sign a prenup that said the channel, the show, and all the intellectual property were his and that I had no claim to any of it if we divorced."

"That's a bit of a mixed message."

Amber said, "I thought it sent a very clear message. He told me he wouldn't marry me if I didn't sign it. I told him I wouldn't marry someone who wanted me to sign it. We argued about whether I was leaving him or he was kicking me out. Either way, I left town, drove down to LA, and landed this job."

"And now he's leaving messages."

"He started when I left."

"He wants you back?"

"I guess. I haven't bothered to read them."

"Good for you."

"Thanks. I'm sorry if I kinda unloaded on you. I don't know why I told you all that."

"Like I said, interviewing people is second nature for me."

"You're saying you made me tell you all that?"

"Yup. I made the assumption that he wanted his stuff back. If I was right, that's good, because that's information. I was wrong, which was even better, because then you felt compelled to tell me the truth. People have a deep-seated need to correct others."

"That's not why I told you."

Jack smiled smugly. "Really?"

"No. I . . ."

Jack turned around and smiled at her.

"Shut up."

"Look, don't feel bad. It's just human nature, uh . . ." Jack stammered and sputtered to a halt.

"It just felt good to get it all off my chest."

Jack said, "Shhhh."

"Don't shush me. Oh God, I was rolling. That entire story's recorded, on two cameras."

Jack turned around and put a finger over his mouth. Amber started to say something, but stopped when she saw surprise and a little panic in Jack's eyes. He beckoned her to come closer, then pointed forward.

Jack had just rounded a bend in the path. She walked to meet him and a long, straight section of boardwalk became visible. At the far end, about halfway to the next bend, stood what, going by earlier eyewitness descriptions, had to be the Eel-Man. He wore no clothes and was completely hairless. His skin was bumpy, irregular, and coated with a glistening yellow-white slime. He stood with his side to Amber and Jack, leaning forward with both arms resting on the handrail. His head bobbed slightly as he stood, oblivious to the fact that he was not alone.

Amber framed the best shot of the Eel-Man she could. She and Jack stood, still and silent, watching as the Eel-Man also did nothing. This lack of action continued for what felt like an eternity but the video's time code would later show was forty-six seconds. Finally, Amber made eye contact with Jack and tilted her head toward the Eel-Man.

Jack shook his head.

Amber tilted her head further toward the Eel-Man to lend her suggestion more emphasis.

Jack shook his head faster and through a wider arc.

Amber frowned, rolled her eyes, and took two steps back, so that now instead of shooting footage of the Eel-Man, she was capturing footage of Jack Owens *not* approaching the Eel-Man.

Jack looked back at her, shrugged, and used his hands to draw attention to the Eel-Man in the distance the way a model in a commercial might do with a revolutionary new soap dispenser. But he stood his ground.

Amber pressed his backside forcefully with her right foot, either shoving him or kicking him, depending on which of them you asked. Jack stumbled forward, glared back at her, then slowly advanced toward the Eel-Man.

Jack took two steps, then stood perfectly still.

He crept forward two more steps and stopped.

He advanced three steps, which brought him within ten feet of the creature, who remained oblivious, leaning on the handrail and looking out into the darkened swamp.

Jack turned back to face Amber and shrugged.

He stood up straight, cleared his throat quietly, and in a loud, clear voice said, "Hello."

The Eel-Man jumped, badly startled. He spun around to face Jack, shouted "Son of a bitch!" and ran away in a slow, gingerly manner, seeming to get very little traction. After a few steps, his feet slid out from under him and he fell hard on his tailbone. Jack and Amber approached cautiously as the Eel-Man rolled on the wooden walkway, moaning in pain, with both hands on his posterior.

Seen up close, he was clearly not so much an Eel-Man as a man who just looked eellike. He had no visible hair, save maybe for eyelashes. As quick an examination as Amber could stomach revealed that he was not naked, or genital-free, as reported, but wore a sort of thong-back speedo. The swimsuit and every inch of his exposed skin dripped with a viscous, yellowish-white ooze that clung to him but rubbed off on the wood wherever it touched. Looking at the walkway, Amber quickly saw that his own oily footprints had caused his lack of traction, and by extension, his fall.

Jack asked, "You all right?"

"I think I broke my tailbone." Speaking a mouth full of braces. He appeared to be a young man, no older than Amber herself. He reached up to his right ear. "And I lost an earbud! Dammit! Why you gotta sneak up on me like that!"

"I didn't sneak up," Jack said. "I said hello."

"Whatever, dude. Look around. Try to find my earbud."

Jack cast his eyes around the walkway for a moment. "Never mind that. I'll get you some new earbuds. Here, let me help you up."

"Really? They're like hundred-dollar earbuds, man."

"Amber, try to find his earbud. Come on, see if you can stand." Jack extended his elbow to help the Eel-Man up without touching the slime. The Eel-Man gripped Jack's sleeve with both hands as Jack pulled him to his feet. Jack scowled at the dark, greasy stains left behind on his tweed coat while the Eel-Man stood, bent noticeably at the knees and waist, still rubbing his behind as he fidgeted. "Yeah, oh yeah. I think it's broken. Jeez, this is all I need. Hey, lady, you found my earbud yet?"

Amber held her camera pointed at Jack and the Eel-Man but had visually scanned the area. "I think it probably went into the swamp. Sorry."

"Fantastic. Fan-friggin'-tastic!"

"Calm down," Jack said. "None of this is her fault. Forget your earbud. We have to get you to a hospital."

"No! No. No hospitals. Hospitals are where people go to die. No, if you'll just help me get home, I'll call my doctor. He'll take care of me."

Jack said, "Okay, well, let's go then."

The Eel-Man gripped Jack's other sleeve with a slime-coated hand to steady himself and began walking at a glacial pace up the boardwalk. Amber followed, capturing the scene.

Jack asked, "What are you doing out here like this, anyway?"

"I have a skin condition. I need to keep the medicine on it and keep it exposed to the air if I want it to heal. I don't go out in the day, but at night sometimes I go for a walk. There's less of a chance of people seeing me like this."

Jack asked, "What is that, some kind of full-body rash?"

"Pretty much."

"That sucks."

"You know it."

"That and the medicine are bad enough, but even without them, I can see why you don't want the neighbors to see you walking around practically naked."

"What are you talking about? By Florida's standards, legally, this swimsuit counts as being fully dressed."

"Of course it does."

The Eel-Man asked, "What are you two doing out here?"

Jack chuckled. "We're investigating. There've been reports of a strange creature that seems to be a cross between a man and an eel that's been spotted walking around the area at night. Pretty funny, huh?"

"Yeah," the Eel-Man said. "It is. The things people believe. So, any luck finding it?"

4

Jack walked slowly. The Eel-Man, whose name turned out to be Trevor, shuffled beside him in his thong-back speedo, one slimy hand clinging to Jack's jacket for support. Amber walked behind, keeping the two of them in frame.

A few hundred feet beyond the bend where they'd found the Eel-Man, the boardwalk temporarily broke free of the swamp and became a cement path with a pond on the left side and a street full of houses on the right.

Amber said, "No shortage of fishing spots in this town."

Jack glanced out over the placid black water and the stars illuminating the outline of foliage behind it. "Yeah, if you're looking to catch malaria."

Trevor said, "I've never heard of anyone getting malaria around here. I'd be more worried about water moccasins."

"Why did they name a deadly snake after a shoe?" Jack wondered.

Trevor said, "I dunno. Maybe one bit a guy on the foot and wouldn't let go. Hey, what's that thing stuck to your chest?"

"It's a camera. We're making a series for the internet."

"Ah. I get it. That's why you're out at night looking for monsters."

"Exactly."

"Sounds like a wild goose chase to me. I go out walking around here every few nights, and I've never seen anything like that." Trevor pointed to a small but very pleasant-looking house a few doors down. "There. That's my place."

"You live with your family?"

"No. I lived with my grandma. It's her place. But she had to go to assisted living, so now I'm flying solo."

"What do you do for work?"

"Phone support. I work from home. Good thing. My current look probably wouldn't fly in an office."

"Yeah, so, about that. I hate to ask. How long have you had this skin condition? What's it called?"

"It started three months ago with a rough, red, itchy spot on the back of my hand. My doctor called it . . . oh, what did he call it?"

"Eczema?" Jack offered.

"No. It was something longer, like a derma-peptic-germ or something. He gave me this salve to put on it, and the itching went away, but then the redness spread. He gave me more, stronger salve, but the crud has spread all over my body. Made my hair fall out. I can't wear proper clothes because they stick to me and hurt when I peel them off. It's kind of a nightmare."

Jack said, "Kind of?"

They walked up the path through the front yard to the door. Trevor pulled a goopy keyring out of the front of his speedo and unlocked the door. Amber and Jack were both very careful not to touch the glistening doorknob as they followed Trevor inside.

A pattering of paws rushed forward out of the darkness. A small beagle ran up but stopped just short of Trevor, looking up at him with its tail wagging.

Jack said, "Cute dog. What's his name?"

"I dunno. He just turned up a couple of weeks ago." Trevor reached down to scratch behind the dog's ears, which the dog seemed to welcome at first, but then it skittered away as soon as Trevor touched it. "I started feeding him, and he sort of stuck around."

Jack and Amber looked at each other. Jack sank down to one knee and said, "Dad? Are you Dad?"

The dog ran to Jack, tail wagging furiously.

Trevor walked across the darkened room as he asked, "You're a big believer in reincarnation, then?"

"No," Jack answered absentmindedly, concentrating on petting the dog.

Trevor said, "You're a weird guy, Jack. Anyway, welcome to my home."

Jack gave the dog an aggressive petting, then looked up to Amber and pointed to the spot behind the dog's ears where Trevor had tried to give Dad a scritch. There was a small bald patch, and the exposed skin was rough and red.

Trevor turned on the lights. The thick carpeting, overstuffed furniture, pastel walls, and landscape paintings suggested a home decorated in the nineties, by a woman who, by this time, would probably also be in her nineties. It took some effort and imagination to discern the furniture, because every piece—the chairs, the couch, and the end tables—was covered by cheap plastic drop cloths that were themselves smeared with the same greasy goo as Trevor. The plastic-draped coffee table sat pushed up against the wall, displaced by a large inflatable children's pool that held no water but had a thick layer of shining ooze coating its floor.

"What's the kiddie pool for?" Amber asked.

Trevor said, "I sleep in it. I don't want to ruin my mattress."

He walked to the recliner in front of the TV, stepping only on a drop cloth secured to the carpet with strips of packing tape. He sat down carefully on the edge of the recliner, avoiding putting pressure on his tailbone. His groan of pain mixed with the squeak of seat springs, the rustle of plastic sheeting, and the squishing sound of slime being forced under pressure out from under his backside.

"Have a seat," Trevor said. "Just pull up the tarps. It should be dry underneath there. I hope you don't mind if I apply more salve while we talk."

"Not at all." Jack sat down, glared at the camera still mounted to the strut coming from his chest, and asked, "Amber, can I take this off now?"

Amber said, "Not yet. Sorry."

"Let me rephrase that. Amber, I want to take it off."

"I know, Jack, but it's important that you don't. We need total coverage."

"You need a close-up of my expression as I sit on this guy's couch? Why, so the audience can sit vicariously through me?"

"It's not important right now, but if we take it off, we'll just have to go through the hassle of putting it on again when we leave, or more likely, you'll refuse to put it back on."

"I look ridiculous sitting here in this thing."

Trevor looked up as he rubbed some of the salve into his armpit. "Who am I to judge?"

Amber said, "I can cut around it in the editing."

"Amber, I don't need your permission to take it off."

"No, but you do need my help."

"I'll take it off myself."

"You can't, Jack."

Jack said, "Watch me," and twisted around at the waist and bent his arm under his jacket and behind his back as if he were attempting to steal his own lunch money. He struggled, strained, and pivoted slightly, trying to extend his reach by even a few millimeters, then stood up, as if that would give his arm the extra flexibility he needed.

Amber said, "It's not physically possible, Jack. You can't reach."

Jack grunted, "Don't tell me ... what I can't ... I'll show you ... almost, almost, damn!" He stopped pirouetting, straightened out, then bent the other arm behind his back, twisted, and spun in the opposite direction, cursing.

Amber said, "Sorry about the drama, Trevor. Jack does this, apparently."

Jack said, "Don't apologize for me!"

"His wife calls it 'going a little bit Donald Duck.'"

Maybe the beagle thought Jack was fighting some unseen opponent, or maybe he thought Jack was playing, but either way, to his tiny dog brain, there was only one thing to do. He helped by jumping up and down in circles around Jack, barking at him as Jack spun in place, grunting and straining.

Trevor said, "I see the Donald Duck thing."

Amber tried to fight her urge to laugh, but she found she was jiggling so violently that she feared the camera's anti-shake mechanism wouldn't be able to keep up. "Stop, Jack. You can't get out of it. That harness is designed to not come off, and you can't remove the camera without a special tool."

"I don't need your special tool. I'm my own special tool!" Jack stopped moving and sagged as if he heard what he said and found it demoralizing enough to snap him out of his tizzy.

The dog continued dancing around him, yapping excitedly.

"Calm down, Dad," Jack said, and started laughing. After a good chuckle and several deep breaths, he looked at Amber. "You're not going to take this harness off me?"

"No. If I had, I wouldn't have gotten all that great footage of you trying to take it off just now."

"I hope it was worth it, because you're never, ever going to get me to put this thing on again."

"All the more reason to make sure I get the most out of it now."

Jack lifted a corner of a tarp and sat on the end of the couch. He leaned down to pet Dad with one hand. Amber stood and moved to a corner of the room where she could frame a good shot of Trevor but still zoom out to Jack if needed.

Trevor reached down beside his chair and pulled up a one-gallon glass jar shaped like a wooden barrel. A partially torn-off label with green letters P and I suggested it had once held pickles. Now it held a partially translucent, yellowish-white sludge. Trevor dipped three fingers in, pulled out a thick dollop, and smeared it on his chest.

Jack asked, "That, uh, that medication. What's it called?"

Trevor said, "Salve."

"What's the active ingredient?"

"I dunno."

They lapsed into a silence while Trevor smeared the glop onto his belly. Jack said, "The pharmacist at CVS must give you trouble, buying so much of it at a time."

"I don't get it at the CVS. Glen saves me money by mixing it up himself."

"Glen's your doctor?"

"Yeah. He says pharmacies have a huge markup, and that the medical industry's full of people who want to rip you off."

"He might be right," Jack said ruefully. "How much does he charge you for a jar of salve like that?"

"Three hundred bucks."

Jack whistled appreciatively. "Three hundred a month. That's pretty steep."

"I wish! No, I go through a tub like this in a week, and it is steep. Damn steep. It's a cliff. My paycheck doesn't come close to covering it, my savings and my college fund are gone, but it's not all bad. One of my credit cards still has some room. What choice do I have? It's medicine, you know? If I need it, I need it. Besides, imagine how much it would cost if I were going to a pharmacy instead of Glen giving me his friends price."

After another long pause, Jack made what Amber assumed was another deliberately incorrect assumption. "He's been your family doctor for a long time, I suppose."

"No. I met him down at the tavern. We got to talking, you know, about our lives and stuff, and he noticed the itchy red spot on my hand. He told me he could fix it. The next night, he gives me a little baby-food jar of this stuff. I put it on and the itching stopped."

"And he gave you his phone number, in case you needed more."

"Yeah, of course."

"Of course."

"I got through the jar and the rash was better, so I called and he brought me some more."

"But he must have charged you money this time."

"Just for the ingredients."

"How much?"

"Not much. Fifty bucks. But that was for a full Miracle Whip jar, and I figured it was worth it, since I knew it worked."

"Well, yeah," Jack said. "Your rash was almost gone."

"Yeah. Right?"

"So, what happened?"

"It started spreading and getting worse. Glen says the infection fights back like that sometimes, and it's just a matter of hitting it even harder."

"By applying more of the salve."

"Yeah."

Jack looked over at Amber, who almost imperceptibly shook her head. Jack nodded his agreement, just as subtly. He looked down at Dad, who gazed up at him with sad eyes, his tail not moving at all.

It seemed the three smartest creatures in the room agreed that this was a bad situation.

Trevor asked, "So, you two were out looking for—what did you call it—an Eel-Man?"

"Yes," Jack said. "There have been reports of sightings of a strange creature that looks like a cross between a human and an eel. Nobody's gotten a picture of it, but there's been some injured livestock."

Trevor said, "Weird."

"Yeah, the reports started around a month ago."

"Well, I haven't seen anything. Do you think it really exists?"

Jack smiled. "Trevor, I'm going to answer your question with a question of my own. Have you ever bitten a live cow?"

"You're a really weird dude," Trevor said, narrowing his eyes at Jack. He turned to Amber. "Is that why you're filming him? Because he's so weird?"

"Yes."

Jack asked, "Do you think we could meet Dr. Glen?"

"It's just Glen. He doesn't make people call him doctor."

"Do you think you could call and have him come over? I'll pay for him to look at your tailbone, but I want to watch, you know, to make sure I get my money's worth."

"Yeah, I guess I could try." Trevor stood up carefully and waddled into the kitchen.

Jack walked over next to Amber and muttered, "We came looking for a monster. We might be about to meet one."

"Yeah," Amber said, pulling out her phone. "Good instinct asking him to come over."

"What can I say? You were right. There's a story here, just not one my listeners will enjoy. They like things that might or might not exist. They know quacks and con artists are all too real."

Amber swiped through screens on her phone. Jack looked down, watching what she did.

He said, "You know, if we're right about this *Glen*, he's a criminal who is not above hurting people for his own gain, and we just invited him over. If he gets violent, can I count on you, Amber?"

"Of course. I'm a professional. If he attacks you, I'll keep rolling."

"Not what I meant."

Trevor squished his way back into the room, holding an old-school cordless phone up to his ear. "Yeah, Glen. They'd like to meet you — hey, what are you doing?"

Jack and Amber both looked up from her smartphone.

Amber said, "Oh, just looking at a text from my stupid ex."

"He keeps leaving messages for her," Jack explained. "It's kinda pathetic."

Trevor smiled and stood a little straighter. "Oh. You're single?"

Jack said, "Amber, I think it's time you told your ex off once and for all."

"That's what I'm doing." Amber began tapping out a text message.

Jack asked, "So, Trevor, is Glen coming over or what?"

Trevor put a slick, glistening hand over the phone's mouthpiece. "I don't think so, man. He sounds like he's packed it in for the night."

Jack said, "Tell him you're injured and I'm paying."

Trevor lifted his hand from the mouthpiece. "Yeah, look, my tailbone is jacked, and he says he's going to pay for the treatment . . . yeah, he looks like he's got a lot of money. He's wearing a nice jacket."

Trevor took the phone away from his face and pressed a button to turn it off. "He says he'll be right here."

5

Ten minutes later, the headlights of a car pulling into the driveway washed across the house's front windows. Trevor pulled himself up out of his seat, peeling away the drop cloth sticking to his back. "That'll be Glen."

Jack looked over at Amber. "Any reply from Brian?"

"Acknowledgment that he got the text, but he's trying to get to a place where he can reply."

"Good," Jack said. "I'd like to get some closure on this tonight."

Trevor, standing with his hand on the doorknob, looked at Jack, confused. "You want closure on her relationship with her ex?"

Jack said, "Yeah, well, I'm emotionally invested. I think she can do better."

Trevor opened the door and said, "Glen. Come on in."

A voice from outside said, "Hey Trevor. So where's this rich friend of yours?"

"He's right here."

Glen walked in. He was a little taller and heavier than Jack, wearing a maroon polo shirt and jeans. His graying brown hair hung long on the sides and back around a bald spot on top and a wispy poof at the front. He held what looked like a 1960s-vintage ladies' makeup case. He extended his right hand, ready for a handshake, but clenched into a fist when he saw Amber with her camera.

"Hey," he growled. "What is this?"

Jack stood up, smiled, and extended his own right hand. "It's an opportunity. Please don't mind my associate. She's here to film me, not you."

Glen absent-mindedly shook Jack's hand, looking at the camera extending from his torso.

Jack said, "Another camera, but it's pointed at me. See? There's the lens, aimed right at my face."

"Oh," Glen said, examining the camera. "Okay, I guess."

"Good. Good. My name's Jack Owens."

Glen blinked repeatedly and sputtered, "What? I'm sorry, say again?"

"My name's Jack Owens."

"I'll be damned. I recognize your voice! I listen to your show all the time!"

"Oh," Jack said. "Really?"

"Oh yeah. I love it. it really helps pass the time when I'm up late at night, mixing up batches of salve."

"I see. Well, the young lady over there checking her phone is my associate, Amber. We bumped into Trevor and he told us about you."

Glen said, "He's not supposed to do that. In fact, I told him not to leave the house at all, or to talk about me if he does."

Trevor said, "I'm sorry, Glen, but I'm sick of being cooped up. I needed to get some fresh air."

"And you see what comes of that." Glen reached down to pet the beagle sitting by Jack's feet, but as his hand approached, the dog snarled. Glen yanked his hand away.

Jack reached down to pick up and comfort the dog. "Okay, okay. Calm down, come here, Da–doggie." He held the dog to his chest as best he could with the camera stalk in the way. "Doctor, we startled Trevor. He wasn't doing anything wrong, and he fell and got hurt. I'll happily pay for his treatment."

Glen said, "It'll be five hundred bucks."

"You haven't even looked at him yet."

"To look at him. Five hundred bucks. Then we'll talk about treatment."

"Fine. Please, just have a look."

Glen said, "Go ahead, Trevor. Lay down. Let's see what you did to your coccyx."

Trevor pointed at his rear. "No, the problem's with my—"

"That's the technical name for your tailbone."

Trevor stretched out in the bottom of his kiddie pool. Glen kneeled down and flipped open the lid of his case. Instead of carrying medicine or instruments, the case was the outer structure of a device. The inner volume was divided into two parts. One had a painted plywood panel mounted flush with the case's opening, holding two black knobs and a square of smooth black plastic. The other half was open space but held only one item, which Glen pulled out. It looked like a microphone, but small and flimsy, like a toy. A fabric-wrapped spiral cord stretched from the end of the microphone into the recesses of the case.

Glen turned one of the knobs. The device let out a deep click, then a barely audible hum. He twisted the knob. The hum grew louder. He fiddled with the other knob, and the hum rose and fell in pitch. When he seemed satisfied with what he heard, he pressed the head of the plastic microphone against Trevor's tailbone. As he moved the microphone around, barely grazing Trevor's skin, Glen pressed his free hand against the smooth plastic square, as if feeling for something specific.

Jack asked, "What is this device? What does it do?"

"You've heard of ultrasound?" Glen asked.

"Yes."

"It's that."

"Fascinating. It looks like it's from the '60s. I suppose not needing a screen makes it a lot more portable."

Glen turned off the device. "You're asking a lot of questions."

Jack said, "Yeah. Look, you've heard my show. I spend a lot of time talking about aliens, ghosts, and monsters. I'm thinking I'd like to talk more about alternative medicine. It seems like a *profitable* topic for conversation. The problem is, all the experts I can get for the show have a book deal and supplements they pitch. That's a marvelous opportunity for them, but all I get is a guest. What I'm looking for is an alternative-medicine practitioner who I can help set up with a book deal and supplement endorsements. I can make him the only medical expert I ever have as a guest, and I'll have an incentive to have him on often, since I'll get a reasonable cut of the deals I help him make."

"That's an interesting idea," Glen said, no longer even bothering to look at his patient. "What would this practitioner have to do?"

As Jack started to answer, they all heard a firm knock at the door.

Glen and Jack both stood up, Glen edging toward the back door, Jack toward the front. Trevor tried to lift himself, but his hands slid out from under him and he wallowed on his belly in the salve-coated kiddie pool.

"Stay cool, Glen," Jack said. "Stay cool. I'll get rid of them. I'm sure it's just a neighbor or something."

The knock came again, louder, followed by a deep voice shouting, "Sheriff's office. Open the door."

Jack sagged. Glen grabbed his device and Trevor's open pickle jar of salve and sprinted out the back door. Dad leapt from Jack's arms and chased Glen, yapping.

Jack yanked open the front door. Sheriff Buck Dalrymple and three deputies stood on the porch. They waited to be invited in, but all three craned their necks and scanned all visible parts of the room.

"We got Miss Cardoza's text," the sheriff said. "It's not strictly probable cause, but we're all curious—What the shit? The Eel-Man's real?"

Jack followed the sheriff's gaze down to Trevor, still struggling to rise from his kiddie pool.

Trevor stopped wallowing, looked up at Jack, and said, "Glen's the Eel-Man?"

Jack said, "That man's a victim. He's being conned by a quack who just ran out the back door."

For a moment nobody said anything, and they all heard the distant sound of Dad barking and running around the side of the house toward the front yard.

Jack pointed toward the sound. "And he's headed that way."

Jack and Amber ran out the front door, Amber watching the world through the screen on the back of her camera. In addition to the sheriff and two deputies on the porch, two more deputies stood next to squad cars parked on the street in front of the house. Both looked stunned to see the popular radio host and his videographer spring out of the house and a middle-aged man carrying a makeup case and what looked like a giant jar of rancid mayonnaise run out of the backyard and across the street toward the swamp with a furious beagle nipping at his heels.

Sheriff Dalrymple shook off his own confusion and shouted, "Stop that man!"

The deputies hesitated for a second when Trevor—in his Speedo, covered in a rash, and dripping with salve—slide-staggered out the front door, but they regained their wits and chased after Glen.

While Dad's interference was slowing him down, Glen had a substantial head start. The deputies fanned out to both sides; when he reached the edge of the swamp, if he attempted to run to either his left or his right, the deputies would easily intercept him.

The plants and water near the edge were visible in the streetlights, but beyond that was an inky black void. Glen threw his device and the salve jar out into the darkness. Splashing noises made it clear they'd gone into the water.

Dad continued to bite at his ankles. The two deputies closest to Glen stopped ten feet short, shined their flashlights on him, and placed their free hands on the butts of their holstered guns. They shouted commands at him, one telling him to freeze, the other commanding him to hit the ground and put his hands on his head. The sheriff and the other two deputies joined the group, forming a sort of semicircle around him, making it unlikely that he would get away without swimming. Jack and Amber stood behind them, her capturing footage of events as they transpired and him getting footage of his own face.

Glen put out his hands, more to signal to the deputies to stay back than in any sort of surrender. "I didn't break any laws!"

Sheriff Dalrymple said, "Just put your hands up and lay down on the ground."

The angry beagle stopped tugging at Glen's pant leg and backed away, head low, growling.

Trevor asked, "What's going on? Why are they arresting you, Glen?"

Glen said, "If the kid doesn't know what I did, how much harm can I really have done?"

The sheriff and his deputies all crept a step closer to Glen, their hands still on their pistols. Behind them, Amber moved to the side to better compose a shot that would include Jack, Trevor, Glen, the officers, and the snarling dog. She thought Dad was looking between Glen's legs, not at them, but it was hard to tell in this uneven light, with Glen the focus of five flashlights and everything else in darkness. She switched her camera to night-vision mode. The world in her viewfinder turned green and grainy. Two points of bright light, very close together, floating in the pond about fifteen feet from the edge, drew her attention.

Amber said, "Uh, you might want to get away from the water."

Glen stood his ground. The deputies moved forward again. Only Jack seemed to hear her. He didn't move, but looked at her, confused.

"Hands up and get on the ground," the sheriff repeated. "I'm not going to tell you again."

Glen said, "I never claimed to be a doctor! I told the kid right up front that I'd lost my chiropractor's license!"

The points of light, which Amber was now certain were eyes, drifted forward, toward Glen's back, but also seemed to rise several inches above the surface. Amber shouted, "Get away from the water!"

Dad barked. Behind Glen, water splashed softly. The glare from the deputy's flashlights spilled past Glen and caught the edges of something. The beams moved instantly around Glen to focus on the thing beyond him, which appeared to be a large alligator, wading ashore on freakishly long legs. Though green and muscular, like a normal alligator's limbs, in length they seemed proportionately more appropriate for a deer or an elk. It paused near the edge of the pond for half a second, stunned by the sudden light in its eyes.

Sheriff Dalrymple shouted, "What the shit?"

Glen spun around to find himself standing eye to eye with an alligator, but he had no time to say anything, or even shriek in alarm. He only just managed to raise his hands in self-defense. The alligator clamped its jaws on Glen's right forearm. Blood gushed and Glen shrieked.

Again, the sheriff said, "What the shit?"

The alligator shook Glen by his arm and pulled back, dragging him into the pond. The sheriff and his deputies darted forward, swinging their flashlights like clubs, attacking the alligator, hoping to make it let go. Beams of light whipped chaotically with each blow.

The alligator walked backward into the pond, dragging a shrieking and thrashing Glen. The deputies continued their flashlight assault, but soon the alligator disappeared beneath the water, leaving them all standing waist deep in the pond. Glen was still shouting, with only his head above the water, as he moved deeper into the pond with enough speed that he left a V-shaped wake. In an instant, his head went under. His voice went silent. Only his feet remained visible. The deputies dove for them. One got a grip and scooted along like a boogie-boarder for a moment, but then stopped and stood up with nothing to show for his heroism but a single waterlogged shoe.

The sheriff cast his flashlight beam across the water, hoping to see Glen swim, or even bob to the surface, but all anyone saw was Glen's ultrasound device and the half-full pickle jar of salve floating on the surface of the deceptively placid swamp.

The sheriff panted, "What . . . the . . . shit?"

Amber kept her camera focused on the deputies in the pond but looked toward where Jack had been when the attack started. Jack was not there. Trevor stood alone, looking slimy and stunned. She spotted Jack jogging to a stop in the distance at least half a football field away, Dad running behind him. When he came to a stop, he hunched over with his hands on his knees, breathing hard as the beagle jumped and danced around his feet. Jack looked to Amber and shook his head in disbelief.

Amber pointed to Jack's right. Jack looked. The same man in a gray suit they had seen earlier stood on the sidewalk, looking as shocked as everyone else. He and Jack exchanged a look that said, *Can you believe this?*

Jack looked down at the dog, jumped when he realized who he had just shared a moment with, looked back to where the man in the gray suit had been standing, and found the spot empty. He looked back at Amber and again shook his head in disbelief.

6

Amber sat beneath Trevor's front porch light, scrubbing back and forth across the same eight seconds of footage—footage that conclusively proved there was something living in the swamp.

Something blurry.

The night-vision mode on her camera was great at increasing the clarity of slow-moving objects in a low-light environment, but was not so good at fast-moving objects lurching out of the dark into the glare of multiple flashlights. On her screen, a greenish blur with glowing eyes darted out of the water and grabbed Glen, who struggled and, in doing so, turned himself into a blur as well. Then both blurs receded into the water and disappeared.

When she watched the footage in super-slow motion, she found a handful of frames where the creature was still enough to provide a clear image, but they looked fake. This disappointed Amber but did not surprise her. She had seen the creature with her own eyes, and it had looked fake then. It was a mutant alligator with big, long, muscular legs. There was no way to make such a thing look natural. It was as if the human brain saw it and said, *No. Nuh-uh. I refuse to accept this.*

Across the street, the sheriff's deputies had the area where Glen last stood cordoned off and lit with portable floodlights, but it was no use. That was the one place in the world they knew for a fact Glen was not, and the crime scene investigators had very little crime scene to investigate. All that remained was a little blood and two troughs where his feet slid into the water.

Jack approached, looking exhausted. He had long since been freed from his camera harness and had removed his tweed jacket, bolo tie, and sweat-soaked dickey. His T-shirt clung to him, as damp as if he had gone swimming. Behind him, paramedics stood in a pool of bluish light spilling out from an open ambulance, but they were clearly packing things in. Amber caught a glimpse of Trevor sitting on a gurney inside as the door swung shut.

Near the ambulance, a white van marked Animal Control pulled away. Jack watched it go.

Amber said, "They're taking Dad back home to Ben?"

"Yeah," Jack said. "But I told them to let him know, if he ever needs to give that dog up for any reason, to call me. I can figure out a way to get him back to Yakima."

"You think Dad would get along with the cats?"

"I hope not. I need an ally. Hey, uh, I wanted to tell you, that was fast thinking, using your clingy ex to cover for contacting the sheriff."

"Thanks. I figured if he wanted me to prove it, I could show him the unread texts."

"Brian's still texting?"

"Yeah."

"And you still haven't replied."

"No, and I know that's not great. I don't feel good about ghosting him."

Jack smiled. "See, and I was over here trying to think of something harsher you could do to the little asshole. Ghosting's too good for him. Take it from me. I know a thing or two about ghosts. Did you get any usable footage of the gator?"

"Maybe three seconds, if I can clear it up. But I can pad that out to six or seven if I cut in closeups of you looking shocked and running away. Good thing you kept the harness on, eh?"

"Yes," Jack said. "Good thing. Now you can pad out the crappy footage of the tall alligator with crystal clear shots of me fleeing like a coward."

"It won't come off that way. I'll make sure it doesn't. I keep telling you, Jack, I'm here to help you, not to hurt you."

"Yeah, and Glen said he was trying to help Trevor with the little rash on his hand."

"How can you possibly compare me to him?"

Jack put his hands up in front of himself and shook his head. "You're right! You're right. That was too far. But what I'm saying is that Glen said he wanted to help Trevor, but he wanted to help himself to Trevor's bank account. You say you want to help my radio show, but you want to help your career."

"There's no reason I can't do both."

"True, but there's also no reason you have to do both, and if you have to choose one or the other, we both know what you'll pick. Just be honest about it. You want to do a good job making these videos because then you'll get other, better-paying work. I want to do a good job on the videos so that if they fail, I won't get the blame. We're working toward the same short-term goal, and that's good. Just stop acting like you're doing this for me. If I've learned one thing about life, it's this: Look out for people who tell you they're looking out for you."

"Anybody ever tell you that you have trust issues?"

"Yeah, but I figured they were lying."

Sheriff Dalrymple walked up, seeming ten years older than when they'd met him that morning. "The paramedics think the kid's going to recover. There might be some long-term scarring. They'll have to play it by ear."

Amber asked, "What's in the salve?"

"Mostly Vaseline and some moisturizer, but they suspect maybe ground up poison-oak leaves, judging from the poor kid's skin. One of my guys got a little on his hand and it's already turning red."

Jack looked out over the pond and muttered, "Bastard."

"Yeah," Amber agreed.

The sheriff said, "I wouldn't wish being eaten on anyone, but in his case, it's about right. We broke open that gizmo of his. All that was inside was an old vibrator with the speed control wired to a knob. The microphone didn't even plug into anything. He just tied the cord in a knot to keep from pulling it out of the hole. How did your video come out? Did you get a clear shot of Stretch?"

"Stretch?" Amber asked.

Jack said, "That's what the deputies call the tall alligator. I suggested 'Talligator,' but that works better in writing than spoken out loud."

The sheriff looked out over the pond and shook his head. "You know, I have to hand it to you, Owens. I always figured your show was just a bunch of bunk, good for a laugh and that's all. You've been in town less than a day and you found the Eel-Man, a con man practicing medicine without a license, and a five-foot-tall mutant alligator. How did you do it?"

"I looked. No sane person would go out looking for an Eel-Man, Sheriff. You didn't. But we did anyway. It was crazy. It was stupid. There was no reason to believe we'd find anything, but we looked, and this time we got lucky."

The sheriff said, "Huh. That's certainly something to think about," and walked away.

Amber smiled at Jack. "That was well said."

"You think so?"

"Yeah. You don't?"

"I hoped you'd find it insulting. All that talk about it being crazy and stupid was aimed at you."

"It didn't come off that way. It just seemed self-effacing. Like you were making fun of yourself."

"Damn. That's the opposite of what I wanted."

The Curse of the
Pennington Portrait

7

Amber said, "When you're ready."

Jack cleared his throat, stepped into the frame, looked back over his shoulder at the grand Victorian mansion at the end of a long, tree-lined driveway behind him, then turned to face the camera.

"Those of you who grew up in Nashville might recognize the building behind me, Hickory Hollow, the stately ancestral home of the Pennington family and their extensive art collection. There, alongside the Rembrandts, the Picassos, the Degas . . .es, is a painting that is famous for very different reasons. One goal of art is to raise questions, and by that measure, this painting is definitely a success. The two most common questions asked by those who have viewed it are 'What kind of person would hang something like that in their home?' and 'Is it really cursed?'"

After an extended moment of Jack staring meaningfully into the camera, Amber said, "Okay, good. Let's do one more."

"No."

Amber arched an eyebrow. "Degas-es?"

"It's fine. A tiny flub. By the time the intro's over they'll have forgotten about it."

Amber rolled her eyes. "Fine. We should get you a change of camera-ready clothes, though."

Jack looked at the sleeves of his tweed jacket. "I had them laundered. They look okay in person. The salve stains are showing on camera?"

"Yeah, on the jacket and the dickey."

"Dickeys aren't easy to find, especially in black. I might have to get a full black shirt. Of course, then I could leave my jacket unbuttoned when it's hot."

"Sure," Amber said. "Live a little. Heck, you could even get a new bolo tie. Where do you buy a bolo tie, anyway?"

"We're in Nashville. I bet you could buy them about anywhere. They probably have them by the cash register at 7-Eleven."

They started walking toward the mansion. Amber sneaked a quick peek at her smartwatch.

"Brian still leaving messages?" Jack asked.

"No, actually. He seems to have stopped."

"Ah. Huh. How do you feel about that?"

"Can we talk about something else, please?"

"Sure. None of my business anyway. So, how did your boss like the Eel-Man video?"

Amber sighed heavily. "I'm happy that Brian has moved on, but it's kind of sad that the relationship has ended, even though I'm glad it's over, which I know makes no sense."

Jack said, "Wow! Okay. She hated the video that much, huh?"

"She didn't hate it. But she isn't going to post it. She said she wants to give me time to find my footing."

"How much time?"

"Her words were 'As soon as possible.'"

"Well, I wish you luck with that."

"You mean it?"

"No. My best-case scenario is that you don't do better this time and they cancel the entire project. But—and I mean this—I hope they just reassign you to a successful project instead of firing you."

"How touching."

"What can I say. I'm a wonderful human being. And, uh, look: don't feel bad about having mixed feelings about that idiot Brian. It's entirely possible to want nothing to do with someone and miss them at the same time."

"Really?"

"Oh, yeah. Way back before I met Renee, I was with this woman. Sarah. We met on the job. I had an afternoon show on a hot talk station in Indianapolis. She read the news on the morning show. We lived together, talked about marriage. I started having her turn up now and then on my show. Then I got sent on a cruise. It was a business trip. The cruise line was a sponsor. I had to record a segment every day about all the fun I was having for the station to air hourly."

"Sounds great."

"Because it was my job to make it sound great. I got a cabin with no windows. I had to eat in the crew's mess, which is called that for a reason. The worst part was they would only send one person, so Sarah couldn't come with me."

"Oh."

"Yeah. But someone had to cover my show, and I said, "Why not give her a shot?" A week later, when I got back, Sarah had moved out of our place and into my old show, and I had the freedom to pursue employment elsewhere."

"Ouch! How did she pull that off?"

"By pulling things off—pieces of clothing, I mean. She moved in with the station manager. That seemed like a clue. What I'm getting at is that I have deep, a genuine feeling for her that will never fade: anger. That said, I spent a couple of months missing her. It felt like everything I saw reminded me of her. Especially the billboards the station put up to promote her show. And the invitation I got to their wedding."

"Sounds like you were better off without her."

"Without her, yes. Without a job, not so much. It was partly my fault. She was always kind of awful, but I overlooked that because she was such a fox. Then I left her in charge of my henhouse. We all do dumb things in our twenties."

Amber furrowed her brow. "I'm in my twenties. I don't do dumb things."

Jack smiled. "In thirty years I'm going to remind you that you said that, and we're going to share a good laugh. Now let's go into that ugly old mansion and report on this bogus curse."

"You're absolutely sure it's bogus?"

"Yes."

"Why?"

"Because it's a curse. Amber, you don't actually believe in curses, do you?"

"I don't believe in magic, but I think it may be possible that there may be some mechanism where enough negative feelings built up might harm other people. Let me ask you this, Jack. When your ex-girlfriend and the station manager got married, did you wish them well?"

"Very much no."

"And how did their marriage work out?"

"Divorced a year later."

"And there isn't a part of you that wants to believe you had something to do with it?"

"Just because I'd like to believe something doesn't mean I do. And frankly, I think their marriage imploding had very little to do with my grudge. Both of the people in the marriage were backstabbers. Their entire relationship must've just been them constantly going around in circles trying to get within stabbing range of each other's backs."

"Maybe there's a self-fulfilling prophecy thing going on with the painting. It's cursed because people think it's cursed. It has a long, creepy history, all the way back to the death of the guy who painted it."

"It was painted in the 1840s. It would be creepy if the artist wasn't dead by now."

"But he died young."

"Again, in the 1840s. People died young back then, and I don't blame them. It was that or continue to hang around in the 1840s, just hoping that if you lived long enough you might get to experience the mass adoption of the flush toilet."

Amber said, "Except for the current owner, everybody who has ever owned that painting has died."

"Except for the current owner, everybody who has ever owned anything old has died. Everybody who has ever lived, or will ever live, will die."

"Good point. Look, I don't believe in magical curses, and maybe the idea that people's negative feelings have affected the painting's owners is far-fetched. There are other ways the painting could kill people. Maybe it's radioactive or toxic. Maybe it has lead-based paint."

"What, and the owners keep licking it?" Jack asked. "I'll grant you that it's possible that the people who own the painting might be prone to irrational behavior. I've seen pictures of the thing, and I can't see any reason anyone would want it. Still, I say curses are just an old wives' tale."

"And I say don't underestimate the wisdom of old wives."

* * *

Amber focused her camera on Jack as he stood in a room that conveyed a sense of overwhelming weight. It wasn't just the weight of the family's long legacy, stifling expectations, and great wealth. The house itself, and every piece of furniture inside, was heavy and overbuilt. A thick Persian carpet lay on a wooden floor as solid as any bowling alley's. The oak paneling looked thicker on its own than the walls in most houses. The copper coffered ceiling didn't hang overhead so much as it loomed.

As part of extensive renovations, a professional cleaning crew had worked through much of the room. Their equipment and supplies sat along the line where they'd stopped for a break.

On one side of the line, the metal shone and the wood had a rich luster. On the other side of the line, a thick layer of dingy residue smothered everything: the accumulated leavings of multiple generations' worth of people who made their livings from the tobacco industry and felt it was their duty to use the family product.

Jack stood next to a slim, neat young man with spiky blond hair and dark brown roots. He wore the high-end designer equivalents of a cloth bomber jacket, a polo shirt, khakis, and sneakers. The ensemble made him look utterly comfortable, both physically and financially.

Amber said, "Ready when you are, Jack."

Jack looked into the camera. "We have the rare opportunity to come inside Hickory Hollow and view the infamous painting. Our guide is none other than Max Pennington, the current CEO of Pennington Partners, owner of Hickory Hollow and the infamous Pennington Portrait. Thank you so much for having us, Mr. Pennington."

"My pleasure, man. And please, call me Max."

"Thank you, Max. We all offer you our condolences for the recent passing of your father."

"Thanks."

"So, before we look at the portrait itself, I was hoping you could give us an overview of its history and the history of your family."

"Sure, Jack. We're in the family portrait hall. It's a good place to run through the highlights. Along this wall are all the former patriarchs of the Pennington family, who also served as heads of the family business and owners of Hickory Hollow. We're supposed to get our official portrait painted within a year of accepting our inheritance. It's one of our family's cherished traditions, along with stoicism, pomposity, and smoking like a chimney. I haven't had mine done yet. I considered trying to have Banksy come spray-paint a picture of me on the wall, but I doubt he'd be into it."

"If these are the owners of the estate, I suppose that means they are also all the owners of the infamous Pennington Portrait," Jack said.

"Yeah. That's true."

"I see. And did they all die young?"

"Not at all, Jack."

"Really? I'd been led to believe they all died mysteriously at young ages."

"No, if you use some critical thought, there's no mystery to their deaths, and they all got to be pretty old."

Jack said, "Oh," trying to hide his smile from Amber.

"Yeah," Max said. "Most of them were in their fifties."

"What? Their fifties isn't . . . ugh. Sorry. There are many of us who would consider dying in our fifties to be premature."

Max said, "This first painting is Percival Pennington, founder of the family business and builder of Hickory Hollow." Max pointed to an oil painting in a gold frame, depicting a man in a bowler hat with eyebrows like the wings of an angry hawk and a cigar the size of a paper-towel tube.

"And the man who commissioned the infamous Pennington Portrait."

"Yes, though they didn't call it infamous at the time. Just creepy."

"But this is not the infamous Pennington Portrait."

"No. This one isn't cursed. It just radiates bad vibes. They say it really captured his essence. Everyone called him Percy, which he hated. The family lore says he decided if they were going to call him Percy, he'd show them, by having the largest purse. I think that sounded cleverer in 1825. He bought a tobacco plantation, then expanded into manufacturing tobacco products; saw the company through the Civil War and the difficult transition from relying on unpaid labor to underpaid labor; and finally died in his seventies, only a month or so after getting the painting you're here to talk about. That's how the rumors of a curse began. He died of what his doctor called an 'illness.' Dad used to joke that he perished from a lack of specificity. Judging from the size of his stogie, it was probably cancer."

Max breezed past the next portrait, a severe-looking man in a gray suit smoking a pipe. "This is his son, Chester Pennington. He died in his fifties during a botched surgery to remove a growth from the roof of his mouth, probably cancer."

Max stopped in front of the next picture, a trim man in a slender suit with a pencil-thin mustache on his lip and a long, thin cigarette in a long, thin cigarette holder in his long, thin hand.

"This is Guillaume Pennington. He saved the company during the Great Depression by making sure our cigarettes were the cheapest. You've probably seen the 'I can still afford a Pennington' ad campaign."

Jack said, "The one with the smoking hobo."

"Bingo. Of course, once the Depression ended nobody wanted to be seen smoking a Pennington anymore. That's when he changed our brand name to Sophisticate. He didn't change the cigarettes, though. They say he died from bad bathtub gin. They weren't sure if the problem was the gin or the bathtub. He had taken to drinking because of a chronic cough. Probably cancer."

Max walked past a painting of a man in a wide-brimmed hat, a wide-shouldered suit, and a thin tie. The smirk on his lips pressed around a cigarette. "His son, Grahame Pennington. He sold a ton of cigarettes to soldiers in World War Two. When the family business went public, Grahame here was in charge. That's when we officially took on the company name Pennington Partners. We have a full board of directors, of course, but a Pennington always sits at the head and has a controlling interest."

"If a single member of your family is still in charge, why call it Pennington Partners?" Jack asked.

"An excellent question. It allowed for the concentration of power but the dispersal of blame." Max turned away from the painting and glanced at the cleaning crew's equipment. "Grahame was also the one who had the mansion modernized, redid all the plumbing, and had HVAC installed. He pioneered many innovative cost-cutting construction techniques, only a few of which had to be reversed later by structural engineers. Aside from some repairs and paint, it's the last real attention the old place got. That's why I started renovations as soon as I took control. He's the only Pennington to die of cancer, officially. He passed away during that sweet spot where it was late enough for the doctors to diagnose and record it as cancer but early enough that the lawyers didn't know enough to cover the cancer up."

The next painting featured a man in a plaid jacket and black pants with a bright red shirt, the top three buttons left open. He had a big, floppy-looking mustache and held a smoldering cigarette in his hand. The glint in his eye suggested he had just winked. "George Pennington. He rebelled against his father by marketing to hippies. We saw an explosion in profits from our rolling-paper subsidiary. He died of a heart attack, but it happened in the hospital while he was recovering from having one lung removed."

The next portrait was of a man sitting in a wicker chair in a pastel suit, with feathered hair and a lit cigar in his hand. "Chad Pennington, transitioned from selling cigarettes to hippies to selling cigars to yuppies. He coined the marketing trademark 'Cubanish.' Official cause of death: natural causes, but by then it was considered only natural that a Pennington would die of the big C."

They came to the last painting in the line. It could have been a painting of Max himself if not for the hair, which was in a race to see whether it would have time to go completely gray before it all thinned out to nothing. Max said, "And this is my father, William Pennington. He passed away three months ago."

Jack said, "I'm sorry."

"Thanks. It was a car accident."

"Oh."

"On his way to meet with his oncologist."

"Do you smoke?"

"Nope. Never have. I'm the black sheep of the family, except for my lungs. Dad was delighted that I never started. He tried to quit many times. But the addiction was too strong, and having an unlimited supply of free cigarettes didn't help."

"I imagine not. So, you're not a smoker, yet you're in the tobacco business."

"For now, but I'm divesting Pennington Partners from all of its tobacco-related holdings. We've slowly diversified over the years, and our expertise in manufacturing and logistics can give us an advantage in other emerging industries. But you aren't here to talk business; let's get to the main event."

They approached a painting hanging on the wall, draped with a sheet. Max said, "I had one of my assistants bring it out of storage and hang it in its original position. I haven't seen it myself in years. Ready?"

Jack looked into the camera. "As ready as anyone can be."

Max whipped the sheet away. Amber reframed the shot to center on the painting, which depicted the room in which they stood, with the unmistakable form of Percival Pennington lying on the floor, limbs bent awkwardly, tongue hanging out, eyes wide open. A second figure, this one semi-transparent, also Percival Pennington, rose from the lifeless body, a look of terror and surprise on his face. On the wall behind the specter was a painting, the same painting, the infamous Pennington Portrait, instantly recognizable though rendered in tiny brushstrokes, hanging exactly where the real painting hung now. The logical inference was that Percival had died (or, when he commissioned it, would die) standing on the very spot where the viewer stood, looking at the very painting at which the viewer, logically, had to be looking.

Jack squinted at the painting. "And you say Percival Pennington actually commissioned it? This is what he asked for?"

"Yup. He had to go to several artists before he found one who would do it. Seems it was his idea of a joke. He would lie down on the floor in the same position as in the painting and wait for someone to find him. Of course, when he really died, it was while lying there, waiting. Nobody knows how long he had been there, but the butler spent at least two hours pretending not to notice him before he finally became concerned enough to break down and check for a pulse."

"That's the one thing that could have happened to make the painting even more disturbing."

"I know, right? Of course, between that and the artist dying young, in unexplained circumstances, it was enough to start people talking about a curse."

"What do we know about the artist's death?"

"He was shot in a brothel, by a sex worker."

"I thought you said it was unexplained."

"It was. She refused to explain why. Anyway, when old Percy's eldest son, Chester, inherited everything, the first thing he did was have the painting put in storage. He felt it was in poor taste and was a constant reminder of the old man's death. Then Chester's son inherited everything and brought the painting back out, both for its historical significance and to show he was different from his father. It's been in and out of storage many times over the years, so much that within the family the power to decide whether it's displayed or not has come to sort of symbolize being in charge."

"And now it falls to you."

"Looks like it, yeah."

Jack said, "My understanding is that you've agreed to let us borrow the painting to have it analyzed scientifically."

"Sure. If the painting is dangerous somehow, I want to know."

"Do you intend to display the painting?"

"Probably. Its history makes it the most interesting thing in the house by a long shot."

"But your father didn't display it."

"No. he said it gave him the creeps."

"But it doesn't give you the creeps?"

"Sure it does, but every painting in the room gives me the creeps. Look at these guys."

8

Amber rifled through a rack of neatly creased Dockers, arranged by color so that they created a sort of spectrum between black and tan with multiple shades of brown in between, like the world's least beautiful rainbow. Behind her, she heard Jack's voice from the fitting room say "None of these shirts fit right."

Amber asked, "Can I see?"

Jack said, "No."

"Why not?"

"Two reasons: I'd have to put them back on to show you, and you're not my mama."

"Yeah," Amber muttered. "If I were, I'd dress you better."

Jack emerged from the fitting room, wearing cargo shorts and a green T-shirt with a painting of a hawk on the front and carrying a stack of black button-down shirts draped over his arm. He hung the shirts on the empty rack beside the door. "Gotta keep looking, I guess."

Amber said, "Cool," and peeked at her smartwatch.

Jack asked, "Anything from the lab yet?"

"No."

Jack arched an eyebrow. "Anything from anybody else?"

"No."

Jack walked out among the racks of clothes. "And how do you feel about that?"

"Fine! I'm fine."

"Good."

"Why wouldn't I be?"

"No reason."

"I'm telling you, I'm fine with it."

"Good," Jack said. "Glad to hear it."

Jack pulled a shirt from a rack and checked the size label. "And you keep checking your messages to make sure that you're still fine. Makes perfect sense."

Amber glared at him.

Jack said, "Off the top of my head, I can think of several perfectly understandable reasons for you to be bothered that he's stopped trying, and none of them make you weak, dumb, or a bad person."

"Thanks. I guess it would cause him less pain if he gave up and moved on. I'm just not sure I want him to feel less pain just yet."

"That's understandable. You loved him. You trusted him. You thought he was a partner. He disrespected you, he used you, and that's all still fresh. If you told me you wished him well, I'd know you were lying. Luckily, the anger at the people who have wronged you fades with time."

"Then you forgive them?"

"Maybe. More often, you just stop caring enough to bother wishing them ill. As you go through life, lots of people are going to screw you, enough that you'll lose track of some of them."

"Have you really had people backstab you so many times that you've forgotten some of the times it happened?"

"No, I never forget a backstabbing, but I have forgotten some of the backstabbers. A long time ago I had the afternoon slot at an easy-listening station in Boise. There was a woman who handled traffic. Do you know what that means in the radio business? Traffic?"

"Was she up in a helicopter over the freeway?"

"No, there's a person at every radio station who keeps track of what commercials the station is obligated to run and at what times. It's tedious, mentally taxing work. They call it traffic. Anyway, there was a lady whose name I don't remember doing traffic at this place, and she decided to screw me."

"Why?"

"What do you mean?"

Amber said, "She had to have a reason."

"Yeah, well, sometimes 'to screw you' is the reason. Anyway, she decided to screw me, so she assigned me to record the voice-overs for all the commercials for embarrassing products. Hemorrhoid cream, impotence remedies, obvious stuff."

"Petty."

"Yes," Jack agreed.

"But funny."

"Yes. She told the guys on the morning team what she was up to. Together, they all started coming up with fake commercials for me to record. The ads looked real to me. After the 'roids and the impotence, they gave me ads for credit counseling, employment agencies, couples therapy, and divorce lawyers. I caught on around the time they got to plasma banks and sex-toy shops. They cut the ads into a long montage that told the story of my life going to hell. It was popular, so they sold it to other stations' morning shows. They named the recording 'Hemorrhoid Jack.' It made the station some pretty good scratch, I'm sure."

"Didn't you get a cut?"

"That's not how it works. Commercials I cut for the station are the property of the station, even if they're fake. They gave me a plaque as a token of appreciation, but it's made out to

'Hemorrhoid Jack,' so I don't display it. Worst part was for years after, when I'd apply for work in larger markets, that would be all the program directors would want to talk about."

Amber asked, "How did they know it was you if you didn't tell them?"

"I told them. I put it on my resume. A credit's a credit. My point is, you can sort people into two groups. There are those you're close to: your family and good friends; and there those you aren't: coworkers, acquaintances, and strangers. The ones who aren't close to you will screw you over, and they won't feel bad about it."

"Maybe, some of them."

"Definitely, all of them. If they get a chance."

"We're not close, Jack, but I won't screw you."

"You already did. You screwed me before we ever met. Our entire partnership is based on me trying to minimize the damage."

"That's a heck of an attitude you've got there, Jack. At least you trust your friends and family—"

"Oh no, they'll screw you too. But they'll feel bad," Jack interrupted. "Or at least they'll go to the trouble to pretend to."

Amber said, "Oh, no way!"

"I know it's hard to hear."

"No," Amber said, stepping behind a pillar and glancing around it to the far end of the store. "Not that. Well, I mean, that too, but we're done with your trust issues for now. We've got bigger fish to fry."

She dug out her phone and pretended to read the screen as she took a quick photo. "Okay, I'm going to hand you my phone as if I want you to read something, but look at the picture I just took."

Amber handed her phone to Jack, who held it up close to his face and squinted at it as if reading fine print and muttered, "Son of a bitch!"

Jack handed Amber's phone back and walked away with purpose. Amber followed, bringing up her phone's video camera and recording Jack as he approached a man in a dark gray suit.

The man seemed to notice Jack's approach and turned his back and bowed his head, trying to appear deeply interested in the garment in front of him: a five-pack of men's bikini briefs.

Jack asked, "Who are you, and why are you following us?"

Seeing the man in the suit up close for the first time, it struck Amber that his large eyes, narrow head, plump lips and protruding ears gave the impression of a fish that had been granted a wish to become human by a sea witch that didn't care very much about the quality of her work.

The man in the suit didn't look up and shied away from the camera. "Sir, I don't know what you're talking about. I'm simply an ordinary man, here to buy . . . undies."

Amber grimaced. "*Undies?*"

Jack said, "A week ago you were in Florida."

"No, I wasn't."

Amber said, "I have video of you."

"Okay, I was in Florida. I was on vacation."

Jack said, "You were wearing a suit."

"It's my vacation suit. I'm dapper."

Amber said, "You're wearing the same suit now."

"I'm still on vacation."

Jack said, "You were in Florida at the same time as us, and now you're in Nashville at the same time as us."

"It's a coincidence."

"It's extremely unlikely."

"That's what coincidence means."

Amber said, "We saw you three times in Florida, in three different places."

The man said, "That's even more of a coincidence, which kinda proves my point? Eh? Eh?" The man in the suit smiled, coaxing them to agree. When they remained uncoaxed, he sagged. "Yeah, okay, you caught me. If you'll stop recording, I'll explain."

Jack looked at Amber.

Amber stopped her phone recording and put it in her pocket. "There. Now, what's your deal?"

"I'm a federal agent. My name's Carmichael."

Jack asked, "What agency do you work for?"

"I'd rather not say."

Amber and Jack both glared at him.

Carmichael said, "I'm part of a task force that's concerned with the kinds of subjects you two are investigating."

"What's this task force called?" Jack asked.

"Never mind that. It's not important. Hey, where are you going?"

Jack said, "I'm here to look for clothes. There's no reason I can't look while we talk. Follow me."

Agent Carmichael and Amber walked behind Jack as he scanned the racks for black shirts and tweed jackets. Jack looked back over his shoulder and asked, "Do you work for Project Blue Book?"

"No."

"Men in Black?" Jack ventured.

"I'm not wearing black."

"It's just a name."

"They don't really exist."

Jack asked, "Monarch?"

Carmichael said, "That's from the Godzilla movies."

"Okay, not Monarch. What was that one from the fifties? It sounded like Monarch."

"Majestic 12," Carmichael said, "and no, I'm not with them. As you said, they're from the fifties. Acronym, okay? My group's name is Acronym."

Amber and Jack both stared at him in silence for a few seconds, pondering this new piece of information. Then Amber asked, "And what does Acronym stand for?"

Agent Carmichael said, "Truth, justice, and the American way."

"Yeah," Amber said, "I'm sure, but that's not what I mean. I just—I assume Acronym is an acronym."

Carmichael said, "Yeah, you'd think. Look, the name isn't important. The job is. Everybody agrees that one of our country's biggest problems is that it feels like half of the citizens believe things that aren't true. Of course, they all believe they see the truth and those who disagree are believing lies. Certain highly placed individuals realized that there are organizations deliberately misleading people to stir up chaos and serve their own ends. These highly placed individuals formed Acronym and tasked us with keeping tabs on any person or group that deliberately spreads misinformation."

Jack checked the size tag on a black shirt, draped it over his arm, and rifled through the others on the rack, looking for other sizes. "So, what do you do, watch cable news all day? Sounds like pretty easy work."

"It was. I'm the agent assigned to your show, Mr. Owens. Does that surprise you?"

Jack said, "Are you kidding? I'd be concerned if you weren't investigating me."

"My job used to be listening to your show every night. I'd do a bit of research to see if the stories on your show were plausible. Since they always weren't, I'd write up a quick report on my findings about the smallcano, or whatever, and call it a day. It was great until Miss Cardoza came into the picture."

Amber said, "Is *everyone* mad at me?"

"No, just everyone in this conversation." Jack draped two more shirts over his arm and walked toward the fitting room. Amber and Carmichael followed.

Carmichael said, "My superiors learned you were going to go out into the field to actually investigate things, and they ordered me to keep tabs on you."

"Is this the part where you warn us not to tell people about Stretch the mutant alligator?" Amber asked.

"If it is, it's way late, since you already submitted that piece to your boss."

"You know about that?"

"I've watched it."

"See," Amber said. "See this? This is why people don't trust the government. Because the government doesn't trust us. You feds watch us like hawks and involve yourselves in every aspect of our lives, when all we want is for you to leave us alone. So, what did you think of the piece?"

"It was a bit dry, but it was accurate, and that's the important thing."

Jack disappeared into the fitting room. Agent Carmichael turned to address Amber more directly as they stood near the door. "The reason monitoring *That's Not Right* has always been such easy duty is that Mr. Owens is clever enough to never claim that the things his guests and callers are saying is true. Heck, our evidence shows that being a guest on the show actually harms people's credibility."

From beyond the door, a muffled voice said, "Please, call me Jack."

"Thanks, Jack."

"What should I call you?"

"Agent Carmichael. Sorry about that, but being a federal agent pays squat. The only perks are getting called 'agent,' getting to sneak around snooping on people while claiming it's your patriotic duty, and an excuse to wear aviator glasses indoors. I'm not giving any of that up without a fight. As I was saying, Jack gives his guests and callers a platform and leaves it up to the audience to decide what's true and what isn't. But now you're going out and investigating. You won't be saying 'This person claims this; isn't that weird?' You're going to be saying 'Here's what we found.' You need to come up with some findings, and if those findings are false, we're going to have a problem."

"But you don't have a problem with the story we did about Stretch?" Amber asked.

"No, because all you did was tell the truth. You found a freakishly tall alligator. You got some grainy, unconvincing footage of it. I know for a fact all of that happened because I was there. I saw it too."

Amber said, "So, we can report any crazy thing we want, as long as it's true?"

Agent Carmichael said, "Yes, and Acronym won't have any problem with you."

"But what if we report something that might cause a panic?"

"If it's the truth, maybe people should panic."

"What if we report something some other agency doesn't want out there? Will you protect us from them?"

"Not even a little. But on the bright side, if you then report that the other agency is after you, we won't stop you. I don't think it'll be a problem. Unless the CIA has some plan to weaponize cursed paintings and very tall alligators, I think you'll be fine."

Amber asked, "And what happens if we do report lies? I mean, we aren't going to, but what if we did?"

Agent Carmichael waved his hand dismissively. "You know, the usual. The standard 'full might of the federal government coming down on your head' package. There's no need to go into specifics. Why should I go to the trouble of threatening you to keep you from doing something you never had any intention of doing anyway?"

From beyond the door, Jack said, "So you're just going to follow us around to make sure we don't knowingly lie?"

"I can't comment on my future activities. My duty to Acronym and the US government prevent me from verifying that yes, that is exactly what is going to happen."

Amber said, "Maybe we should just carpool then. Make it easier for everyone."

"Nope, no dice. My orders are to keep my surveillance as covert as possible, and it's hard to hide from someone when you're riding shotgun."

Amber said, "You'd be in the back seat."

"More reason not to carpool. Besides, the sneakiness is the fun part. Surveillance without sneaking is just hanging around."

Jack said, "You're deliberately speaking up so I can hear you through this door. You call that sneaky?"

"I'm off to a poor start, but don't you worry. I'll raise my game. I've only just begun to sneak. You'll see."

Amber said, "If you really do improve—"

Agent Carmichael waved a hand dismissively. "Yeah, yeah, you won't see. You know what I meant."

Amber said, "I have one more question."

"Sure."

"What does the name Acronym stand for? You never answered before."

"It doesn't stand for anything. Acronym is not an acronym."

"What?"

"The plan was for us to have an acronym for a name, but they didn't think up the name first. They wrote up the paperwork to create Acronym, but when they came to the name, they just wrote 'Acronym' as a placeholder until they could think up something later. They kept putting it off. People started referring to us as Acronym, and when it came time to finalize things, nobody had a better idea."

Amber shook her head. "But even if they wanted to call it 'Acronym,' they could've come up with a name that kept that acronym. I mean, Agency Concerning . . ."

Jack said, "Reality . . . Or?"

Amber muttered, "N-Y-M."

Agent Carmichael said, "Most attempts never get past the O."

Jack said, "Or. Or. Or . . . uh . . . Nailing Your Mama."

Agent Carmichael said, "And the overwhelming majority of those that get past the O end in 'Your Mama.'"

9

Jack and Amber stood facing each other, his back to a glass and steel building, hers toward that building's parking lot. He wore his new not-salve-stained shirt, jacket, and slacks. She used both hands to hold her camera steady.

Jack cleared his throat and looked into the camera. "Behind us is the charming campus of the institution known to locals as NCC but officially named Nashville Community College. Long a welcome option for those looking to better themselves, students hoping to accrue enough credits to move on to a four-year university, or young people who aren't yet sure what they want to do but who know that it isn't the military. It is also, in our case, an inexpensive source of scientific equipment and people who are eager to use that equipment on a project with practical, real-world applications. Say, for instance, seeing if an infamous cursed painting is chemically toxic."

Amber said, "Good. Another?"

"Nope."

"I figured. Let's head in."

Jack shrugged and began walking toward the building, took three steps, and stopped to look back at Amber. "Aren't you coming?"

"Yeah, right behind you, so I can film you walking around on campus."

Jack rolled his eyes and kept walking. "Sounds riveting. What, are you hoping I'll trip?"

From behind him Amber said, "Not at all. I'm just getting some B-roll. You want a change of scenery and some motion. It breaks up the monotony of just people talking into the camera. Trust me, I know what I'm doing."

"Just because you know what you're doing doesn't mean I want you to do it.'

"It should, Jack. We're a team."

"*Team* is just a word people use to get you to do things you don't want to."

"That's not true."

You been on many teams?"

"A few."

"Been captain of any?"

"Not officially."

"And how often did you get to do what you wanted?"

"Not often, but I had to do what was best for the team."

"Yeah, what the captain or the coach thought was, at least. Look, sometimes your interests align with other people's, but at the end of the day we all work alone."

"Does Renee know you feel this way?"

"No, and the fact that I hide it from her proves my point, not yours. Besides, she's my wife. That's different. Our finances are interlocked."

"And you've never been partners with someone you weren't married to?"

"Of course I have. That's why I know it doesn't work. Back in the nineties, I was part of a morning team in Sacramento. *Dumbass and Jack.*"

"Your partner's name was Jack?"

"Funny. No, his name was Rob Dumas. Everyone mispronounced his name as a joke anyway, so he turned it to his advantage. He was always a little too clever."

"What happened?"

"He decided *Dumbass and Jack* would be a better show without Jack there dragging him down. He started sabotaging me. He'd mess with my volume, introduce a delay into my headphones so I'd stumble over my words. One time he told me we were interviewing the Everly Brothers, but we were actually talking to the Righteous Brothers. They didn't have much pleasant to say when I asked them about recording 'Wake Up Little Susie.'"

Amber said, "I don't know who any of those people are."

"You've never heard of either the Everly Brothers or the Righteous Brothers?"

"No. But I think I've heard of Little Susie. She's from the snack cakes, right?"

"That's Little Debbie."

"Oh. Okay, then I haven't heard of any of them." Amber cast one look back at the parking lot as they entered the building. "I assume you spotted Agent Carmichael too."

"Red sedan, third row back. He tried to duck when I saw him."

"Tried to?"

"His shoulder belt was still fastened, and it tightened up on him. Snapped his head forward pretty good."

That explains why he was rubbing his neck when I noticed him. Poor guy, he got whiplash from a seat belt in a stationary car."

"Yeah," Jack said. "I don't envy him having to file that workers' comp claim."

* * *

Jack stood at the front of a college science lab full of students. Most appeared to be between the ages of eighteen and twenty-five, but two stood out as different. A woman in her forties sat in the front row, leaning slightly forward, smiling, and taking in her surroundings with great enthusiasm. In the back row, a man in his seventies leaned back in his chair with the air of a man who has seen it all, done it all, and didn't enjoy any of it.

Along with a sink and several pieces of scientific equipment, each lab table had a PC, but not the standard big-manufacturer bulk-purchase boxes Amber expected to find at a community college. Some looked like hot rods, others like Megatron's internal organs. Most had glass panels showing off their components, and all of them pulsated with colored lights.

Amber checked her shot framing on the camera's screen and nodded to Jack. "Ready when you are."

"This is Professor Duane Fiscus." Jack gestured toward a portly man in a lab coat. "A lab instructor here at NCC. How long have you been teaching science, Professor?"

"Twelve years, but only five as my primary occupation."

"Teachers are underpaid, even at the community college level. You finally started making enough to support yourself as an educator five years ago, then?"

"No. I gave up trying five years ago. Teaching has been a sideline since then. My main gig is building custom gaming PCs and selling them online."

"Good for you," Jack said. "I certainly appreciate you and your class analyzing the infamous Pennington Portrait. Have you found anything unusual?"

"Yes. It's very interesting. Who would like to share our findings with Mr. Owens?"

The younger members of the class remained still and silent; the old man at the back sank down further in his seat and folded his arms; but the woman in her forties raised her hand with such enthusiasm that Amber feared she might dislocate her shoulder.

Professor Fiscus said, "Ramona."

Ramona kept her hand up for several seconds as she said, "Thank you, Professor. Where would you like me to start, Mr. Owens?"

"At the beginning, wherever you feel that is, Ramona. And please, call me Jack. I can't help but notice that you have a plastic tarp draped over the painting. Does that mean you found it to be toxic?"

"No, Mr. Owens, just ugly. We took a vote and agreed we'd rather not have to look at it more than necessary. But with the professor's help, we ran several tests to see if we could detect any toxicity."

The old man in the back lifted his hand just slightly above the level of his own eyes and began talking before anyone even had time to consider calling on him. "Of course, now, this kinda thing might fly here in your fancy college, but I spent fifty-odd years out there in the real world doing real work, and I'm here to tell you, out there ain't nobody gonna do a job like this for you for free, I don't care how good of an educational opportunity it is."

Professor Fiscus said, "You've said that already, more than once, Bill."

"Yeah, but I ain't said it to him." Bill pointed at Jack.

The professor said, "And now you have. Please continue, Ramona."

"Thank you, Professor. First, we got to use the school's Geiger counter. The painting wasn't radioactive. Then we put it in an airtight chamber to capture any fumes it might be letting off."

"And the result?"

"Now the airtight chamber stinks of cigarette smoke, but we found no toxic vapors. We wondered, though, maybe you can answer a question for us. The painting's supposed to have killed several of its owners. How many of them were smokers and died of cancer?"

Before Jack could answer, Bill grumbled, "And I told you, even if they died of cancer, you can't blame it on the smoking. Cancer comes for all of us, eventually. Life's just a race to see if anything else can kill you before cancer does. If you live long enough, you'll die of cancer."

A young man with stiff hair and dead eyes who also sat at Ramona's lab table muttered, "There's something to look forward to."

Ramona said, "I know you're kidding, dear, but you shouldn't joke about your death like that."

The young man jerked a thumb back toward Bill. "I wasn't talking about mine."

Jack said, "So, Ramona, it sounds like you found nothing."

"But I'm not done yet, Jack. We did a spectrographic analysis of the paint itself, and that's when we found something very interesting."

Professor Fiscus said, "I have the results here on my computer."

"Excellent. Please tell me about it."

"It's one of my powerful but reasonably priced bespoke gaming rigs. It has an ASUS motherboard—"

"The findings, Professor. Please tell me about the findings."

Professor Fiscus led Jack to his desk. Amber followed to get a shot of the results as well. On the desk sat a massive PC, with a screen three times wider than it was tall, a pair of speakers like glossy black shoe boxes, and a PC case the size of a tombstone, painted with flames coming up from the bottom as if it were burning up upon re-entry. Fiscus pressed the space bar, which made a loud clack like a tiny shotgun blast. The PC case came alive with spinning fans, their blades glowing with LED light that pulsed and changed color in unison. FISCUSTOMS.COM and a QR code appeared on the screen before the professor pulled up a window with an image of the painting and a list of chemicals. In the image, the painting's colors looked much darker than usual, except for the very light areas such as the man's shirt, the ghost, and other highlights, all of which glowed bright red.

Ramona said, "Using spectroscopic analysis, the professor showed us how to find out what materials are in the paint, and as you can see, we found titanium. They use titanium in white paint, but Becky said that they didn't start using it until the 1920s."

Ramona pointed at a young woman in a dark gray sweatshirt who seemed to get smaller when the room's attention turned to her.

Ramona said, "We looked it up, and she was right!"

Jack said, "And you just knew that off the top of your head, Becky?"

Becky said, "Mmbuh."

Jack said, "Well, that's very impressive."

Becky shrunk down even further, rolled her eyes, and said, "Mmbuh," a little louder than before.

Ramona said, "So, do you see what this means, Jack? The painting is supposed to be from the 1840s, but there's paint in it that wasn't available until the 1920s. It isn't just retouching either. All the whites and highlights have titanium. That made us suspicious, so we did some internet sleuthing, and if you look at the back of the canvas, the color is too uneven. That suggests it was made in the twentieth century, then hand stained, we think with tea. This isn't the original painting. It seems like if the guy who owns it now knew that it wasn't the original, he would have mentioned it, or if he knew and was hiding it, he wouldn't have let us analyze it, so someone stole the painting and replaced it with this forgery without the owner knowing."

Jack said, "That really is quite a finding! Well done, everybody! Thank you."

Bill pointed a crooked, gnarled finger at Jack. "Yeah, you're welcome I'm sure, but you just keep in mind, this all might seem cut and dried here in this nice little college lab, but out there in the real world, where things are serious, the things that seem so clear in the lab usually don't hold up."

Ramona snapped, "Damn it, Bill, what makes you think this lab isn't serious?"

Bill said, "This computer on my table has a steering wheel."

Professor Fiscus looked into the camera. "That's a popular add on for your high-end custom gaming PCs. It's great for driving games."

Jack said, "And many other things, I'm sure."

Professor Fiscus said, "No. It's only good for driving games. It's pretty much useless for anything else."

10

Jack stood in front of a low, wide house made mostly out of stacked stones and vast sheets of glass behind a lawn of uniform green grass with shrubs sculpted into perfect cubes.

Jack looked into the camera. "I have often found that many amazing revelations are waiting in plain sight, undiscovered, simply because nobody has bothered to look. For example, public records show that somebody stole the infamous Pennington Portrait and several other items from Hickory Hollow in the early nineteen-seventies. They recovered the other items later and convicted a household servant for the theft, but a local artist returned the painting much earlier, in exchange for a twenty-five-thousand-dollar reward, claiming a guilt-ridden thief gave it to him. The man who returned the painting used to live in the house behind me. Many years later, the authorities discovered that he was an art forger, but nobody ever connected the dots—until now. We're here to meet the forger's grandson, Marvin Partida."

Amber stepped back and to the side, changing the camera's point of view enough to include Marvin Partida, a tall man with thinning gray hair and a pencil-thin mustache.

Jack said, "Mr. Partida, thank you for agreeing to talk to us. I want you to know we don't plan to drag your family through the mud. We're just trying to get to the truth."

Marvin Partida said, "Of course. No worries. Grandpa has been dead for many years. If it's time for the world to hear his story, then so be it. Please, come in. I'll take you to his studio and we can talk about the wonderful old scoundrel in the room where he scoundred."

Marvin and Jack walked to the front door. Before she followed, Amber waved to Agent Carmichael, whose head was poking out from behind a tree three houses down. He waved back, grimaced, and pulled his head back out of view.

The inside of the house matched the outside: a beautiful, well-maintained example of what seemed tasteful and luxurious in the late nineteen-sixties.

Marvin beckoned them forward. "Grandpa's studio is this way. My father never cleaned it out. He said it felt disrespectful to his father. I always thought he was being silly, but now that I'm the one who could clear the room out, I find it feels disrespectful to both of them. Perhaps that's how traditions begin."

They passed through a door into an expansive room brightened by north-facing windows and multiple skylights. An easel stood next to a table holding a palette and dozens of tubes of paint, all of which looked as if they had been used as a restroom by a flock of technicolor pigeons. A couch draped with various velvet and satin throws and pillows sat opposite the easel. A few paintings in various styles hung on the walls. Amber saw landscapes, still-lifes, elegant black-and-white line drawings, strikingly colorful modern pieces, and even a portrait in the style of the old masters. Completed canvases leaned against the wall in deep stacks. The paintings at the front of each stack all appeared to be nudes.

On the easel was a framed black-and-white photograph of a tall man, impeccably dressed, with a perfectly styled mane of jet-black hair and a pencil-thin mustache.

Marvin Partida looked at the photograph. "That is my grandfather, Servando Partida: fine artist, master forger, and seducer of women. This is the studio where he did all of those things."

Jack turned to look at him. "Seducer of women?"

Amber said, "That's not what we came to discuss."

Jack said, "We're here to follow the clues, no matter where they lead; and get to the truth, no matter what it might be. Now, Mr. Partida, please tell me the truth about your grandfather seducing women. How many women are we talking about?"

"A great many. He would offer to paint them, bring them here, pour them some wine, then render them not as they were, but as he saw them, as he knew they wanted to be seen. He said that it was his pleasure to send each young lady home with a beautiful painting and a beautiful memory. After they left, if he . . ." Marvin looked warily at the camera. "How do I put this? If he found the encounter to be, let's say, complete and successful, he would paint another copy of the portrait for himself."

"As a trophy."

Marvin looked taken aback. "As a keepsake."

"Did the family keep them?" Jack asked.

Marvin gestured toward the stacks of canvases on their sides on the floor, leaning against the wall.

Jack looked at the countless artworks and asked, "Those are—?"

Marvin said, "Yes."

"How many of them?"

"All of them."

Jack looked at the paintings, then at Marvin, then back to the paintings, then at Amber, a look of uncertainty and temptation on his face.

Amber shook her head.

Marvin said, "Please, feel free to have a look at them."

"Well, if you insist!" Jack hurried to the canvases.

Amber said, "Jack, this isn't why we're here."

Jack began flipping through the canvases one by one. "Maybe it's not why you're here."

"We came to find out if Mr. Partida's grandfather might have forged the Pennington Portrait."

"My priorities have shifted."

Marvin said, "If by the Pennington Portrait you mean that ghastly painting of the man's ghost rising from his body, then I can tell you for a fact that my grandfather forged it."

"Good," Jack said, absentmindedly. "See, Amber? We're getting to the good stuff here. The really good . . . good . . . stuff."

Amber asked, "Did your grandfather steal the original?"

"Never! My grandfather was not a thief. He would never steal a painting. Why would he bother? If he saw a painting he liked, he could paint a copy himself, and it would usually be better than the original. If he had stolen a painting, I can promise you it wouldn't have been that hideous thing. No, he heard it was stolen and that there was a fat reward, so he got his hands on a few photos of the original, whipped up a copy, returned it to the Penningtons, and accepted the twenty-five thousand dollar reward that they never missed."

"Which is fraud," Amber said.

"I said my grandfather wasn't a thief. I never claimed he wasn't a fraud. He said it was the easiest money he ever made. The hardest part was replicating the nicotine staining. He used up all of his ochre."

"But weren't they suspicious when an art forger just happened to find their painting?"

"They didn't know he was a forger yet. He was in the yellow pages as a portrait artist. Whenever someone came in to hire him, he'd quote them an outrageous price. If they accepted, he made good money. If they didn't, he had more time to forge and entertain his lady friends, and his reputation for being expensive explained to the neighbors how he lived so well."

As Amber considered this, the conversation lapsed for a moment. She turned to Jack, still standing with his back to the others, head bowed, staring at the paintings. Amber asked, "Hey, Jack. Do you have any questions for the man you're here to interview?"

"Yes! I do!" Jack pulled up a painting of a blonde woman with a bob haircut, stretched out nude on the same couch that still sat in the corner. "This painting. It looks a lot like—"

Marvin said, "It is."

"No!"

"Yes. She was filming a movie in the area."

"Seriously?"

"The names and dates are written on the backs. Lower right corner."

Jack whipped the canvas around and read the back. "Wow!"

Marvin smiled. "Look at the third stack from the left, ninth painting in."

Amber said, "Mr. Partida, you said nobody knew your grandfather was a forger yet."

Jack blurted, "Holy crap! It can't be!"

Marvin said, "It is."

Jack let out a groan. "Oh man, when I was a kid, I used to watch reruns of *Charlie's Angels*. Now here I am, looking at this."

Amber ignored him. "Your grandfather was caught, eventually. How did that happen?"

"Some insurance company finally tracked him down. Grandpa never went into specifics about it. In exchange for him telling them all of his secrets and never forging a painting again, they let him off without prosecuting him. He told them about most of his forgeries, but they kept it quiet."

"Why?"

"If you tell a wealthy customer that their painting is a forgery, they lower their insurance policy, or cancel it entirely. If, on the other hand, you sit on that information until after the forgery is stolen or destroyed, you can keep the premiums high but not pay out if there's a claim, saying that in your investigation of the loss, new information has come to light. And yet my grandfather was the one facing prosecution, eh?"

"Did he keep his word not to paint fakes anymore?"

Marvin looked at the camera and smiled for a second. "Yes. He never painted another forgery. That said, his earlier works hang in museums around the world with other, more famous names attached."

"What did he do then? Did he have to start actually painting portraits for a living?"

"Heaven forbid. No, he sold a few paintings under his own name, but he also created two fictional artists who painted in styles different from his own and sold paintings under their names as well. I remember once he told me, 'These days it's hard for an artist to make ends meet. But three artists can do pretty well.'"

Amber said, "It's a shame he never wrote a book or anything. You know, told his story. He probably would have been famous. He was living a lot of men's dream."

"Yeah, he was!" Jack said while continuing to flip through the paintings. "What? You didn't think I was paying attention? Hey, I don't suppose you'd be willing to sell me any of these?"

Marvin said, "Come talk to me in twenty-three years. Grandfather stipulated in his will that none of the paintings were to be sold until fifty years after his death. He figured that would be long enough that most of the ladies would be deceased as well, or old enough not to care if it went public."

Jack pulled out his smartphone. "I'll put a reminder in my calendar."

Amber shook her head. "He was so worried about embarrassing these women, but he wanted to be sure people knew he had been with all of them."

"Not at all," Marvin said. "Or else he'd have displayed them when he was alive. No, he just understood that these paintings have less and less sentimental value for the family, but at a certain point, some of them will still have quite a bit of monetary value. That money can help benefit his family for decades after he's gone. My grandfather didn't want fame, but he knew it could add a couple of zeros to a painter's fee. That's why he used other, long dead artists' fame for himself."

"It seemed to work out well for him."

"Very well indeed. As you said, he lived his dream, many young men's dream. And when that ended, he lived a mature man's dream. In his forties, he married a lovely woman who adored him, stayed married, and as far as I know was faithful to her until he died, an old man with grandchildren constantly running around underfoot, pestering Grandpa to paint them a picture. He was nefarious, disreputable, and successful; and he was beloved, respectable, and successful. He led two charmed lives, and he managed all this because he fought the urge to tell people about it."

"And," Amber added, "just to put a fine point on it: he never had possession of the genuine Pennington Portrait?"

Marvin shook his head. "As far as I know, he was never even in the same building with it."

Jack said, "You say he married. How'd he meet his wife?"

"He painted her portrait."

Jack withdrew his hands from the stack of paintings he'd been perusing. The canvases tilted back against the rest of the stack with a soft whump. He pointed at the stack tentatively. "She's not in here, is she?"

"Lord, no! Grandpa removed her painting when they became engaged."

"Good," Jack said. "Glad to hear it. Me standing here oohing and aahing over these paintings, then finding out one of them was your grandma? That would have been uncomfortable."

Amber said, "Oh, like this hasn't been."

* * *

Jack stood on a sidewalk in front of a rusted chain-link fence, a patchy lawn, and wildly overgrown trees that dominated the property and hid a small house in shadows.

Looking into the camera, Jack said, "As we now know, someone stole the infamous Pennington Portrait in 1973, along with several other items of value. The Penningtons believed they recovered the painting, but they got a skillful forgery. After the fraudulent return, the case grew cold until 1975, when the other stolen items turned up at a local pawn shop. The police tracked the items to Andrew John Withers, a former groundskeeper and handyman at the Pennington estate. Easily convicted, Mr. Withers served five years, and passed away of a heart condition in the early 2000s. The police assumed that he felt remorse for stealing the painting and gave it to Servando Partida anonymously to return for the reward. We now know that assumption to be false, which makes Andrew Withers and his progeny our best lead in the questions of what happened to the painting and whether it is cursed."

The hinges groaned as Jack swung the gate half open, the furthest it would swing before scraping to a halt on the ground. He stepped sideways through the narrow opening and held the gate for Amber as she steered the camera through.

As they approached the screen door, a shadowy figure moved inside. A woman in her sixties in bare feet, well-worn jean shorts, and a white sweatshirt advertising Corona beer pushed the screen door open and said, "Come on. Ain't got all day."

Jack thanked the woman, and after he and Amber had both entered the house, he turned to the camera.

"This is Ellen Donavan, formerly Ellen Withers, the daughter of Andrew Withers. Thank you for agreeing to speak with us, Mrs. Donavan."

Ellen said, "Uh-huh."

"As I told you on the phone, we want to talk about your father and a painting. It's one of the items they say he stole from Hickory Hollow when he worked there in the seventies."

"Uh-huh. The one with the ghost, right?"

"Yes. That's the one. Do you know what happened to it?"

"No. I don't. No idea at all. Saw it once when I was a little girl and never saw it, heard about it, or even thought of it again."

Jack said, "That's a shame."

"Yup," Ellen said.

"Because we've contacted Max Pennington, the painting's rightful owner, and he said that since the man who stole it is long dead, he wouldn't pursue any legal action against whoever has it, and that if they returned it to him, he'd even be willing to match the original reward of twenty-five-thousand dollars."

Ellen said, "I've got the painting."

"Oh," Jack said. "May we see it?"

Ellen shrugged and walked out of the room.

Jack looked at Amber, amazed. Amber leaned out from behind her camera and mouthed, "I know!"

Ellen's distant voice called out, "You coming or what?"

As they followed, Amber filmed the inside of the home, which was packed with furniture and other things, but not as if Ellen were a hoarder or a collector. The impression was that over Ellen's entire life, whenever someone said "I've got something I'm looking to give away," she took it without bothering to ask what it was.

Ellen stood in the hallway, reaching up to grasp a pull cord dangling from the ceiling. A trapdoor above her opened and unfolded—accompanied by an off-key chorus of squeaking hinges and groaning springs—into a rickety wooden ladder leading into the attic.

Ellen pointed up at the rectangular hole above them.

Jack nodded, signaling that he understood that the painting was in the attic.

Ellen stared at him for a moment, then again gestured toward the attic.

Jack's shoulders sagged as he came to truly understand what she was telling him. He climbed onto the ladder. Halfway up he asked, "Where is it?"

She said, "Up there."

"Yeah, where up there? What part of the attic?"

"It's not a big attic."

"Fine, I know, but what am I looking for?"

Ellen said, "A painting."

Amber kept Jack in frame as he half-disappeared into the dark rectangular hole overhead. Just as he crested the ladder, she heard a loud thump, followed by Jack muttering curse words.

Ellen said, "Yeah, the rafters are pretty low. You'll want to watch out for that."

They heard another bump, then a series of thumping noises that went on for several seconds before ending in a dull rattling crash.

Amber called out, "You all right?"

Jack's voice came through the black rectangle in the ceiling. "Ugh! I'm okay! Hit my funny bone!"

Ellen said, "Well, don't do that."

Jack said, "Okay, look, where's the light up here? I can't find it. Is there a switch? Is there a pull cord? Help me out."

Ellen said, "There isn't a light. No need. You just bring a flashlight up."

The sound from the ceiling suggested Jack turning around and returning to the trapdoor. "You could warn a guy! How am I supposed to—" A loud snapping noise ended Jack's sentence. Instead of speaking, he yelped in surprise and pain.

Ellen said, "And watch out for the mousetraps. I don't wanna have to go reset all of 'em."

Judging from the combination of thumps, thuds, and crashes, Amber surmised that Jack had pulled the trap off his foot and thrown it across the attic before stomping his feet and hitting the rafters as hard as he dared. He let out a stream of sounds interrupted occasionally by recognizable bits of sentences.

"*Bah, gah! How am I, ugh, just tell me, aaargh . . and she's worried about the mousetrap!*"

Amber said, "He does this sometimes."

"Of course he does. He's a man, ain't he?"

The sound died down, replaced by heavy breathing. Amber asked, "Jack, do you have your phone?"

"Yeah."

"Does it have a flashlight?"

After a long silence, Jack grunted out a strained "Thanks." He fumbled around for a moment, and then the attic grew slightly lighter as he activated the flashlight.

Ellen shouted up, "It's on the floor, to your left. It's wrapped in a garbage bag."

Jack called down, "Yeah, I see it."

Amber asked, "The garbage bag is to keep the dust out?"

"It's to keep the smell in," Ellen answered. "The damn thing reeks of cigarette smoke. I don't want my attic to stink."

Jack appeared in the attic trapdoor. "You wouldn't want to make all the dust and mouse turds smell bad."

"Okay," Ellen said. "I don't want the attic to stink more. Pass the painting down, smart guy."

Jack passed the painting down. "I should really be wearing a respirator."

"You should be wearing a diaper, crybaby." Ellen took the painting through the kitchen and out to the backyard, leaving Jack to fold the ladder up and close the trapdoor. Amber held the ladder steady with one arm as he descended and helped him pat the dust off his new tweed jacket.

By the time Jack and Amber made their way to the backyard, Ellen had removed and discarded the dusty garbage bag and propped the painting on a picnic table. It seemed identical to the one they'd seen at Hickory Hollow.

Jack said, "That's it! Amazing!"

Ellen said, "Yeah. Isn't it? Now, about this reward. Do you think he'd be willing to pay it under the table? I don't want the taxman to come take it all."

Jack said, "You'll have to take that up with his lawyers."

"So that's a no. Fantastic."

"Your father, he must have seen the painting hanging on the wall there at Hickory Hollow, and he . . . how do I put this?"

"He swiped it."

"Yes. Did he ever say why?"

"He had to have it. He thought it was the best thing he'd ever seen, and he wanted it for himself. I don't have any idea why. I think it's awful. Mom always said that it just goes to show, you never know what worthless piece of crap you're gonna fall in love with." Ellen shook her head and laughed bitterly. "It figures that would be the one thing she was ever right about."

Jack asked, "Was she talking about your father and the painting or her and your father?"

"Both."

"So your dad decided he needed the painting. How did he take it? Was it spur of the moment, or did he have a thought-out plan?"

"Do you think a man who would steal this thing ever thought anything out? He waited till he was alone with the painting, yanked it down off the wall, and split."

"Was he a thief before that?"

"No. If he had been, he probably would have been better at it."

"But the painting's not all he took."

"He thought if he just took the painting it would be more likely that they'd suspect him, so he grabbed a bunch of other stuff on the way out. Some silver. A vase."

"But they did suspect him."

"Of course they did. He tried to cover up stealing something by stealing other things too. It didn't occur to him that each crime was another chance to get caught. He wasn't exactly Danny Ocean. That's why I told my boys, if you're gonna steal something, just steal one thing."

Jack let out a short laugh. "But do sons ever listen to their mothers?"

"No, they don't," she said. "The Penningtons knew he'd done it, but they couldn't prove it at first, so instead of arresting him they fired him and made sure he couldn't get a decent job anywhere else."

"That must've been hard."

"We scraped by. Mom worked. He did odd jobs. But the bills kept coming. When the heat seemed to die down, he risked trying to pawn the other stuff he'd took."

"And the cops found out and arrested him?"

"Within twenty-four hours. He went off to prison and left Mom alone to support me and my big brother until he split too."

"He got a job and moved out?"

"He got caught boosting a car and went to juvie."

"That's terrible."

"Eh, Mom didn't have to pay for his food or clothes for a while. But two mouths were still one mouth more than she could handle. I saw that my family pretty much sucked, so I got pregnant, got married, and got out. Of course, nine months later I was right back in a sucky family, but as the mother this time around instead of the kid."

"When your father got out, I hope he was some help."

"He tried, but he wasn't exactly the belle of the ball at any job interviews. They'd see that he'd been in prison for stealing from his employer, and their next question would be 'How soon can you leave?'"

Jack said, "In a way, this painting is as important to your family as it is to the Penningtons."

"The day Dad decided he had to have it was the day the whole family went to shit, so yeah, I suppose you could say it's important."

"You understand, in order to collect the reward, you're going to have to return the painting."

Ellen laughed. "What a shame. The attic won't be the same without it."

11

Amber and Jack stood in the portrait gallery at Hickory Hollow, looking at the two versions of the infamous Pennington Portrait as they waited. Max Pennington talked in hushed tones to a grim-faced contractor, who shook his head, shrugged, and looked down at Max's shoes. Max put his hand on the other man's shoulder. It struck Amber as odd, seeing a small man in an immaculately clean tracksuit comforting a large man in well-worn work clothes and a hard hat. The contractor handed Max a small cardboard box, and the two parted with a handshake. The contractor left, and Max approached Amber and Jack.

Jack said, "Architects sell you a dream. Contractors wake you up."

Max chuckled, then stifled a cough. "He's a good man, with bad news. The price tag for the renovation just doubled. It seems the hollow part of Hickory Hollow is filled with asbestos. In the old days, they used to insulate heating ducts with the stuff; back when Grahame Pennington had the HVAC installed, he saved money by just making the ducts themselves out of asbestos. Turns out it's possible to be too innovative."

"Is it safe to be in here," Amber asked, "you know, breathing?"

"The real danger was when the system was new, or any time any of the ducts gets jostled. Still, I'm told we should wear these." He reached into the box and pulled out three respirators. They all put them on.

Amber said, "I'm sorry. That's terrible news."

Max shrugged. "It just means more money and more time. It's a minor inconvenience."

"Minor?" Jack asked. "Where will you stay while they fix this place?"

"Probably our vacation house, after I've had it checked for asbestos as well."

"Where's that?"

"On the beach in Miami."

"Yeah, okay," Jack said. "That is a minor inconvenience."

Max rubbed his hands together. "We can't let that bring us down. This is a happy day! You've returned a priceless family heirloom and given me a great story to tell. To thank you, I'd like to buy a whole bunch of advertising space on your show and sponsor this video when it gets posted."

Amber said, "I'm sure we can work something out."

"Excellent," Max said. "Since we're getting out of tobacco, I'll have to talk to the marketing department to see which of the businesses we're diversifying into will be the best fit for your demographic: the dispensaries, the legal marijuana farms, or the flavored vape cartridges."

Jack said, "I suggest the dispensaries. Talk radio draws more than its share of glaucoma sufferers."

"We'll take that under advisement," Max said, then coughed.

The three of them looked at the paintings side by side.

Max asked, "The original is on the left?"

Amber and Jack both said, "Yeah."

Max sniffed the air, turned his head toward the original, and sniffed again. "You can tell by—"

Amber said, "By the smell, totally."

Jack said, "Can't miss it. Even through a respirator."

They looked for a few moments more, until Max said, "And you can tell by looking at them. They're the same image, but one of them is painted much more skillfully."

Amber said, "The forgery."

Max said, "Yes."

* * *

Amber sat in the driver's seat of their rental car, playing with one of her cameras, as Jack sat in the passenger seat, staring down at his laptop. After a quick burst of key presses, he said, "Okay, just let me look this over one more time and I'll be ready to record the outro."

Amber said, "Good! I mean, don't rush. But good." She took a quick look at her smartwatch and frowned.

"Brian still hasn't texted?"

"No."

"Good. You don't want to talk to him anyway. I say good riddance."

"You're right. Totally. I have nothing to say to him, and I don't want to hear anything he wants to say to me."

Jack said, "But?"

"I'm over him. Completely. I'm just not quite ready for him to be over me. Does that make sense?"

"You still care about him, in that you want him to suffer."

"Yes. I'm a terrible person, aren't I?"

"Yes, just like the rest of us. That said, you should try to get over your instinct to hope that he's unhappy."

"Yeah, I know it doesn't make me a better person."

"That's not what I'm getting at. To hell with being a better person. You're already good enough. I'm saying if you really want him to be miserable, the best way to make that happen is to not actually care what happens to him at all. The best revenge is not giving a crap. Look at me. Plenty of people have screwed me in my career, but I've won. I've won because they all know that I'm more successful than they are, so they assume I'm happier, too. And the thing they know, deep down in their bones, the certainty that keeps them awake at night, is that I have forgotten all about them. I don't remember their names, remember their faces, or know if they're alive or dead."

Amber stared at Jack. "Really? You're being serious about this?"

"Of course. Why wouldn't I be?"

"Because you're clearly still furious at all of them, Jack."

"True, but they don't know that, and you're not going to tell them! Understood?"

"Jeez."

"Understood?!"

Amber rolled her eyes. "Yeah, yeah, understood!"

"Good! Don't screw me on this, Amber."

"I won't! You know, it's possible that your lack of trust in other people leads you to always get shafted, like a self-fulfilling prophecy."

"Or I don't trust anybody because everybody bones me eventually."

"Could be. Which one do you think it is?"

Jack thought for a few seconds. "The second one, because that wouldn't be my fault."

Amber lapsed into a momentary silence before asking, "You ever notice how many of the words we use to describe ripping someone off or sabotaging them are also words men use to refer to having sex with women?"

"Yup, and what does that tell you about our self-esteem as a gender? Okay, I'm ready to go."

They got out of the car. Jack stood in the exact spot he'd stood in for the introduction, with Hickory Hollow in the background, only now the asbestos abatement workers were busy covering the old mansion in plastic sheeting.

Amber took a moment to compose her shot. "Start whenever you like."

Jack looked into the camera. "In the end, of course, there is no scientific evidence that supernatural curses are real. Normally I would point out that there isn't proof that they aren't real and leave it at that, but now I think perhaps the words 'scientific' and 'supernatural' may both be limiting our thinking."

Jack paused a moment, as if thinking about what to say next.

"I ask you, what is a curse? We've met members of three families affected by the actions of three men, all long dead. One left a legacy of affluence and power enjoyed by his progeny, at the cost of their consciences and their health. Another man made a mistake that has reverberated through time, harming himself, his children, and his children's children. The third man changed his life and struck out in a more positive direction. That man's grateful offspring venerate and celebrate him to this day. To those who want a supernatural explanation, I point out that the family with the positive outcome was the only one that never had possession of the painting. Is it a coincidence, or the curse of the infamous Pennington Portrait? Either way, we seem to end up paying for our ancestors' mistakes, and *that's not right.*"

Amber said, "Very nice."

"Thanks. You don't think the 'that's not right' was a little forced?"

"Eh, no more than usual."

"That was not a compliment."

"It was very good, Jack. Thought-provoking. And every word of it was true, so the agent from Acronym should approve."

"You think so?" Jack raised a hand to his brow to shield his eyes and scanned the distance. He saw Agent Carmichael stand up from inside a bush, easily two football fields away, and give him a thumbs-up.

Amber pointed her camera at him and zoomed way in for a better view. "Can he hear us?"

Carmichael nodded, then used two fingers to point at his own eyes and then at Amber and Jack to communicate that he was watching them.

Jack shouted, "Yeah! We know!"

Carmichael pulled out his earpiece and winced in pain.

Battery Boy

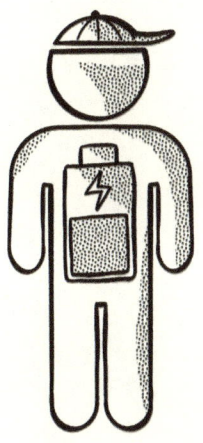

12

While Jack sat in the passenger seat, working on his intro, Amber reread the email she'd received from her immediate supervisor, Ivy Atkins.

Amber,

This will not be pleasant for you to read. It isn't pleasant for me to write. But I'm showing you the respect and courtesy of being honest. You are out on a limb. That limb is cracking. If you think I'll be able to grab your hand and keep you from falling, you're wrong, because I followed you onto the limb.

I hired you because I believe in you. I've watched every drunk-guy-golfing video you made. You did brilliant work then. We both need you to do some now. Shoot Owens as if he were a drunk guy golfing. Hell, get him drunk and take him golfing if you have to.

You hear about people begging for a second chance? The video you just turned in was it.

You also hear people talk about a third strike. Don't make the next video yours.

There are no common phrases I can think of about fourth chances.

Amber didn't like the idea that she had done her best work documenting the antics of her ex-boyfriend and his drunken buddies. All she'd done was point a camera at them and wait for stupid things to happen, then edit all of those moments together. She'd never suffered a shortage of material.

Jack said, "The intro's ready to shoot when you are."

Amber put her phone away. "Cool. Let's do it."

They got out of the car. Amber turned on her camera and composed a shot of Jack standing on the sidewalk in front of a lawn, dotted with trees, that led to a substantial two-story red brick building.

Jack looked into the camera and, after receiving the nod from Amber, began his introduction.

"Behind me is the prestigious Breckwood Academy of New Milford, Connecticut, an expensive private school for the diligent children of ambitious parents. One such parent is Dr. Erin Frolick, a neurobiologist with many bold ideas and a willingness to take risks. Of course, to be truly groundbreaking, ideas need to work. Risks must pay off. We're here to find out if hers do, because she has risked the most precious thing in the world to any mother: her child. A young lad my listeners like to call Battery Boy."

Amber said, "Very nice."

"Thanks."

A woman and a young boy roughly nine years old waited in front of the door. The woman wore slacks, a stylish sweater, and a black beret tilted jauntily to the side. The boy wore a school uniform of shorts, a blazer, and a striped tie but had a rainbow-colored terry cloth sweatband on his head. Both stared at Amber and Jack from a distance.

Jack said, "Now let's see how convincing this kid is in person."

"You've interviewed him before," Amber said. "I listened to the show. He seemed pretty convincing."

"Yeah, but that's over the phone, on the radio, with a skilled host making him sound good. There's a world of difference between that and keeping the act up with a camera pointed at your face. There's a reason cheap lunch meat comes in a package that only has a little window on the front. It's harder to sell baloney when people can get a good look at it."

"You don't believe the Battery Boy is real?"

"I believe there is a boy, and I'm reasonably sure there's a battery. Beyond that, I have my doubts."

"So you're calling him a liar."

"I'm calling his mother a liar. It's possible that he believes her lies and passes them along, thinking they're true. I'll give him the benefit of the doubt and call him a stooge."

Amber said, "Doubt doesn't have much benefit."

"This doubt doesn't."

"But do you really think a parent could talk their kid into believing they have superhuman abilities?"

"Parents have to talk their kids *out* of believing they have superhuman abilities. The day a child discovers Superman is the day their parents start listening for the sound of footsteps on the roof. Kids are gullible. It's one of the things their parents love about them. And all kids are prone to believing that they're special anyway, because life hasn't taught them they aren't yet."

Jack and Amber walked up a brick path to the school. The entire facility projected an effortless air of old-money respectability.

Amber hung back to catch Jack approaching the school and greeting the doctor and her son, the Battery Boy.

Jack said, "Hello. I'm Jack Owens," and extended a hand.

As the woman stepped forward to take Jack's hand, the boy looked up at Jack with his head tilted slightly to the right and said, "Dupe."

Jack said, "I'm sorry, what?"

The boy said, "*Dupe*, Mr. Owens. If Mother had tricked me into believing a falsehood so that I would help her spread it, that would make me a dupe. A dupe is someone who has been fooled by falsehoods and subterfuge into doing things they otherwise would not. A stooge is a dimwitted oaf who follows another's orders."

Jack glanced all the way back at the sidewalk where he and Amber had conversed, then back to the boy. "Oh, you heard that."

"Yes. My hearing is excellent, but within the normal range for a person my age. That said, I also have 30/20 vision and above-average mental focus, which allowed me to combine the faint sound of your voice, the movement of your lips, and other context clues to parse every word you said. Hardly what I'd call superhuman abilities—just excellent-human abilities, and evidence that Mother is not fabricating her results."

Jack said, "I, uh, I suppose you might be right."

"I am."

"You certainly have a tremendous vocabulary for someone your age."

"Thank you. I read at approximately the level of someone in their mid-forties."

Jack smirked. "I'm in my early fifties."

"Yes," the boy said. "Reading speed and comprehension peak when a person reaches their mid-forties. After that it declines."

"Oh."

"Rapidly."

"Kid, do you ever blink?"

"Of course, Mr. Owens, when it's necessary."

The woman shook Jack's hand. "That's enough, Balthazar. Mr. Owens, I'm Dr. Cynthia Frolick. I apologize for my son. He's perceptive enough to never miss an insult, sensitive enough to take them rather badly, and smart enough to retaliate, as you just learned. It's nice to meet you in person, Mr. Owens. I have to admit, you didn't seem so skeptical when you interviewed us for the radio."

Jack said, "My job is to allow you to state your position and let my listeners decide. That's what I did on my show, and that's what we're going to do in the video. That doesn't mean I don't form my own opinions. You've made some big claims. I think it's understandable that I'm skeptical."

Dr. Frolick tilted her head slightly to the right as she looked at Jack. "Openly calling me a liar goes beyond skepticism, Mr. Owens. I'd say it's a sign that you've made up your mind. But no matter. I'm glad you're here to see my results in person. I look forward to your apology. Please follow me."

They followed Dr. Frolick into the school. Amber, as usual, stayed well behind, capturing Jack walking with the scientist and her child. Even if she hadn't already known where she was, Amber would have instantly recognized the hallway as an elementary school. She had expected something fancier from a private academy like this, as compared to her relatively rural California public school, but here was the same basic architecture finished with the same linoleum tile floor and acoustic ceiling. She supposed that even rich and gifted children were messy and loud.

Dr. Frolick said, "I don't blame you for having your doubts, Mr. Owens. The results I've achieved sound too good to be true, and sound is all you've had to go by—a conversation with me and Balthazar on your show. Now you're here. You can see for yourself and understand the importance of my work."

"You're confident of that?"

"Completely, because it's happened before. The parents of Balthazar's classmates, many of them were skeptical as well, until they saw Balthazar's work and the results when their own children attempted to compete with him. Soon, they were lining up to ask that I allow their children to take part in my study."

"Wait," Jack said. "You're saying that you've started experimenting on other people's children too?"

"Balthazar," Dr. Frolick asked. "Is that what I'm saying?"

"Of course not, Mother. You would never say something that narrow-minded and prejudicial. You're saying that at their parents' request, you are allowing other children to take part in your exciting and highly beneficial work."

Jack laughed. "If nothing else, Balthazar, you have a great future ahead of you in advertising."

Balthazar said, "Take that back."

Dr. Frolick said, "He and his classmates are destined for great things, Mr. Owens. Here, look at this bulletin board. Every month, a different class decorates this board to call attention to something they think the other classes and grades will find interesting."

They had done something similar at Amber's school. She remembered coming home with ink on her fingers because she and her class had all drawn and cut out hand-turkeys that they'd stapled to a field of green construction paper in such a way that they spelled out the word "Fall." They tried to spell out autumn first, but they didn't have enough kids in their class, and thus not enough turkeys.

Jack, Dr. Frolick, and Balthazar stood looking at the bulletin board in silence. Amber walked around beside them to give the audience, and herself, a good look. What she saw only confused her. At the top of the bulletin board, many index cards formed a pyramid, with all the cards connected in a web of red yarn. The top card read, Asia: The World's Only Source of Natural Rubber. The next layer of the pyramid down, three cards bore the words Tires, Belts, and Assorted Latex Products. Below that, five cards bore the names of five industries: Shipping, Manufacturing, Automotive, Technology, and Healthcare. Below, many cards listed individual products made of rubber, and the next layer listed products that had those products as components.

By the fifth row down, there were too many cards to fit, and they had to be fanned like playing cards. Beneath the pyramid, blood-red letters spelled the words Total Economic Catastrophe.

Jack asked, "What am I looking at here?"

Balthazar looked up at him, disgusted. "Isn't it obvious? We made it as clear as we could. This chart demonstrates that all it would take is one rubber blight to cause the complete collapse of our entire civilization."

Jack looked at the board, then at Balthazar, then at the board again, then at Dr. Frolick. "Is that true?"

"What do you mean?" she asked. "Is it true that that's what the board says, or is it true that mankind is that dependent on one crop that we all take for granted?"

"I guess both!"

"The answer is yes. Though I see why you had to ask. The kids ask the viewer to make some logical leaps that might not be as obvious as they think. What do you expect? They're fourth graders. Come. Meet them."

"You brought some in on a Saturday?"

"They're already here. Class is in session, Mr. Owens. The school recently changed to a six-days-a-week schedule."

"How did the kids react to that news?"

"They thanked us for agreeing to their proposal."

Dr. Frolick walked to a door, peered into its window, then quietly swung the door open and put a finger over her mouth to tell the others they needed to be quiet.

Twenty children sat at little desks facing the front of the room. Balthazar left his mother's side and slid silently into his desk. The teacher stood at the dry-erase board, which bore a surprisingly detailed illustration of a sailing ship and a whale.

The teacher was a man in shorts, a yellow ball cap with a black B, and a yellow T-shirt that said Breckwood Bees with a cartoon drawing of a bee holding an A+ report card. He nodded to Dr. Frolick as she entered the back of the room but continued addressing the students, all of whom were sitting perfectly straight with their hands on their desks and wearing headbands.

"Okay," the teacher said. "So we know that in the end Ahab failed in his goal and died. Do any of you have any ideas why?"

Most of the kids' hands shot up. The teacher said, "Donald."

A boy said, "Lack of flexibility. He became too fixated on one goal."

The teacher said, "Good. Any other ideas? Vicky?"

"He delegated too much to Starbuck."

"Perhaps. What else, Lisa?"

"He offered a bounty to the first man to spot Moby Dick. That rewards luck, not skill, and was bad for morale."

"Valid. Raymond?"

"He became emotionally involved. He forgot that whaling is, at its core, a business."

"Very good! Gold star for Raymond. Now, class, we have visitors." The teacher beckoned Jack, Amber, and Dr. Frolick to come to the front of the room. "You all know Dr. Frolick, of course. She has brought Jack Owens. He hosts a show called *That's Not Right*, on radio. Have any of you heard of it?"

A boy raised his hand.

The teacher pointed to the boy and said, "Nathan?"

The boy said, "Radio is a communications medium, Mr. Hardin. Modulated electromagnetic waves are used to transmit sound."

Jack chuckled under his breath, but not far enough under, as everyone in the room stared at him. Amber noticed that many of the children tilted their heads to the right, just as Balthazar did.

Jack smiled. "I'm sorry. It's nothing. I liked your answer— Nathan, is it? Your description of radio is right on, but I think your teacher meant to ask if you'd heard of my show."

Mr. Hardin asked, "Is that what I meant, class?"

In perfect unison, all the children said, "No, Mr. Hardin."

Mr. Hardin said, "Don't feel bad, Mr. Owens. It was a trick I pull on them from time to time. I phrased that question in such a way that most people would jump to the conclusion that the word 'it' referred to your show, but if you really think about the way I worded the sentence, 'it' referred to radio. I do this to teach them not to make assumptions. Why, class?"

In unison, the children said, "Because assumptions are almost always bad."

"Almost always?" Jack asked.

Mr. Hardin asked, "Why do we say 'almost always,' Raymond?"

A boy said, "To believe that all assumptions are always bad would, itself, be an assumption, and would be bad, probably."

"Correct. Mr. Owens is here to learn about Dr. Frolick's work, so let's explain it to him. Where to start? Kelly, please tell Mr. Owens what flow state is."

A little girl said, "Flow state is a condition most people occasionally experience where ideas come easily, problems that are normally difficult seem simple, and memories are both created and retrieved with above-average clarity and ease."

Mr. Hardin pressed a switch on the wall that caused a projection screen to extend down from the ceiling. The lens of a projector hanging in the center of the room lit up. "Very good. What is a famous example of someone in flow state? Tim?"

A boy thought for half a second, then blurted, "Albert Einstein. He was sitting on a train, saw a clock tower out the window, and had a series of ideas, one right after the other, that led him to his theory of relativity. He said the thoughts came so quickly that it felt as though a storm broke in his mind."

"Very good. What's another example, Becky?"

"Jack Kerouac," a girl said. "He wrote the first draft of *On the Road* in three weeks, doing little else but sleeping and writing. It is believed that he kept himself in an artificial flow state by breaking open asthma inhalers and chewing on the drug-infused felt plugs he found inside."

"Correct," Mr. Hardin said, leaning over to tap the touchpad on his laptop while still grilling his pupils. His computer desktop appeared on the projection screen. "Is there a glaring difference between these two stories that stands out to you, Vanessa?"

"Yes. Albert Einstein waited for flow state to happen naturally. It occurred while he was riding a train. Kerouac created and sustained his flow state at a time and place convenient for him through the unauthorized use of dangerous pharmaceuticals."

"And what does that make Mr. Kerouac, Sal?"

"Brave?"

"Perhaps. What do you think, Kenny?"

"Smart?"

A girl raised her hand. The teacher pointed at her. "Bonnie?"

The girl said, "Both brave and smart."

Mr. Hardin smiled, "I like that answer. Now, who can tell me what this is?" He tapped his touchpad. On the screen, an image of a semi-transparent brain appeared. Brief flashes of blue light blinked at random inside the brain like a tiny lightning storm.

A sea of hands shot up. The teacher said, "Kelly."

A girl said, "That's an MRI of a person's brain performing mental tasks under normal circumstances."

"That's right." Mr. Hardin smiled at Jack and said, "They've seen these slides before."

The image changed to a different brain. This time, the blue lights blinked in a much more regular pattern. The synchronization was not perfect, but the overall effect was of a pulsing blue wave working its way from the back of the brain to the front.

Mr. Hardin asked, "And what's this? Kyle."

"That's an MRI of a person's brain while performing the same mental tasks while in flow state."

"Very good. And class, what is this?" The image of the brain disappeared, replaced by an exploded diagram of a terry-cloth headband like all the children wore, along with some other electronic components.

The children almost shouted in delight, "The Normalizer!"

"Yes," Mr. Hardin said. "Very good."

Dr. Frolick said, "We've given it that name because it normalizes the brain's activity. And it's catchy."

Jack said, "I certainly won't forget it."

Mr. Hardin said, "Nathan, please take the laser pointer and talk us through the Normalizer's components."

A boy walked to the front of the class, lifted a laser pointer from the dry-erase board's gutter, and pointed it at the screen.

"It is a simple device. These electrodes press against the user's right temple. They are connected to this printed circuit board, which generates a low-voltage electrical wave that normalizes the brain's activity, inducing and maintaining the flow state indefinitely. And this component is the battery that powers the apparatus. It is a rechargeable lithium-ion battery, though the original prototypes used a store-bought alkaline nine-volt battery, which was inexpensive and readily available but bulged visibly and caused part of the headband to slide down. The headband houses and conceals the apparatus. Though terrycloth is suggested, the style and color of the headband is left up to the choice of the child who wears it."

"Why are you allowed to choose your own headbands, class?" Mr. Hardin asked.

Again in unison, the children said, "To express our individuality."

13

Recess for Balthazar's electrically augmented class involved less shouting than one would expect from a group of playing fourth graders, but Amber didn't notice. She leaned against the wall next to the school's rear entrance as she reread that morning's email from her boss. Ivy Atkins had managed to strike an interesting balance between encouragement and threat, as if she knew in her heart that Amber could do the job—and if she was proved wrong would make Amber pay dearly.

Amber understood that the next video needed to be entertaining as well as informative. She thought back over the footage she'd captured so far that morning: Jack's intro, the conversation with Dr. Frolick in the hall, and the children explaining brain scans. Her heart sank.

At that moment, she received an email from Brian. Maybe he was still trying to get her back, both to his channel and into his life. Maybe he'd finally learned a lesson. Maybe losing this job wouldn't be the end of the world after all.

The email's subject was "You were right!"

That surprising admission, coupled with her low emotional ebb, was enough to get her to open one of his messages for the first time since they broke up.

Amber,
I know you probably aren't reading this, but if you are, I want you to know you were right. I can see that now.

Amber smiled.

The guys all took a stab at shooting and editing some content, and not one of them was even half as good as you. I finally had to face facts, swallow my pride, and hire a professional. He's great! He should be. He's charging me more than you asked for. That probably makes you happy.

Amber's smile had already faded away, and she couldn't imagine it coming back soon.

The channel is going to look so slick and professional! And because he's an employee, he has to listen to my ideas and do what I say. You always made us look like idiots, and because you were the one who did the editing and uploaded the videos, it was hard to stop you. Also, we were getting lots of subs, so why rock the boat? But when you left, you tipped the boat over, and now I've put it right, the way I think it should have been to start with. Here's a link to the first of our new, good videos. It goes out to the patrons tomorrow. I'm really proud of it. This wouldn't have been possible if it weren't for you, and I will always be grateful.

Amber followed the link. She recognized the back forty of Brian's parents' farm, but the blaring electric guitars and the girls dancing in swimsuits were new. As the opening titles ended, Brian stood on a back wheel of his father's John Deere as if it were a pile of his vanquished foes. He wore a ball cap and shorts and a thick layer of coconut oil on his bare torso. The camera angle caught his pelvis from the side, but he twisted at the waist to exaggerate any V-shape he might have. His usual gaggle of sycophantic buddies gathered around to look up at him, but several young women in bikinis also gathered around, and there was a large group of spectators, most of whom looked to be under eighteen.

"All right, men." Brian spoke in a tone nearly an octave deeper than his normal speaking voice. "Today's course is nine holes. Our usual rules apply, but the prize is new. The guy with the best score gets to lick whipped cream off of Kristen."

Kristen—a fit, outgoing blonde Amber remembered less than fondly from high school—jumped up and down in a swimsuit, holding a can of aerosol whipped cream while the spectators cheered.

Brian continued. "That's only part one of the prize. Part two is after the winner licks up the whipped cream, he baby-birds it into the guy with the worst score's mouth!"

Amber stopped the video, put away her phone, and muttered, "That's what he does when he's trying to not look like an idiot."

Jack came out the door smiling. "A different state, a different tax bracket, and forty years later, but the soap in the elementary school bathroom is still the same. Here, smell my hand."

"No, thank you."

"Yeah," Jack said. "I could tell that sounded bad as I was saying it. Never mind. Did you get footage of the battery boys . . . and girls . . . the battery kids playing?"

"Some, from a distance, you know, establishing shots, but I figured it'd be better to go in for a closer look while you're here, so you can make comments, interact with the kids."

Jack nodded. "They give you the creeps, and you didn't want to have to deal with them alone."

"Yeah, that too."

"Fair enough. Let's go."

From a distance, at a glance, the busy playground looked like those at schools all over the world. Things only seemed unusual when you looked closer, and not just because all the children wore headbands.

Four kids played catch, but each rode on a skateboard-like device that had two wheels and moved forward when the rider moved his or her rear leg back and forth to cause a propulsive force. The four kids rode in a circle with the precision, and joyless expressions, of a military drill team, all facing inward, throwing and catching four balls as easily as if they were standing still.

Nearby, on the playground equipment, children slid down the slide, swung across the monkey bars, walked the balance beam, and clambered up the net ladder. All the children did all those things, in that order. They formed a great circulating loop running from station to station and executing each activity so close to one another that each could have reached out and touched the kid in front of them.

Amber got footage of Jack watching, looking confused and amazed, but he hesitated to interrupt either group of children.

Off to the side, in the shade of a tree, one kid stood running through scales on a bassoon that was taller than him.

Jack approached the boy, who stopped and removed the reed from his mouth. "Can I help you, Mr. Owens?"

Jack said, "I was just wondering: This is recess. Shouldn't you be playing?"

"I am playing. I'm playing my bassoon."

"Yes. Okay. But why?"

"I need to practice."

"Fine, I guess, but why the bassoon specifically? Why pick that instrument? It isn't exactly a chick magnet."

"I'm nine, Mr. Owens. I'm too young to be thinking about chicks."

"Still, there must be a reason you picked the bassoon."

"College admissions. The best schools have orchestras, and there are very few bassoon players. Proficiency can help you get into your preferred school and acquire scholarships."

"The lad's right," Mr. Hardin said as he and Dr. Frolick approached, smiling. Amber had to crab sideways and rotate while zooming out to get them into the frame with Jack, the child, and the bassoon.

"I don't doubt it." Jack pointed to the kids still circulating around the playground equipment. "What are they doing?"

Mr. Hardin said, "Playing."

"Yes, but why are they playing like that, running around in a line?"

"It's the most efficient way. They all get an equal chance to enjoy all the facilities with the least amount of wasted time. You don't approve?"

Jack shook his head. "It's not my place to judge. It just doesn't look like they're having much fun."

"But they are having fun, Mr. Owens. The most fun possible. I'll show you the spreadsheet when we go back inside."

Dr. Frolick cocked her head to the right. "You seem troubled, Mr. Owens."

The adults left the boy to his bassoon and walked far enough from the playground to not be overheard.

Jack said, "I understand what you're doing. Well, 'understand' isn't really the right word. I don't understand what you're doing, but I do get why you're doing it. You want to give your kids every advantage. Fair enough. But what are you doing to their childhoods?"

"We're enhancing their childhoods," the teacher said. "These children are having the most efficient childhoods in history."

"Childhood isn't about efficiency."

"Perhaps yours wasn't, but who's to say that's better?"

"I feel like it was."

"Yes," Dr. Frolick said, "but you're the product of an inefficient childhood. In the end, only these children will be able to judge whether our experiment is a success, but they won't have the opportunity to make that determination if we don't perform the experiment. Besides, you've spoken to them, seen them at work and at play. You can't deny that our results are impressive."

Jack laughed. "You underestimate my ability to deny things."

Neither the teacher nor Dr. Frolick laughed back.

Jack cleared his throat. "But in this case, yes, I will grant you, what I've seen looks very impressive. But all kids can do things adults can't. They absorb information like sponges. They pick up languages by osmosis. And as for the physical stuff, when was the last time either of you tried to cross some monkey bars or a balance beam?"

The teacher said, "What these children are doing out here on this playground for fun demonstrates focus and intelligence far beyond what normal kids their age are capable of."

I'm not so sure," Jack said. "I mean, this all looks amazing, but when I was a kid, my friends used to play tag while riding full speed on bicycles, shooting each other with lit Roman candles."

The teacher said, "I'm not sure that would require focus or intelligence."

Dr. Frolick said, "Quite the opposite, I'd argue."

Jack said, "I give you the intelligence part, but trust me, we were plenty focused. I'm not saying you're wrong, or that you're lying, but some of my listeners—I'm sorry, viewers—will. They'll point out that everything we saw in the classroom could be achieved through rote memorization. I don't know how often you drill them on that stuff. As for what we're seeing right now, I don't know how long they've been practicing these games . . . tricks . . . whatever you want to call them. All we're looking at here, really, is juggling."

Dr. Frolick asked, "What would impress your viewers, Mr. Owens?"

"That's a good question. Something less prepared. Something that calls for thinking on their feet, improvisation, some real-world problem solving."

* * *

Ten minutes later, Jack sat on a too-small chair at a too-small table, across a chessboard from a too-small adversary, a girl from

Balthazar's class. The game table sat in the center of the room. Amber stood to the side, capturing both competitors in one shot. The rest of the class, Mr. Hardin, and Dr. Frolick sat around them in a circle, watching.

Jack turned to Amber. "Are you sure we can't use an adult-sized table and chairs? She could sit on a booster seat or something."

"Booster seat? We aren't at Denny's. Besides, this looks better."

"Really?" Jack asked, arching an eyebrow. "This looks better?"

"It depends on what you're after. It looks better for the drama of the situation, not for your dignity."

"And you wonder why I have trust issues. Okay, Kelly. I drew the light piece, so I go first." Jack moved the pawn in front of his king.

Kelly moved one of her pawns.

Jack nodded. "Ah, the Sicilian Defense."

Kelly furrowed her brow.

Jack spoke as he moved a knight. "You see, kids, when the player with the dark pieces moves that pawn, it's the beginning of what's called the Sicilian Defense."

Kelly moved another pawn.

Jack gave the board a quick once-over and moved a bishop. Kelly moved a bishop. Jack barely noticed. "When you see the other player start the Sicilian Defense, you just nod sagely and say 'Ah, the Sicilian Defense.' If the other player doesn't know about the Sicilian Defense, it'll make them think you know more than they do. If they do know about it, they'll think you're on to them."

Kelly said, "It's your move."

"Yes, I know." Jack peered down at the board and moved a bishop. Kelly moved one of her bishops.

Amber asked, "Jack, how do you counter the Sicilian Defense?"

"Dunno. I've never needed to. Frankly, I don't even know the rest of it. I figure if you identify it right off the bat, they'll abandon it anyway, and you'll be in their head. Remember, kids, that's where the game of chess is always won or lost: in the head."

Kelly repeated, "Your move."

"Yeah, sorry. Okay, let's see." Jack moved a pawn.

Kelly moved her queen. "Checkmate."

Jack's eyes darted around the board, his lips moving as he muttered "I go there, she goes there" several times in a row while looking at different pieces and squares. Finally, he leaned back in his too-small chair and said, "Huh. She's right. She's got checkmate."

Amber asked, "But does she have checkmate in your head?"

* * *

Jack sat in the same chair, at the same table, across from a different student, playing a different game, Go. Black and white pebbles covered the board. Amber didn't understand the rules, but she understood body language and context clues well enough to know that Jack was losing and had been since the third move. Finally, Jack leaned back and said to the headbanded boy, "Well played. Congratulations."

The boy said, "Thank you. I had an advantage."

"What's that?" Jack asked.

"You're not very good at Go."

Jack looked down at the boy, bit his lip, then in a voice that was only barely audible muttered, "Yeah, I'll tell you where you can go."

* * *

Jack loomed over the same table, now accompanied by three of the children, a girl and two boys, all peering down at a Monopoly board, the kids with their heads tilted slightly to the right. Jack rolled the dice. "Ha! Seven!"

None of the three children reacted at all.

Jack moved the little metal Scottie dog. "I avoid your row of houses on Kentucky, land on Chance, take a card, and look at that! I advance to Go and collect two hundred dollars!"

Jack moved his token to Go and said to the boy acting as the banker, "Instead of the cash, I'll just take four houses for Oriental Avenue."

The little girl playing said, "That word is considered a slur."

"I didn't name it. I just own it, and now I'm building houses on it."

The banker said, "You can't do that."

"What? Oh, I see. That's how you play it here, huh? Okay, I'll take the four houses and spread them evenly over all three blue properties, but the extra goes on Oriental too."

"No," the banker said. "You can't buy any houses. All the houses are taken."

"What?"

"There are thirty-two houses in the set. Other players have all of them, so you can't build any houses. None are available."

Jack laughed. "Oh, is that your problem? That's easily fixed."

"Is it?" the banker asked.

"Sure," Jack said. "Do you have any LEGOs? The little two-bump ones. My brother and I called them camels. They're a good size to use as a house."

The girl said, "The plural of LEGO is LEGO. The LEGO company prefers that you refer to multiple LEGO bricks as 'LEGO bricks.'"

"What? So one LEGO is a LEGO, but five LEGO is still LEGO?"

"No," the girl said, "Five LEGO *are* still LEGO, or preferably, LEGO bricks."

"Maybe that's what the LEGO company wants—*or companies, I suppose, since it's plural*—but people call them LEGOs."

"Yes," The girl said, "People are often wrong."

Jack laughed. "I can't disagree with you there. But anyway, not all LEGO pieces are bricks. Some are planks, or wheels, or little heads."

The girl said, "Now you're being pedantic."

"Oh, am I?" Jack asked. "Whatever. They make great houses. Do you have any? They don't have to be green."

The banker said, "That's not the way it works. There are only thirty-two houses, and if all of them are taken, nobody can build any more houses until someone either sells theirs back or upgrades to a hotel."

"Says who?"

"The rules."

"If you're gonna make up crazy house rules, you have to tell us at the start."

"It's not a house rule. It's in the official rules that come with the game."

Jack said, "You've actually read the printed rules that came with your Monopoly set?"

All three of his competitors, and all of the other kids in the room, said, "Yes."

"Why? Fine! Fine. Whatever. I'll just save up and jump straight to building hotels."

"You can't," the banker said. "The rules state that you must build houses, then build a hotel. You can't jump straight to a hotel without building houses first."

"So, you're telling me that all of you have houses, I don't, and as long as none of you slips up and lets one of the houses go, I can never get a house or a hotel?"

All three opponents said, "Yes."

"But my highest rent is, like, fifteen bucks. As soon as you got all the houses I was doomed to lose."

"No," the banker said. "When you agreed to play a game without knowing the rules, you were doomed to lose."

* * *

Jack sat in a chair, an adult-sized one this time, at the head of the class, next to four of the students, all sitting in chairs their own size. The teacher said, "The next word is for Mr. Owens."

Jack stood up.

Mr. Hardin said, "The word is 'chiaroscurist.' Chiaroscurist."

Jack thought for a long moment. "Can you please use it in a sentence?"

"The artist's exquisite use of chiaroscuro gained him a reputation as a fine chiaroscurist."

Jack thought for another long moment. "I pass."

Mr. Hardin said, "I'm sorry, you pass?"

"Yes."

Mr. Hardin looked to Dr. Frolick and to Amber before shaking his head, shrugging, and saying, "Okay. Kenny. Your word is chiaroscurist."

Jack sat down. Kenny, sitting next to Jack, stood up. "Chiaroscurist. C-H-I-A-R-O-S-C-U-R-I-S-T. Chiaroscurist."

The teacher said, "Correct."

Jack nodded. "Yes, that is correct, Kenny. Very good."

* * *

Balthazar stepped to the dry-erase board, drew an O in the lower right-hand box of the tic-tac-toe board, and then drew a line through three Os in a row.

Jack sputtered, "How? How did that happen? I went first! It's tic-tac-toe! The person who goes first always wins!"

Balthazar shook his head. "No. The person who goes first almost always wins."

"But how? How do you win if you go second!"

Balthazar pointed at the finished game board. "You do that."

Jack said, "Please excuse me for a moment."

Amber kept recording as Jack stepped out of the room, walked down the hall, and entered the restroom, where he could be alone. Because he still wore his radio microphone, she heard everything he said through her headphones. She stifled a small giggle as she reached down to her audio recorder and adjusted the volume so that Jack's shouts wouldn't top out the input.

When he finished, he left the restroom, walked back up the hall, and reentered the classroom.

"I think the problem," Jack said, "is that we're still just playing games they can win by memorizing strategies. We need something more chaotic. Something that will test the kids' ability to think on their feet. Something that you can't plan or study for."

"You want a game that requires no thought or strategy," Mr. Hardin said.

Jack said, "Yes."

"I don't know. Maybe the first-grade class has something. I could go check."

"Please do."

"Even if you win, what will that prove?"

"I don't know yet. But I'm willing to give it a shot and find out."

14

Jack stood in the hall, head hanging low, shoulders hunched, leaning against the wall, massaging his sore right wrist with his left hand.

Amber stopped recording to switch memory cards and asked, "How did they beat you ten times in a row at Hungry Hungry Hippos, Jack?"

"If I knew that, they wouldn't have beaten me ten times, would they, Amber?"

"Maybe. I don't know. If you had found a way to counteract whatever they were doing, they probably had a plan B waiting that would beat you even worse."

Jack shook his head. "Man, I really wish that weren't true."

Amber looked through the window in the classroom door at the children, sitting at their desks like disciplined military officers, facing the front, engaging with their teacher as he asked questions and wrote numbers on the dry-erase board. "These kids, they're impressive, but I don't like it."

"You don't like it? I hate it. I think the whole thing stinks."

"I'm not talking about the fact that they humiliated you, Jack."

"That's not what I'm talking about, either. The Normalizer clearly works, despite its cartoonishly sinister name. But at what cost does it work? Is it damaging their brains? And if it isn't doing physical damage, what's the result of spending your childhood in this altered state? And I was not humiliated; I was chagrined. Humbled at worst."

"No," Amber said. "You were definitely humiliated, but I agree with everything else you said. I think the best thing to do, both for the kids and for the video, would be to get a Normalizer and take it to some other neuroscientist. Maybe talk to a child-development specialist. And if it seems warranted, get the police involved."

"Yeah, that sounds about right. I think the best way to get one would be to just ask if we can have one. Maybe I say I want to try it."

Amber said, "I think it would be better to tell them the truth."

"I know you do, but I'm the one doing the talking. You rolling?"

Amber said, "One sec," powered up her camera and her sound recorder, and nodded at Jack, who opened the door and entered the classroom.

Mr. Hardin and Dr. Frolick stood at the front of the room with the dry-erase board, on which was written a line of seemingly random percentages. "Ah," the teacher said, "our guests have returned."

"Yes," Jack said. "And I think the best thing to do next would be—"

"If I may," Mr. Hardin interrupted. "While you two were out in the hallway, we were discussing the situation, just as an exercise for the class. Now, before you say anything, we'd like to explain our thought process and tell you our conclusions. We'll start with why the doctor and I agreed to let you meet the children and see their abilities. Lisa?"

Lisa said, "Because Mr. Owens and Ms. Cardoza will make a video that may gain many views, and even if it doesn't, Mr. Owens will talk about what he sees here on his radio show. When he reports that Dr. Frolick's work is genuine and yields these results, that will lead to increased funding for her work."

Mr. Hardin asked, "But why not just approach sources of funding directly?"

"Psychology. If you approach a backer, they see you as someone asking for their help. They hold all the power. If the backers find out about you in a public manner, you become a discovery to be secured, or a prize to be fought over, allowing you to negotiate a better deal."

Mr. Hardin said, "Very good. But there is a potential downside to showing them what we've all done here. What is that, Kenny?"

"They may suspect trickery, as is the habit of the slow-witted, because they are used to being tricked. They also may take a narrow-minded moralistic view that our choice to improve the functioning of our own brains is somehow wrong."

"And now that we've spent the morning with Mr. Owens and Ms. Cardoza, what do we think are the odds that they intend to produce a negative story?" Mr. Hardin asked.

The class, in unison, said, "Seventy-three percent."

Jack said, "Meaning that seventy-three percent of you think we're slow-witted or narrow-minded?"

Mr. Hardin said, "Stevie?"

A boy said, "No, Mr. Owens. That math would not work out in a class of twenty children. The percentage is not a measure of how many of us think you are slow-witted, and note, I did not say *or*; I said *and* narrow-minded. It is instead indicative of just how gullible and narrow-minded we all believe you to be."

"Oh," Jack said. "That's not any better, is it?"

Stevie said, "No. It is worse."

Mr. Hardin said, "Once we decided you probably intended to produce a negative story, we gamed out what your next move would be. Balthazar, please walk them through the permutations?"

Balthazar rose from his seat, walked to the front of the class, and picked up the laser pointer, which he used to draw attention to the first entry in the row of percentages written on the board.

"We determined that there was a seventy percent chance you would try to leave with one of our Normalizers to have it examined by lesser minds or to use as evidence against us. The percentages describing your more specific actions broke down thus: a forty-five percent chance you would pretend to want to try the Normalizer yourself, then attempt to make off with it somehow. A twenty-five percent chance you would simply ask if you could take an example with the stated intention of having it examined, and a thirty percent chance you would be so unnerved by what you've witnessed here this morning that you would simply flee."

Jack said, "I see."

Balthazar said, "Not yet, you don't. I'm not done. Upon our refusal to give you a Normalizer and your realization that you will not trick us into handing one over, we are certain your instinctive reaction will be to flee anyway. If you were to manage to escape the school, there's a ninety-five percent chance everybody will dismiss your story out of hand, because people expect your stories to be nonsense."

Jack said, "So there's no reason to stop us."

"On the contrary. If you flee from the school, it will represent only a five percent risk of harm but a one hundred percent certainty of missed opportunity. You're going to leave here eventually, one way or the other. It's to our advantage to make sure that you leave the right way: the way that gets us increased funding and possibly interest from the military."

"And how are you going to make that happen, kid?"

Balthazar said, "By giving you what you want, old man: a Normalizer of your very own. Only instead of having it analyzed, we're going to let you experience it firsthand."

"No, thank you. I look terrible in headbands."

Balthazar said, "There are other options," and motioned toward the teacher in his baseball cap and Dr. Frolick in her beret.

"No, sorry. Never been a hat guy."

"We know you're apprehensive about altering the function of your brain."

"Yes, I am, very much. I don't want your headband messing with my mind."

Balthazar blinked at him. "That's what I just said. Never mind. The point is, Mr. Owens, we know you're scared of altering your brain, but we're convinced that if you just try the Normalizer, it will change your mind."

Jack said, "So am I."

"Then you'll try it?"

"No!"

"Why not?"

"You said it would change my mind. That's specifically what I don't want."

"Mr. Owens, you might just be too dumb to outwit."

"How awful for you. What do you do about that?"

Balthazar said, "Stop bothering to try. Get him!"

All the kids stood up and walked toward Jack and Amber. Without a word, the two of them bolted out the classroom door. Amber hustled out into the hall. This being a small school, there was only the one hall, a long, straight passage with the large main entrance at the nearer end and the smaller rear exit at the other.

Jack immediately cut to his left, toward the main entrance, but slowed to a near stop and looked over his shoulder at Amber, who had bolted across the hall and stopped. He asked, "What are you doing?"

Amber stood by the wall, camera pointed at him, and shouted, "Getting the shot! You escaping! Go! I'm right behi—"

But they had delayed too long. A flood of headbanded fourth graders burst out of the classroom between Jack and Amber, who had little choice but to run in opposite directions, both shouting words the other could not hear as the fire alarm bell went off, drowning out all other sounds.

Amber ran as fast as she could, and luck was on her side. Her end of the hallway contained the cafeteria and the gym. It was not lunchtime, and the PE class was outside that day. She ran down the empty hall toward the doors at the far end. She reached a door and took the risk of pausing to get a quick shot back behind her as she exited the building.

The fire alarm had brought the other classes out of their rooms. They engulfed and surrounded Jack. All the children wore headbands. Jack stood, head and shoulders visible above the roiling sea of children, countless tiny hands gripping his arms and preventing him from fleeing or defending himself. She saw Dr. Frolick walking toward him, holding a headband high for all to see, and then she saw nothing but children running toward her.

The kids had the boundless energy of youth, but Amber was a full-grown, long-legged woman in her physical prime who had lettered in cross-country. As she accelerated to a run, the kids got within five feet of her, but she pulled away as she sped around the side of the building and to the parking lot. By the time she reached the car, half of the kids following her had stopped and were bent over, breathing heavily, and the other half were only close enough to be in danger of getting run over as she drove, tires squealing, out of the parking lot.

She nearly hit a guy on a scooter with the name Nice-Slice Pizza Delivery on its side. After that, she split her attention evenly between the windshield and the rearview mirror, but saw no cars leaving the school parking lot. She drove as quickly as she could without endangering anybody or drawing attention, about five miles per hour faster than the posted speed limits, which was the same speed she always drove anyway. Of course, she seemed to hit every possible red light, which is always the way when one is in a hurry, fleeing from a prepubescent mind-control cult.

She put the time waiting at lights to good use. First, she checked Jack's audio feed. Of course, she was well out of range of the radio mic now, but it had gone dead before she made it to the car, deactivated by the children.

As she drove to the next light, she considered where to turn for help. She had few options. She briefly considered contacting her boss, Ivy Atkins, for help or guidance, but Atkins was a marketing executive for a radio conglomerate. What help could she possibly offer? The best she could do would be to send a news crew from the local AM talk station. Besides, Amber's job was on thin ice already. Calling her boss with information that things were going badly and she didn't know how to handle it seemed counterproductive. At the next red light, she used her phone to get directions to the nearest police station. She had video footage of Jack being taken against his will. She figured that should be enough to get some sort of help.

The police station consisted of a red brick box with a set of glass doors, four large windows on the front, and a stripe of beige bricks around its middle to add style points. Amber parked, grabbed her camera and sound recorder, and ran through the front door.

She stopped running two steps into the lobby. An officer in a full uniform and hat sat at the front desk behind a long counter and a thick sheet of Plexiglas. She looked up at Amber and cocked her head slightly to the right. "Hello. Is there some problem, miss?"

"Uh," Amber sputtered. "I, uh, I want to report…something."

"What would you like to report?"

Amber looked around the lobby. Four other people sat in the waiting area on chairs bolted to the floor. All of them stared at Amber. Two of them wore hats.

Amber said, "Uh, you know what? I'm sorry. I think I'm in the wrong place."

Behind the reception officer, two more cops walked into view, both in full uniform, including hats. One asked, "Is there a problem?"

"No," Amber said. "No, sir. Nothing to waste your time with. Just that I'm in the wrong place, and that's no crime. Even if it were, I wouldn't report myself! Ha! I'm still here, and still talking! That's a . . . uh, that's crazy! Well, I'm going to go now. There's certainly nothing strange about that! Bye-bye!"

She backed out the front door and stood there as it closed, noting that the three officers were still staring at her through the glass door. She waved goodbye, saluted out of sheer awkwardness, then walked at top speed to her car. Inwardly, her mind screamed at the desperation and stupidity of her situation and the embarrassment at having said "bye-bye."

Schoolchildren had taken Jack, intent on forcing him to wear a mind-altering headband, and she was now actively avoiding the police, the very people she should be going to for help, because they wore hats. She put a hand against the roof of her rental car and sagged there for a moment, not knowing where to turn.

She stood up straight, and did not shout, but in a clear, loud speaking voice said, "Agent Carmichael?" She looked around. The police station sat at one end of the town's main street. A few pedestrians dotted the sidewalk on both sides of the street. Cars drove back and forth in both directions. Across the way and two doors down, the Nice-Slice Pizza scooter sat idling in a McDonald's parking lot. The rider took off his helmet. It was Agent Carmichael. He waved, then beckoned her to come over to him.

15

Amber sat in a booth across from Agent Carmichael as he watched the footage from the school on her camera's screen, picking at his burger and fries.

She said, "Please don't get grease all over my gear."

"I'm being careful."

"Not careful enough. Did you really need to get food?"

"It's part of the cover, and besides, it's wrong to take up a restaurant's table and not buy anything."

He watched a few more moments in silence, then put the camera down and leaned back. "Wow! Yeah, I can see why you're freaking out. And why you don't trust anyone wearing a hat. If I had left my helmet on, would you have come to me for help?"

"No. Even after you took it off, I looked for a headband. Where'd you get the scooter?"

"I have access to the full resources of the US government. Every time a local field office has to make something for a covert surveillance operation, they keep it, and if I can make a good enough case, I can use it. You wouldn't believe some of the stuff they have just gathering dust in storage lockers."

"Like what?"

"I can't tell you."

"What, or you'd have to kill me?"

"Of course not. But I might have to use some of it to hide from you one day. I will tell you this: the next time you meet a cute young guy in the park walking a large dog, be careful. It might be me."

"They can convincingly make you look like a cute young guy?"

"Or a large dog."

"And yet you really didn't know what was going on inside the school?"

"Nope. There are limits to my ability to monitor your conversations. I can't keep tabs on you in most buildings at the moment."

"At the moment?"

"Yeah, but once my requisitions go through, I'll know things about you that even you don't know."

"What kinds of things?"

"I have a friend who got reprimanded for congratulating a woman on her pregnancy before she knew about it."

"Ew."

"Yeah, not good. But it all worked out. He learned to be more careful, and according to the ongoing surveillance reports, she's a great mother." Carmichael took a drink from his large soda. "Diet Coke always tastes better from McDonald's. You ever notice that? Maybe you should investigate that. They might put drugs in it or something."

"I'll discuss it with Jack—you know, after his kidnappers release him."

"Huh. Kidnappers. 'Cause they're kids. I like that."

"You've had too much caffeine."

Carmichael looked at his large beverage. "That's the first I've had all day. This is all adrenaline. Riding that scooter is terrifying. It's like whizzing around in traffic on a barstool. Okay.

I'll focus. As you know, this falls outside Acronym's purview. That said, if you can edit together a greatest-hits version of the video you shot, I can send it to my superiors and we might get some help. Just include the important parts. The kids explaining how the headbands work, some footage from the playground, them taking Jack hostage . . . and I suggest you throw together a quick montage of the kids beating Jack at all of those games."

"To show that the kids are a threat mentally and physically." Amber pulled her laptop out of her bag, put it on the table, and cracked her knuckles.

"Yeah, and also to make sure they watch the video and share it around. Jack getting madder and madder as the kids keep demolishing him? That's gold right there."

* * *

Three hours later, camera rolling, Amber and Agent Carmichael—still in his pizza delivery uniform—stood on the sidewalk in front of the school, accompanied by two representatives of the CIA, four agents from the nearest FBI field office, three scientists from DARPA, seven Army Rangers, four Navy SEALs, and truckload of Marines. Aside from being representatives of the US government, they all had three things in common: they all wanted to save Jack, they all wanted to discuss the applications of the Normalizer with Dr Frolick, and they all wanted Amber to know how much they had enjoyed the montage of the kids repeatedly beating Jack.

When so many representatives of so many agencies and branches of the armed forces arrived, there seemed to be a genuine risk of a vicious battle between them just to see who would get to confront the schoolchildren. After several phone calls, it was decided that the CIA would take charge. They and DARPA would take joint custody of Dr. Frolick. The FBI would get the school faculty, the Army would transport the kids to the local authorities, and every agency and service branch represented would get at least three Normalizers to analyze and reverse engineer.

One of the Army Rangers asked, "Okay, so what's the plan?"

A CIA agent said, "S-O-P. We call the school to negotiate. If we can talk them out, great. If we can't, we go in."

The Ranger asked, "And what if they resist?"

The CIA agent shrugged. "They're kids."

A Marine piped up, "They should be easy to subdue."

The CIA agent said, "I was going to say that we don't want to hurt them."

The Marine said, "Yeah, of course. We don't want to hurt them. But if we have to, it'll be easy."

A Navy SEAL said, "Typical jarhead. Shoot first and ask what's for dinner."

The Marine said, "The school has a swimming pool. You SEALs can go secure that while we do the real fighting."

"Against the schoolkids, you mean?"

"If they resist."

The CIA agent handed Amber a phone. "You should make the call. They know you. I'll be listening in, but I won't say anything at first. Don't make any requests or any threats. Just tell them who you are, ask if your friend is all right, then introduce me, and I'll negotiate. Okay?"

Amber handed her camera to Agent Carmichael. "Would you mind?"

Carmichael said, "Eh, what the hell." He took the camera and pointed it at Amber.

Amber pressed Dial and put the phone to her ear. It barely had time to ring at all before the other end picked up the call.

Jack said, "Hello, Amber."

"Jack! Are you okay?"

"I've never been better."

"Are you wearing a Normalizer?"

"Of course I am."

"Will they let you take it off?"

"I haven't asked, and I don't want to. I was a fool to resist it, Amber. Just wait. You'll see what I mean."

"Jack, I've brought help."

"I know. We have windows. We can see. I'm impressed at how much backup you got in such little time, especially considering how frazzled you seemed at the police station. Your instincts were right. One of the officers you talked to was Lisa's father."

"Jack, just say the word and we'll come in and get you out of there."

"Why would I do that? I don't want you to come get me out of here. I have much to discuss with Dr. Frolick about her next appearance on my show. Besides, I can leave anytime I want to."

"Then leave."

"I don't want to."

"I don't believe you, Jack. I think that's the headband talking."

"That's just silly, Amber. The headband can't talk. It's nothing but some terry cloth, a simple circuit board, and a battery. I'm doing the talking. The headband's just helping me decide what to say."

"That's what I was getting at."

"Yes. I know. One moment." The line went silent, then Jack returned. "How's this? I have no intention of leaving the school until I'm good and ready, but I will come out and meet you all at the gate. The school is private property, so none of your new friends can come onto school grounds without probable cause. I'll be alone, nobody forcing me to say anything, and you and your friends can be sure I'm staying of my own accord."

The CIA agent listening in nodded.

Amber said, "Okay. When?"

"At precisely midnight." Jack laughed. "Don't be so dramatic. I'm going to the door right now."

The school's main entrance opened. Amber took her camera back and used the zoom to watch Jack backing out, pushing the door open behind him while talking to a crowd of headband-wearing students and hat-wearing faculty in the hall.

Agent Carmichael, pressing one finger to his left ear and staring down at his smartphone, muttered, "He's saying that there's a forty percent chance he'll just get rid of us but a sixty percent chance he can convince several of us to come back with him to try on the Normalizers."

Amber asked, "What kind of microphone does that have in it?"

"A laser mic. I use the camera to target some flat surface, like a window, near the person speaking, and the laser translates the vibration into sound. Government tech—pretty cool, eh?"

One of the CIA agents snorted. "Twenty years ago. They're obsolete now. They only give those to easily impressed agents who would most likely screw up anything more complicated."

Jack walked up the path across the school's lawn. Behind him, Balthazar held the door open so the students and faculty could watch.

Amber and her entourage of armed government officials stood against the outside of the gate. Jack wore a rainbow headband that clashed terribly with his customary tweed jacket, black shirt, and bolo tie. His head tilted slightly to the right. Soon, he and Amber stood, face to face, separated by the school's front gate.

"Hello, Amber."

"Jack, are you okay?"

"Yes. All things considered, I think I'm quite well."

The CIA agent asked, "Mr. Owens, are you in distress? Do you need our help?"

Jack looked at the agent and blinked. "Yes. I am in distress, and I need your help. I've been taken and held against my will and forced to wear a headband that is altering my brain function and looks ridiculous."

"That's not what you said on the phone."

"I was lying."

So is the Normalizer not working?" Amber asked.

"No, it's working perfectly. I'll admit, when I saw them coming at me with the headband, I was terrified, but as soon as they put it on my head, all of my panic and confusion melted away, and I saw the situation clearly. I was up against children, and as I said earlier, all children share the same weakness: gullibility. They are prone to believe almost anything you tell them, especially if you also tell them they are special. I just had to claim that the Normalizer made me see that they were correct, and they believed anything else I said."

"And the teachers?"

"They bought it too. My theory is that while the Normalizer makes one's thoughts more focused and efficient, it also suppresses feelings of self-doubt. As long as I told them they were right, they saw no reason to disagree."

"So you've just been lying to them nonstop ever since?"

"Yes, and I still am. They think I'm out here trying to talk you all into trying the Normalizer for yourselves. I suggest that all of you act as if you are listening to me and occasionally nod your heads, like I've made a good point. They think that a Normalized person can convince anybody of anything. In a moment, I'll lead all of you but Amber into the school, where you can apprehend the little sociopaths."

"Why should I stay behind?" Amber asked. "You don't have to protect me."

"I'm not. If you follow us, you can get a better shot."

16

Jack looked back over his shoulder at the school's empty hallway, then turned directly to the camera and arched an eyebrow.

"Here, our tale comes to an abrupt end. After the children took me hostage and my producer returned with help, the US government seized all the existing Normalizers as evidence and escorted Dr. Frolick away for questioning. If the Pentagon announces the addition of sweatbands to military uniforms, we'll know why. Medical professionals are examining the children, who seem to be in good shape but very sleepy. They will release the children immediately, but any parent who shows up to collect their child while wearing a hat is liable to face some questions."

Jack paused for a moment, looking pensively at the floor before continuing.

"You know, we often get so focused on what's best for children that we lose sight of what's good for them. Dr. Frolick tried to help them learn facts and figures, names and dates, and the importance of the Oxford comma. She prevented them from learning other lessons: how to make friends or deal with enemies, that stoves are hot and knives are sharp, and that Band-Aids and aspirin only do so much. If you neglect those lessons, kids go out into the world believing that they know everything and are invincible, and will soon learn, to their terrible cost, that that's not right."

Jack stared into the camera for a moment, then sagged, eyes drooping, limbs heavy, and shuffled to a chair sitting against the wall. "How was that?"

Amber lowered her camera. "Good, but a little low energy."

Jack scoffed. "Really? What a shock."

"You want to try another take?"

Jack just stared at Amber until she said, "No, I guess not."

Jack looked beyond Amber to Agent Carmichael and one of the CIA agents and asked, "And does that meet you two's approval?"

Carmichael said, "Everything you said was true, so Acronym is satisfied. How about you?"

The CIA agent said, "We've declared the explanation of how the Normalizers work a state secret, and we erased the footage of the children being apprehended for public relations reasons, but as for everything else you shot, yeah, go for it. Just be prepared for the agency to claim that you made the whole story up."

Agent Carmichael said, "And the CIA should be prepared for Acronym to lodge a formal complaint when you spread inaccurate information."

"We always are. We have a whole office staffed with agents whose entire job is to ignore Acronym's complaints and mock you behind your backs. Also, just for the record, they won't add headbands to military uniforms. They'll probably just build Normalizers into the helmets."

Carmichael said, "That's true."

Jack nearly nodded off, jerked his head back, and forced his eyes open wide. "What happened to Frolick?"

Carmichael said, "The DARPA scientists hauled her off to answer some questions, though I got the feeling it wasn't so much an interrogation as a job interview."

Amber shuddered. "Was I wrong for hoping the feds would look at what she was doing, be horrified, and want nothing to do with it?"

"No," Carmichael said, "you were right to hope. But you would have been wrong to expect that. Any time America hears about something potentially disastrous a government can do, we always rush to do it first. If we don't, someone untrustworthy might beat us to it."

Amber said, "I just hate to see her rewarded for this."

"It's not that much of a reward, if you think about it. I mean, sure, they'll fund her work, but it won't be hers anymore, and as soon as she fails to do exactly what her new bosses tell her, they'll toss her out on her butt with a legal penalty if she tells anyone about their secret project."

"But she'll get paid with our tax dollars."

Carmichael smirked at the CIA agent. "Yeah, and we all know how lucrative working for the government can be."

The CIA agent laughed bitterly. "We've all heard that old expression 'As rich as a federal employee.'"

Amber extended a hand to Jack, who sagged against the wall, nearly asleep in his chair. "Come on, let's get you back to your hotel room so you can rest."

Jack said, "Yes, please," and allowed Amber to help hoist him to his feet. "Geez, I only wore the damn thing for a few hours and I'm wasted! I can't imagine how those poor kids feel."

They walked past the door to the gym and saw the entire student body lying on the floor napping, some on small rugs, others on gym mats. Some lay on the hardwood floor but looked to be sleeping peacefully all the same. In the cafeteria, government agents were questioning teachers who blinked back at them with half-closed eyes, spoke in sleepy voices, and suffered severe cases of hat hair.

As they walked out to the parking lot, Amber said, "To think: even with their brains juiced up, they were still vulnerable to a simple lie."

"Hell," Jack said. "They were more vulnerable. As I said, kids are already prone to thinking they're special. These kids had a respected scientist who explained at great length why they were. Once they thought I was special too, I could use their arrogance to my advantage. The way the morning had gone, their confidence was riding high, and their fear of me as a threat couldn't have been lower."

"Yes." Amber opened the rental SUV's passenger door for Jack. "They played right into your hands by beating you all those times."

"Thanks," Jack said as he climbed into the passenger seat.

"For making fun of you, or for getting the door?"

Jack said, "The door," as she pushed it shut.

After she'd walked around the SUV and got in on the driver's side, Jack continued his thought, talking to her though his seat was reclined, his head flopped back on his headrest, and both his eyes were closed. "And for saving my neck. I could have kept fooling those brats a while longer, but I was going to have to come up with some way to get out of there, and I wasn't having a lot of luck. Things would've been bad if you hadn't come back with so much help. Thank you, Amber."

Amber paused before she started the engine and turned to face Jack. "Of course, Jack. You're welcome. But what did you think I was going to do?"

"Go to the cops, sure. But when they were no help, I figured you'd get out of town to somewhere safe, then call your boss and then let her handle it. You surprised me. You could have just gotten yourself to safety, but you came back."

"You would've done the same for me."

"I'd like to think I would, but you definitely did. I can add you to the list of people I know have my back. The list is now three names long, and the other two names are me and my wife."

"Thank you, Jack. Now get some sleep."

"I will. I can, because I know you're driving, and I can trust you."

＊ ＊ ＊

Four days later, on a Wednesday night, Amber sat alone and bleary-eyed in front of her computer, the only light coming from the screen. She had to submit her edited video to Ivy Atkins. Her deadline loomed, and the next day she would be traveling to meet Jack for their next story.

Editing had taken much longer than usual—not because it was difficult. Parts of it had come so naturally, she reflected with some amusement, that on this, of all projects, she had experienced a naturally occurring flow state.

The editing took a long time because she had edited two versions of the video.

The first was a test edit, made after Agent Carmichael's offhand comment that the footage of Jack losing repeatedly to the children was "gold," Brian's suggestion that her best work had come from making him and his friends look like idiots, and Ivy Atkins's urging to make the kind of videos she used to. Amber indulged every instinct she had for making her subject, in this case Jack, look foolish. The idea was to make the first video as an exercise in brainstorming. Then she could decide what material was usable and what was too mean, then take the acceptable bits and sprinkle them throughout a more sober edit, like chocolate chips in a cookie.

She named the first video file "Batteryboy One." It started with a text crawl reading "Later this episode" under footage of Jack being defeated at Go by a fourth grader who told Jack he wasn't good at Go and Jack threatening to tell that child where he could go. What followed was a severely truncated version of Jack's intro, edited together with B-roll of the school's exterior so that the cuts would not jump out. The next scene was a shortened version of the conversation Jack had with Dr. Frolick and Balthazar in the hall, emphasizing the doctor's accomplishment and mentioning that the other class members were now participating. Then footage of the kids on the playground with Jack expressing skepticism that they could perform as well in any tasks that didn't involve memorization or physical dexterity.

That all was the first sixty seconds of the video. The rest was a montage of Jack being repeatedly beaten at various games by fourth graders. The first version just showed the moments where he lost, but that was over too quickly, so Amber added in every time he lost an important piece, made an error, received an insult from one of the children, or simply looked embarrassed or angry. She wondered if the background of dopey tuba music was gratuitous, but she left it in, because if she was going to do this, she should do it all the way. In the end, the video was ten minutes long, with the montage of Jack's failures taking up most of that. After the montage, Amber cut to a thirty-second edit of Jack's outro: only the final paragraph about the kids missing out on the best parts of childhood, but cut in such a way that it sounded more like sour grapes than any sort of deep thought.

She knew in her bones that the video was funny. She also knew Jack would never forgive her if he saw it.

The second video she labeled "Batteryboy 2." It featured Jack's intro in its entirety, followed by a sober but gripping retelling of the portion of the day's events the CIA would allow them to report, followed by Jack's summation in its entirety.

After a great deal of agonizing, Amber edited in highlights of the Jack's Repeated Defeats montage throughout the video, adding dashes of humor at regular intervals. Making the second video was hard work, but she was proud of the result, and cautiously optimistic that Ms. Atkins would not entirely hate it.

As soon as she stopped concentrating on editing, Amber realized how tired she was, again, disturbingly like the kids who had been pulled out of their artificially induced flow state. She felt her eyelids drooping and her thought process growing muddy. She dragged and dropped her work to the corporate cloud drive and allowed auto-complete to suggest most of a quick email to Atkins, telling her the file was on the server.

As she started stand up to shuffle off to bed, she noticed that her computer was uploading both video files, not just the one she wanted to send. An instant spurt of adrenaline jolted her brain. With all the speed and grace of a panicked idiot swatting at a wasp that has landed on his own forehead, Amber seized her mouse and deleted the first of the two ongoing uploads listed.

As the file continued to upload, she walked away. She imagined Atkins watching the first edit and, God forbid, loving it. She'd never be able to talk Atkins out of using that video and running the more sober version instead. Amber congratulated herself for averting disaster.

The Fantastic Files of
Professor Frederick Franks

17

Amber glanced at Jack, who was sitting in the passenger seat working on his intro. He seemed to be engrossed in his work and oblivious to her. The coast thus being clear, she opened the email from Ivy Atkins. The reaction Amber was hoping for was light disappointment. A sort of "This isn't what I wanted, but it's good enough, I guess."

Amber,
This!

Seeing the exclamation point made Amber's shoulders tense. In this situation, excitement was not a good sign. She continued reading.

This video is exactly what I wanted! I never doubted that you could do it. I was just concerned over whether you would.

Amber didn't understand. The video she'd sent was not at all what Ivy Atkins wanted, and she knew it. Either Atkins was toying with her or something was desperately wrong. Amber pulled up the corporate cloud app on her phone and looked at her upload log. She felt her internal organs drop to the floor as she read the file name "Batteryboy One." In her haste the night before, she had failed to notice that the files were listed in alphabetical order. The sorting algorithm put numbers before letters, so "Batteryboy 2" came before "Batteryboy One." When she stopped the first file's upload, she held back the one she wanted to send—and sent the one she didn't want her boss to see.

It would not be fun explaining to Ivy Atkins why they couldn't use the exact video she had wanted in the first place, but Amber would have to do just that, and fast, if she was going to head this disaster off before the video was posted. She read on.

We posted the video at midnight.

Amber's organs drilled a hole into the earth's crust. She gritted her teeth so hard the roots hurt. She briefly entertained the notion that they could pull it down before too many people saw it, before she continued reading.

I came in early this morning to find that it's already our most viewed video, just from the night owls, the UK, and Australia. I can't wait to see what happens when most Americans get far enough into their day to start goofing off and passing it around.

Regardless of how this first video does, know that I am happy with it. Your job is safe, as long as you keep delivering videos this good. Please re-edit the two earlier stories to be as close to this in style as possible. I know you didn't shoot them with that in mind, and it will be hard to make them funny, but I'm sure you're up to it. When in doubt, lean into anything embarrassing.

I'm glad I hired you, and glad we paired you with Jack. He seems like perfect fodder for your style.

Ivy Atkins

Amber turned off her phone, closed her eyes, and waited for her heart rate and breathing to return to normal. She hadn't meant to betray Jack's trust—not this much, at least. Creating the insulting video in the first place was a betrayal, but it was a private, secret betrayal. This was much worse, because it was a big public betrayal, one that he would find out about. On one hand, her job was safe. On the other hand, her relationship with her one coworker was probably ruined for good, and Atkins had just ordered her to re-edit the first two videos to make Jack look foolish, ruining it even more, twice. It didn't help that Amber already had several good ideas for how to do exactly that.

She found that the worst part about being a bad person was discovering that she seemed to be pretty good at it.

Jack glanced over at her and saw her frowning at her phone. "Email?"

Amber mumbled, "Yeah."

"From Brian?"

"No."

"Atkins?"

"Yeah."

"Reaction to the Battery Boy video?"

"Uh, yeah."

Jack winced. "Ooh! She didn't like it, eh?"

"We'll talk about it later."

"That bad, huh! Well, don't worry. We'll turn it around. Did you set up the interviews I suggested for this afternoon?"

"Yeah, they're both on. The fact that they're both at the same university made it easier."

Jack said, "You don't seem very excited about it. Come on, you've finally got me fully on board! Don't you run out of steam! Now I see that we've actually found something interesting in all three of the stories we've done. Not necessarily what we thought we would, but something. We have an opportunity here to break some real ground."

"And that's what turned your attitude around?" Amber asked.

"That, and realizing that I can trust you."

Amber said, "Oh. Good."

"You don't think the stories I found are interesting? We're talking about legitimate research here, that fits my show's subject matter."

"No, that's not the problem. The opposite. They're both very interesting stories. I just don't think we'll have enough time to do them justice, since the morning is already full."

"No problem. We'll just cancel this morning. Dump the BS we had set up and do the new stories."

"Jack, your listeners are going to want to meet Professor Franks."

"Yeah, but I don't want them to."

"You have him on your show all the time."

"Whenever I can't think of a better idea. Amber, it's hard to make him seem credible on the radio. I doubt letting people get a good look at him will make it easier. He's just going to make the entire show seem . . ." Jack trailed off, searching for the right word, and eventually settled on "laughable."

Amber said, "We should definitely interview him. We should get as much footage of him as possible, you know, so I have a lot of options to make him look the way we want him to."

Jack threw up his hands. "Okay. You're the professional. I trust you."

Amber bit her lip.

Jack said, "Just promise me we'll ditch the professor in time to go do the two serious stories."

Amber muttered, "I promise."

"Good enough for me. Okay, let's shoot the intro."

Amber crouched on the grassy strip between the sidewalk and the road, holding her camera low and tilted upward to capture Jack and the house behind him in the same frame. A winding set of concrete steps, cracked and slanted, worked back and forth up a steep incline. The house sat at the highest point of the lot, a once-beautiful example of an Arts and Crafts-style bungalow buried under many years' accumulation of dirt. The front porch held a couch and two chairs, none of which was designed to be outdoor furniture. A cluster of satellite dishes of various sizes, manufacturers, and vintages sprouted like a colony of mushrooms from the roof.

Jack loomed over the camera, one eyebrow raised. "I stand in the suburbs outside Washington, DC, predictably—or perhaps alarmingly—close to our nation's decision makers and secret keepers. People often ask me how I find the subjects for my show. I am not sure how I manage it sometimes. There's no shortage of bizarre occurrences and uncanny events in this world, but most of us are unaware of them. After all, if too many people become aware of a strange phenomenon, it is no longer strange. Therefore, I need—indeed, *society* needs—people who seek the unusual, and who, predictably, tend to be unusual themselves. Behind me, looking exactly as one would expect, is the home of one such person, Professor Frederick Franks."

Amber said, "One and done, as usual. Good work."

"Sure you don't want another take or two?"

"No, I think we're good."

"Are you sure? I could easily run through it a couple more times."

"Are you stalling, Jack?"

"No, not at all. If anything, I want to get this over with. I just want to give you options, make sure I do my best to set you up for success."

"Don't worry about that," Amber said, looking at the ground. "Seriously. How the edit comes out is on me, okay? You should never blame yourself for the final edit."

"Sure."

Jack carefully climbed the steps. Several of the slabs rocked beneath his feet. He reached out for the handrail to steady himself, but it bent and wobbled with his weight. Huffing and puffing before he reached the halfway point, he stopped for a moment and noticed for the first time that Amber was still filming him from the sidewalk below. After half a second of confusion, he said, "Okay, yeah. I get it. Getting the shot. I'll wait for you when I get to the top. It's a shame this won't be usable, footage of me looking scared and out of shape."

Amber said, "You just do what comes naturally. I'll worry about if the footage is usable or not."

Jack fought his way to the top of the path and waited as Amber made the same climb, noticeably faster but no less nervously. When she reached the top, she immediately hoisted her camera back up and started shooting again. Jack put his foot on the first step up to the porch, which creaked alarmingly. He moved up to the second step, which broke under his weight, causing his foot to fall straight through to the ground beneath. He cursed under his breath; looked at the porch itself, judging whether he could trust it to support him; and finally just shouted, "Fred! Fred! We're here! Fred!"

The front door creaked open, and Professor Frederick Franks came out. Amber didn't know how she had imagined he would look, but at a glance she knew that this was what she should have expected. If she met this man at random, somewhere out in the world, she might have assumed he was Professor Frederick Franks. He wore shiny black shoes, rumpled black slacks, and a short-sleeved button-down shirt just thin and sheer enough for her the clearly see the thick white undershirt beneath. Wispy brown hair like a cloud of smog clung to his scalp and his forearms. He had sharp, bright eyes and dull gray teeth. His inquisitive nature was reflected in his physicality, in that he had the posture of a question mark.

He looked down at the man standing in the shattered remains of his front steps and cried out, "Jack! Jaaack! Jack, Jack, Jack, so good to meet you in person, Jack!" Fred lurched forward toward Jack, both of his hands outstretched.

Jack extended a hand up. "Hi, Fred."

Fred reached down, grasped Jack's hand with both of his own, and shook it vigorously for an extended period, gushing, "Hello, Jack! Hello! Welcome! Welcome, Jack! So good to have you here!"

Jack stood, knee deep in the broken steps, watching the professor whip his arm up and down like it was a rope at a CrossFit gym. "Fred, yes, good to see you, Fred. Look, uh, could you— Stop shaking my hand, Fred! I don't need a handshake right now!"

Fred said, "You're right, of course. We've known each other for so long! No need to be formal!" He dropped to one knee, leaned forward, and took Jack in a heartfelt embrace.

Through gritted teeth, Jack said, "Fred, your step broke. Please help pull me out."

Fred let go of Jack, looked down, and amid a flurry of apologies offered a hand to steady Jack as he extricated his right leg from the ruined step and then pulled himself up onto the porch.

"I'm sorry about that, Jack," Fred said. "I hope you're not hurt."

"I don't think I am. No, no harm done, to me at least. Sorry about your step."

"Don't worry about it. It's been threatening to fail for a while."

"Then why didn't you fix it?"

"Too busy with my work. In a way, you did me a favor by breaking it completely."

"Now you'll have to fix it."

"Someday, yes, but in the meantime, nobody else will try to step on it now. Come in! There's so much to talk about, so much to do."

Fred disappeared into the house. Jack stood on the porch, stammering, "But wait, I should introduce you to Amber. She's my director."

Fred said, "Yes, of course. We talked on the phone."

Amber said, "It's good to meet you, Professor Franks."

"Oh, come now. That's far too formal. Please, call me Fred. Professor Fred. Now please do come in."

Jack helped Amber step up over the broken stair and they both entered Fred's home. Looking around, Amber reflected that the difference between a hoarder and a researcher might just be their filing system. Had she not known that Professor Franks studied the occult, she might have assumed he collected various historical methods of document storage. Filing cabinets of every description lined the walls. Anywhere there was not a window, the cabinets supported towering collections of cardboard document boxes. Lidded plastic bins littered the floor in front of and around the cabinets, leaving barely enough space for Fred to access the one available chair and the TV.

The few horizontal spaces left open held a strange assortment of objects, only some of which were recognizable as anything other than a cry for help. Amber saw jagged, bent, and scorched hunks of metal and sealed mason jars containing twigs, dirt, ashes, and something that might be genuine cinnamon bark, or perhaps very rough old leather. One area held several models of spaceships, some carved from wood, some made from various toys and model kits combined together. She saw one craft that consisted of the wings and engines from an X-wing fighter glued to the saucer section of the *Enterprise*-D, which offended her for both aesthetic and narrative reasons.

Fred pulled on a puffy waterproof overcoat and flitted around the room, picking up various items and stuffing them in his pockets. "Come in, please. I'd offer you coffee, but we don't have time."

Jack reached down into a bin sitting open and pulled out a heavily modified stuffed toy of Barney the dinosaur. The soft plush horns and tusks of various stuffed elephants, bulls, and unicorns protruded from its mouth so that its teeth were larger than the rest of its head, and someone had glued the claws from two Wolverine action figures to the dinosaur's hands and feet.

"What is this?" Jack asked.

Fred glanced at the toy as he buzzed around the room. "That's a chupacabra. The Mexican goat sucker."

Jack said, "I've heard of the chupacabra, just not a purple one."

"Well, there are no photos of one. You have to afford some leeway. It's an artist's rendering."

"Are you the artist, Fred?"

"Never mind the chupacabra. We have much stranger things to discuss today."

"Stranger?"

Amber said, "Hey, Jack, hold the chupacabra up for the camera."

Jack scowled as he held the stuffed toy aloft, its limbs quivering as he spun it one way, then the other, so the camera could capture it from all sides. "This is a waste of time."

Fred said, "I agree. We have to go."

"No," Jack said. "Not until we talk about the plan for today. Now look, we came here to interview you."

"You can do that in the van."

"We can do it here. That's the plan. Where do you think we're going?"

"I've lined up something much better than an interview for you, Jack."

"What?"

"Proof!"

"Proof of what?"

"Ghosts! Monsters! Conspiracies at the highest levels of the government! Doesn't that sound better than just talking to me?"

"Yes, I admit it does, but you have one thing that proves all that?"

"No, not yet. That's why time is of the essence! We have several stops to make today. We gotta get going!"

"Hold up, Fred! Look, you can't just spring stuff on us like this. We have other appointments this afternoon."

"With who?" Professor Fred asked, stopping abruptly and looking more than a little hurt.

"A couple of scientists doing interesting research at the university—"

"Oh, that's no problem."

"It's not?"

"No, just cancel them. Those 'legitimate' scientists at the universities, their stuff always sounds promising, but they never deliver."

"You can't say legitimate science never produces anything! What about penicillin?"

"Penicillin's a placebo."

"I don't think so."

"Exactly. That's why it works. Cancel on them. If you don't want to be the bad guy, I'll do it." Fred pulled out his smartphone. "What's the number?"

Jack said, "We're not canceling on them. We're doing the simple interview with you that we agreed to, and then we're leaving to make our other appointments."

Fred rolled his eyes. "Fine. Go waste time at the university, but trust me, first you want to come with me and see what I have lined up."

Jack bit his lip and looked over to Amber, who pictured the nice, dignified interview she and Jack had planned, then tried to imagine the sorts of things the professor might have in store for them. "You know, Jack, you two talking out in the field while investigating things would be more interesting, and who knows? He might have something."

Fred said, "Who knows? I know! And I do have something! It's settled then. Everybody into my van. Chop-chop!"

Jack followed slowly. "No, Fred. We'll follow you."

"Nonsense. How can you interview me on the way if we're not all together?"

"Then you can ride with us. I'll drive, you ride shotgun and give me directions, and Amber can sit in the back and film."

"Why cram into your little rental car when I have the van?" The professor patted all of his pockets, looked stricken, then bolted to another room, muttering, "Wallet."

Jack turned to Amber and quietly said, "Please, don't make me ride in his van. You never let a crazy person drive."

"Why not?" Amber asked. "Are you afraid he'll crash?"

"No, because if he's our only ride back here, we're at his mercy. Look, you're the director. I'll follow your lead on this. But I'm telling you, if we get in that van, it'll be a fiasco."

She looked at their clean, reliable rented compact four-door. Then she looked at Fred's van, a white, mud-splattered monstrosity he'd apparently bought as surplus from a moving-truck rental company that hadn't quite managed to kill it. Amber took a moment to imagine what kinds of misadventures he might subject them to and how easy it would be to edit the footage of them into an amusing video.

Amber said, "More elbow room in the back seat would make it easier to work the camera."

18

Amber had too much elbow room in the back of the van. She struggled to keep her shot stable as she sat in a lawn chair completely unconnected to the van's metal floor, and she had very little in arm's reach to hold onto in hopes of steadying herself. There was no seat belt, but she didn't really want one. In an accident, it would only have held the chair to her rear as she went flying.

Behind her, in the back of the van, a dozen mismatched toolboxes of various sizes and weights slid around on the ribbed steel floor.

Amber would have described Professor Frederick Franks's driving style as "zestful." He took turns fast, braked hard, and talked nonstop at the top of his lungs.

"It was short notice, but I agreed to meet the guy," Fred said, looking at Jack in the passenger seat instead of at the road. "Because proof that werewolves exist would be a huge deal, and I don't want to wait a month for the next full moon. Who's got time for that? So I get there. The guy invites me in, and right off the bat he ties me to a chair."

"How'd he tie you to your chair?" Jack asked.

"With rope."

"Well, yeah," Jack said. "But didn't you fight back?"

"Not until it was too late. At first I didn't want to be rude, but then he had my right hand tied and had a good hold on the left. That was pretty much it."

Jack turned and looked directly into Amber's camera. "That's an important life lesson. When someone tries to tie you up, fight! Don't worry about offending them."

Fred also turned and looked back into the camera. "Wise words."

Jack shouted, "Eyes on the road!"

"What? Oh! Right. Sorry. So anyway, I ask him why he tied me up."

"A fair question."

"I thought so. And he says, 'Because it's a full moon.' I tell him there's no need, on account of I'm not a werewolf, and he says he knows that, but he is, and he doesn't like to have to go chasing after his food."

"Not what you wanted to hear." Jack said.

"Not at all. Anyway, he leaves me there and goes into the other room. I hear a lot of grunting and struggling, a couple of crashes like he knocked something over. I'm getting pretty scared."

"Sure."

"And then he comes out."

Jack said, "I'm betting he wasn't a werewolf."

"No," Fred said, disappointed. "He was wearing a big furry wolf costume, like you'd see at a theme park. And he had a boom box."

Jack nodded. "Not the worst outcome, but not the best either."

"I know. It could have been a lot worse than it was. He didn't rub on me or anything. He just giggled and danced around to Duran Duran."

Jack again turned to look at the camera and raised one eyebrow. "'Hungry Like the Wolf.'"

"No, that's the disturbing part. It wasn't 'Hungry Like the Wolf.' He put on a wolf costume and danced to 'The Reflex.' I mean, who does that? You end up dealing with some real freaks working in this field."

"Yes," Jack said. "All you wanted was to meet a werewolf, and you ended up dealing with a weirdo. You're taking us to meet the werewolf, are you?"

"No, not at all. This is a totally different deal."

"Good."

"Yeah, this is a lady I know. She's going to freak you out, man."

"How so?"

"She has ideas. Lots of ideas."

"What kind of ideas?"

"The kind that make you question the world and your place in it."

Jack pressed his fingers to his temples and squeezed his eyes shut. "You understand none of what you said are necessarily good things."

"Jack, this lady, she has a theory. It's not just one theory, but it is. It's a bunch of theories that explain other people's theories, and it all leads back to one big theory, her theory, that explains everything and throws everything into doubt, and it all makes sense."

"That description didn't make sense."

"No, but the description wasn't the theory, just a description of the theory."

The van rolled a little too fast down a residential side street and stopped abruptly, tires letting out a small chirp, in front of a four-story brick building. After they'd gathered their gear and gotten out, Professor Fred studied numbers next to a rectangular grid of buttons by the glass front door and pressed one at the bottom, marked 15.

A terse voice crackled through the speaker. "Who are you?"

"Hi, Carrie, it's Professor Franks. Remember, we arranged for me to come by today?"

"You alone?"

"No. I told you I would have guests. These are the people I told you about. Jack Owens, the famous radio host, and Amber Cardoza. She's working with Jack to film a documentary for the internet."

"Yes. I remember, and so do you. That was a test. You've passed. Your reward is that you get to come in. I'm on the fourth floor. You'll want to take the stairs."

"Is the elevator broken?"

"No, but if they stop it between floors, they'll have you trapped."

"Who?"

"I don't know, but do you want to risk finding out?"

The buzzer sounded, and Fred pulled the door open. Once inside, they took the elevator, their fear of capture by unseen forces losing out to their fear of walking up four floors' worth of stairs.

They reached the door marked 16. Professor Fred raised a fist to knock.

Amber said, "I think this is the wrong door. You buzzed fifteen."

Fred said, "This is fifteen. She swapped the numbers with a neighbor so if people come after her, they'll be fooled."

The door opened abruptly. A woman in her forties, heavy, with large wet eyes magnified behind thick glasses, stood in the doorway and hissed at Fred, "It won't fool anybody if you keep blabbing about it! Get in! Quick! Before they see you!"

As Professor Fred, Jack, and Amber hustled past the woman into the apartment, Jack asked, "Who? Before who sees us?"

The woman said, "Any of them!" She shut the door, turned the knobs and keys to four different locks, and connected a tripwire to a box with an ominous-looking red light.

Jack asked, "If people are after you, aren't you worried about your neighbor?"

"No," the woman said. "If he were working for them, he'd have made his move years ago."

"That's not what I meant. I mean, you switched apartment numbers with him to throw off attackers. Wasn't he concerned about them going after him instead of you?"

"Not as concerned as he was about me going after him if he refused. You ask an awful lot of questions."

Jack looked at Fred, then into Amber's camera, momentarily at a loss, and finally said, "I'm here to interview you."

The woman studied him for a moment, then slowly nodded. "Okay, yeah, I buy that. My name's Carrie. Have a seat. Can I offer you a drink?"

Fred asked, "What have you got?"

"Distilled water."

Jack and Amber waited a second for her to list other options, but she did not.

"That's all you have to drink?" Jack asked.

"That's all I trust, because I distill it myself."

Jack asked, "You distill tap water?"

"No," Carrie said. "I don't get it from the tap. That's where they expect you to get it. You've got to learn to zag. Get your drinking water from the last place they'd expect, and don't tell anybody where that is. You want a glug or not?"

Fred said he'd like a glass, but Jack and Amber said no, thank you, rather quickly.

The apartment wasn't so much a home with an office in it as it was an office with a bed. A desk and computer dominated the main room, with an old couch and a couple of chairs included as an afterthought. Amber panned around the room and found no disorderly stacks of documents, no bulletin boards holding photos and red yarn, no dry-erase boards covered with indecipherable writing and question marks—none of the stereotypical hallmarks of a paranoid conspiracy theorist. The only physical manifestation of Carrie's paranoia Amber could see was the table next to the bay window at the front of the apartment, which held telescopes, cameras, several pairs of binoculars, a parabolic microphone, and what appeared to be a crossbow with a telescopic sight.

Carrie returned carrying water in two colorfully painted glasses, the kind that fast-food places used to sell to promote movies and now thrift stores sell to clear out shelf space. She handed a glass to Fred, kept one for herself, sat down in her desk chair, and swiveled around to face her guests.

Jack said, "I apologize. Usually I do research on my guests before I interview them so I have some idea what they're going to say. But in this case, all I know is that Professor Franks says you have many provocative ideas."

Carrie said, "That is not true."

"It's not?"

"No. I have one provocative idea, with implications so far-reaching, so profound, that it affects every aspect of our society."

"I see. And what is that idea?"

"Stated one way, my thesis is that virtually every conspiracy theory, from the most obscure to the most well-known, is, in fact, false."

"False?"

"Yes. False."

"You're saying they aren't true?"

"That's correct."

"Bigfoot. Ancient aliens. Atlantis."

"Nothing but fairy tales."

"That's not what I expected you to say."

"I know, Mr. Owens, but just hold on. That's not the good part. The core of my theory is that long ago, even before the days of Machiavelli, the people in charge realized that the best way to hide a secret truth was to put it next to a much larger falsehood."

"I don't follow."

"If they tell a huge, obvious lie, it will distract from the much smaller truth they want to hide."

"Can you give me an example?"

"Many, but I'll start with one of my favorites: the moon landing."

"What about the moon landing?"

"It happened."

"I suppose some people might consider that a shocking revelation."

"Yes! Some would, because there's that conspiracy theory that the government hired Stanley Kubrick to fake the whole thing, right?"

"I'm aware of it."

"Everybody is. The CIA made sure of that. They started the provably false story that the government and Stanley Kubrick faked the moon landing to divert attention away from the true secret: the moon landing was real, and the government faked the existence of Stanley Kubrick."

Jack's face froze in an emotionless neutral expression that, to anyone who knew him, spoke volumes. He looked over at Amber, who tried her best to hide the huge smile on her face.

Fred said, "Told you. Mind blowing! Right?"

Jack said, "Oh, my mind's blown. I'll give you that. Why would they do that? And how would they do that? But mostly, why. Why would they do that?"

Carrie said, "How is easy. They create fake identities for people all the time. A name, some documents, a few blurry black-and-white photos of a random toddler. It's not a problem. As for why? Psyops. Propaganda, if you like. Why mess with leaflets, commercials, and rumor campaigns when you can get people to voluntarily sit in a dark room and subject themselves to two-plus hours of your message and fund the program with the box-office take?"

"But people don't just mindlessly go see any movie they're offered. They'd have to want to see it, and they don't want to see government propaganda."

"Unless, Mr. Owens, that propaganda is disguised as the latest work by the greatest living artist in his field. If you see an ad for a movie that looks so-so but everyone you know says the director is a genius, you give it the benefit of the doubt. You watch it, if not in the theater, then in your home later, which is even more insidious if you think about it."

"But people love his movies."

"They believe they do. Here's a fun exercise to try, Mr. Owens. Google the words 'Kubrick' and 'hypnotic,' and see how many people use that word to describe his movies, how often people talk about how his films lull you into a trance, how you walk out of one of his films feeling more like you've had an experience that changed you instead of just watching a movie."

"But once people see the movie, even if it lulled them into a stupor, it has to be a work of genius or the entire operation goes down."

"No," Carrie said. "The movies don't have to be brilliant. They just have to plausibly seem like they might be brilliant. They need to be shot beautifully, acted well, and the editing and special effects need to be top-notch. Those are all things you can get by hiring the right people. But the story doesn't need to be good. In fact, the story needs to not be so good, so that the audience won't understand it. That's the key! Because Kubrick is such a genius, the audience blames themselves for not understanding."

"That's not—"

"Explain the ending of *2001: A Space Odyssey.*"

"Well . . . I mean . . ." Jack sputtered. "I'll admit that one's confusing, but they explain it—"

"In the sequel?" Carrie asked. "*2010: The Year We Make Contact?*"

"Yes!"

"Which wasn't directed by Kubrick." Carrie stood up to emphasize her point.

"I know, which is another problem for your theo—"

Carrie took a step forward, pointing at Jack. "It was directed by Peter Hyams, who also directed *Capricorn One*, the film that—even though it was about a faked Mars landing—first brought the idea that the moon landing took place on a sound stage into the mainstream. I never said Kubrick was the only director they faked."

"Huh."

"And aside from the confusing ending, what was *2001* about? The first part shows one version of intelligent design, and the middle bit glamorizes space exploration, which directly benefited the military-industrial complex."

"But that's just one movie in a whole catalog—"

Carrie took another step toward Jack. "Back in the Eisenhower administration, he made *Paths of Glory*. Ike was a World War Two general, and the movie painted the French army as suffering from cowardly, dishonest leadership, leaving the audience primed to see our European allies as less effective than us and giving the US Army credit for victory in the second world war."

Jack said, "I haven't seen that one."

"No, they never show it anymore, because it did its job. And *Spartacus* helped the nation recover from McCarthyism."

"Yeah, maybe."

Carrie stepped forward again, now looming over Jack as he remained sitting, her knees nearly touching his. "The Kennedy administration made *Dr. Strangelove*, which looked like a vicious send-up of the military but reinforced people's fear of nuclear war and incentivized them to fund our military."

"That's a bit of a stretch."

"Or is it just subtle? *A Clockwork Orange* made people simultaneously more fearful of violent crime and less trusting of people who sought to rehabilitate criminals instead of punishing them. It also made people distrust youths who dressed funny and used impenetrable slang—like hippies, perhaps? And it boosted the dairy industry."

"It didn't make milk look that good."

"Yeah, I might have overreached on that one. But *The Shining* sold the idea that cutting yourself off from society, from TV and radio, would drive you insane and destroy your family. Also, it had an anti-alcoholism message, because Jimmy Carter was concerned for his brother, Billy."

"Billy Carter was a much smarter man than people gave him credit for."

"*Full Metal Jacket* was about how military training makes normal young men into killers, and then it demonstrates why that's a good and necessary thing. A useful message to get out there if Reagan and George Herbert Walker Bush knew we were about to embark on several decades of undeclared wars in the Middle East."

"R. Lee Ermey was very good in that movie."

"R. Lee Ermey was assigned to keep the actor who played Kubrick in line and parlayed it into an acting career for himself! And he used his fame to boost the military for the rest of his days."

"What about *Eyes Wide Shut*?" Jack asked. "What possible pro-American political subtext can you find in *Eyes Wide Shut*?"

Carrie shrugged, deflated a bit, looked around as if surprised to find herself standing so close to Jack, and walked back to her desk chair. She said, "By then Clinton was in the White House. I figure he just wanted to see Nicole Kidman naked."

"Yeah," Jack said. "That sounds about right. You lay out an interesting case. Do you have any proof?"

Carrie looked at Jack as if he were stupid. "If I had proof, I'd be dead. Look, don't humor me. I can see you're not taking this seriously."

Jack said, "I'm sorry. I understand that you believe what you're telling me. Maybe it's just the example you chose. You say this is a tactic the government has used more than once. What else have you got?"

"I know you've heard that some people believe the Earth is flat."

"Yes. I've had people on my show promoting that idea."

Professor Fred said, "Yeah, me!"

Amber said, "I heard that episode."

Carrie said, "They claim the North Pole is the center of the disk and Antarctica is an ice wall around the rim."

Jack nodded, smiling. "Yeah, and the sun and moon are about the same size and spin around in a circle over the disk."

"Which," Carrie said, "I think everyone in this room will agree is ridiculous."

Fred said, "Well now, one sec—"

Jack cut him off. "Utterly ridiculous. Because the sun and moon don't whiz around in a circle. They rise and set."

Carrie added, "And anyone who has ever gone on a long drive in the western United States, or gone out to sea on a ship, has seen things rise up over the horizon."

"Yeah," Jack said. "I mean, if the Earth were flat and you had a powerful enough telescope, you'd be able to see the Rockies from New York, and you can't."

Carrie said, "Exactly. It's a silly, easily disproved falsehood that is just intriguing enough to draw people's attention away from the truth: that the Earth is round, but the sun is flat."

"The sun is flat?"

"Yes."

"The sun?"

"Yes."

"Why would the sun be flat?"

"Why would it be a sphere?"

"We can see that it's a sphere."

"If the sun's a sphere, Jack, then explain why the middle of it isn't brighter than the outside edge."

"What do you mean?"

"Think about it." Carrie held her hands up, fingers splayed and bent to approximate a sphere. "If the sun is a ball of fire, like you say, then from the Earth's point of view, the center of the sun is a thicker mass of fire than the outer edge. Shouldn't it be brighter? And the surface of the sun at the center would be closer to the Earth. That would make it brighter, too. And if light radiates off the sun in all directions, then the light from the center would be aimed more directly at the Earth than any light coming off the rest of the surface. That's three different reasons that if the sun is a sphere, its center should be noticeably brighter than the outer rim, but it isn't brighter at the center. It's a uniform glowing disk, isn't it, Jack?"

Jack said, "I can't really say. I've never stared directly at the sun long enough to see for myself."

"None of us has, Jack. That's a big part of how they can keep it a secret. And think about this: you never see a photo of the sun taken from the side, now, do you?"

"It's a featureless ball. It would look exactly the same from the side. The Earth orbits around it. We see it from a different angle every day, and it always looks the same, like a sphere would."

"Isn't that convenient?"

"Yes," Jack said. "The fact that anyone can see that the sun is a sphere is convenient for those who would claim that the sun is a sphere."

"Appears to be a sphere, Jack, because it doesn't change. But, given its uniform brightness, wouldn't it make more sense for the sun to be a flat disk that rotates once every three hundred and sixty-five days to stay aimed at the Earth? Look, this will make more sense if I have a visual aid. One second. I'm going to go get a plate."

Carrie rose from her seat and left the room.

Jack spoke quietly to Amber. "This is a waste of time. We should go."

Amber said, "I don't think she's right, but I do think she's interesting."

"If you use her, you will be obviously taking advantage of a mentally ill person."

"If that's true, Jack, then you've been taking advantage of mentally ill people for years."

"Yes, and if you use any of this footage, people will figure that out!"

19

Amber struggled to find a shot tight enough to show the facial expressions of the people holding the séance yet wide enough to give a sense of the graveyard in which they stood. The bright daylight helped with the camera work, if not the desired spooky ambiance.

The fact that it was a pet cemetery didn't help on that score, either.

On a field of leafy trees and lush green grass, studded with stone plaques set into the ground and several statues of dogs and cats or the occasional tombstone with a cartoon bone shape carved in it, Jack and Professor Fred stood next to a psychic, a man in his forties whose appearance disproved the idea that black clothes are slimming; a man in his sixties who looked sad; and a woman in her thirties who looked skeptical.

The man in black directed everyone to stand in a circle around a grave marked "Bosco." Amber looked at the camera's screen and adjusted her shot as the others all joined hands and stood silently with their eyes closed.

Satisfied that her framing was as good as it was going to get, Amber left the camera alone and peeked at her phone. Her smartwatch had alerted her to incoming messages far more than usual that morning, but she had not bothered to acknowledge any of them, partly out of fear that Jack might notice and ask her what was up—especially if he saw a slightly guilty smile on her face.

One hundred and forty-one notifications waited for her. She scanned them: emails, DMs, texts, and mentions. She didn't have the time to read them now, and might not ever.

As near as Amber could tell, all her messages were congratulatory. The first few told her how great it was that one of her new videos had finally been posted. After that, many spoke about how funny the video was. Eventually, all the messages expressed amazement at how the video was blowing up, many suggesting that she had made Jack the star of the internet for the day.

"Now we are ready to beckon Bosco forward from beyond the veil." The psychic in black squeezed his eyes shut in intense concentration, lifted his head as if calling out to the heavens, and said, "Here, boy! Bosco! Where's Bosco? Where's Bosco? Come'ere boy! Bosco!"

After that, he whistled and made clicking noises.

Amber had to be selective about which emails she would read right now. She opened one from Ivy Atkins. It expressed surprise and delight at how the video was performing. That episode was already not just the most viewed of any that Live Air's channels had produced, but its views alone dwarfed the views for all their other videos put together, and the pace was still accelerating. Ivy ended by saying she looked forward to seeing the re-edits of the first two videos.

The psychic said, "There's a spirit present. It's . . ." He grimaced with concentration. "It's . . . I think . . . Yes! It's a dog."

Jack glanced at the camera. Amber had to stifle a laugh.

The psychic asked, "Is it Bosco?"

"Yes."

"Are you sure?"

"I think it is, but I'll see if there's some way to prove it. Yeah, uh, I'm getting something. Something about Frisbees. He says he loved chasing Frisbees."

The man in his sixties sagged. "Bosco didn't like Frisbees."

"Yes," the pet psychic said. "That's right. I'm getting it clearly now. He hates Frisbees."

Amber noticed a message from Brian. He said her first video with Jack was hilarious and that she had a talent for making men look stupid. She could always tell when a compliment from Brian was sincere, because it was invariably meant as an insult.

She looked at Jack, who was barely containing his impatience as a charlatan asked a sad old man leading questions. She had finally gotten him to trust her, just in time for her to accidentally betray that trust, and the worst part was, it was already done. There was nothing she could do about it now but wait for the inevitable fallout.

Maybe she was being overly pessimistic. Maybe he'd understand. Or maybe he'd see the humor in the entire situation. She reflected on how well he had handled adversity and feeling foolish in the past, and gave up on that hope immediately. In the end, she had to just pray that he took as long as possible to discover that she had achieved success by making him the butt of the joke. Realistically, she thought it was likely that she could at least make it until the end of the day. Once they went to their separate hotel rooms, he'd probably turn on his laptop, and then the jig would be up. But until then, they were busy working. He probably wouldn't think to look it up on his own, and she doubted anyone would remind him. The video was a big deal to them, but she figured it wasn't like everyone on the planet was watching it.

To her right, she heard someone make a quiet hissing noise to draw her attention. She looked and saw a groundskeeper. He had turned to face her. It was Agent Carmichael. He put down his clippers and held his smartphone up. She recognized her video, tiny though it was on his screen. He smiled broadly, pointed at the screen, gave her a thumbs-up, and mouthed the word *hilarious*.

✳ ✳ ✳

The three of them sat in a booth at a Denny's they had found just off a freeway off-ramp. Amber ate her fried chicken fingers alone on one side, next to a camera on a tripod that covered Jack and Professor Fred sitting side by side opposite her. The rationale had been that they hadn't really interviewed the professor, and that was the initial reason they met him in the first place. Unfortunately, Jack was in a bad mood, and Fred was the reason for it, so there had been little conversation. Jack ate his Reuben sandwich with one hand and pulled out his phone with the other.

"Huh," he muttered.

Amber asked, "What's up?" To her own ears, she sounded far too eager.

"I have an email here with the subject line 'great vid,'" Jack said, putting his phone in his pocket. "I'll look at it later."

Amber squirmed a bit in her seat. "Uh, Jack, we should talk about the Battery Boy video. I had a challenging time editing it."

Jack said, "I'm sure. After the CIA said you couldn't use a bunch of the material we shot, it must have been a bear trying to get the story to make sense. I'm sure whatever you came up with was great."

Fred picked a cracker and a piece of cheese out of a segmented clear plastic tray. "Wow, Jack must have a lot of faith in you, young lady."

Jack said, "She's earned it. And you probably shouldn't call her 'young lady.'"

"Why not? Both of those words are compliments."

"Yeah, but you use them together and you sound like a father about to ground her for coming home late. Besides, we should all stop talking and eat. We've wasted enough time today."

Fred said, "Hey, you're the one who wanted to stop, not me."

"For lunch. We needed to eat lunch, Fred."

"I know, but I told you, I had a cooler with lunch for all of us."

"Lunchables, Fred. You had Lunchables for all of us."

"And what's wrong with that? Lunch is what Lunchables were designed for."

"Lunchables were not designed to be good for lunch. Lunchables were designed to be good for busy parents who need to pack their kids a lunch but don't have time to make and bag up the sandwich, chips, and stack of Oreos the kid really wants."

Professor Fred said, "Lunchables are fun! They're like a deli platter for a party of one."

Jack shook his head. "That's the saddest thing I've ever heard."

"Nonsense! Look at my Lunchable. What's not to like? You've got crackers; you've got cheese; you've got salami. Who doesn't like salami? Here, Jack, you want a piece of salami?" Fred held up a disk of cured meat. "Come on. You know you want a piece of salami."

Jack said, "What the hell?" and took the slice of meat and popped it in his mouth.

Amber said, "They are for kids, though."

Fred said, "You, my friend, are trapped in a self-made mind prison! It doesn't matter how old you are. If you want to eat a Lunchable, you should. Or if you want to drink a Capri Sun, you should."

"I don't."

"Good. More Capri Suns for me." Fred reached down into his cooler and pulled out a Capri Sun.

Jack said, "They make things like Lunchables for adults, you know."

"Yes! My point exactly! And what's the difference between the kids' and adults' versions? A boring name, a drab cover, and it's bigger. I just eat three Lunchables, and I get the same meal, have more fun, and I feel like I'm being a glutton when I'm actually eating sensibly."

"Doesn't that get expensive?" Amber asked.

"It would if I bought them new."

Jack stopped chewing his salami. "What?"

"I refill the trays myself," Fred said.

Amber said, "But you have to buy the trays to begin with."

"No! I salvage the trays out of the trash at the elementary school down the street."

Jack made a sound that could only be described as a closed-mouth scream, and continued making the noise as he flapped his hands and looked frantically around the table until he found a napkin, which he pressed over his mouth, and spat the partially chewed salami out.

"Oh, calm down," Fred said. "I wash them before I use them."

Amber, who couldn't have been happier that she had a camera running, asked, "How do you reseal them?"

Fred beamed with pride. "Glue stick! I always look for the ones where they didn't peel the top completely off."

Jack drank a mighty swig of his Diet Coke and swished it around in his mouth before spitting it into his water glass. "Okay, look, Fred, I appreciate you trying to help us drum up material, but I think it would be best if we just went back to your place after lunch so Amber and I can pick up our rental car and go to the university."

"No," Fred said. "That's a mistake. You'll miss out on the best story I have lined up."

At the same instant, Jack said, "I don't care," and Amber asked, "What's that?"

Jack glared at Amber as Fred said, "Have you ever heard the name Polybius?"

Amber said, "No."

Jack rolled his eyes. "The story is that in the early eighties, I think in Portland, Oregon, this video game nobody had ever heard of just turned up in an arcade. The game was called Polybius. Kids lined up to play it, but nobody could describe what the game was actually like."

"Almost as if," Fred said, "the game messed with their memories."

"Or," Jack said, "it never really existed, and they're confusing it with Tempest or something. Anyway, they say kids started suffering headaches, nausea, and personality changes. Then one guy had a seizure while he was playing and died right there on the sticky arcade floor. Workmen in black jumpsuits came and hauled the game away in an unmarked van, and to this day nobody's ever seen the game again."

Amber looked at Fred, her eyes wide. "And you know someone who's found it?"

"No."

Jack laughed. "You're right Fred. That's a great story."

"He hasn't found a Polybius machine, but he has evidence that the technology Polybius tested is being built into modern games right now."

"And that evidence is?" Jack asked.

"His own teenaged son."

"Who is having seizures?"

"No, but he says the boy spends all of his money on video games, plays them nonstop. Apparently, the kid's become sullen and moody and doesn't seem to be interested in anything."

"So, the mind-controlling Polybius technology has caused his teenage boy to act like a teenage boy. Come on, man. Most of us go through a phase like that. That's why Doors albums still sell."

"He says his son's personality has totally changed, Jack."

"Because he's developing one."

Amber said, "Or he's broken on through to the other side."

Jack laughed. "Very good! Check out Amber with the classic-rock reference!"

"He says the kid doesn't want to do anything," the professor said, "even something fun. This winter he tried to take the kid ice fishing, like, four times, and each time his son refused to go."

"It's ice fishing, Fred! Most people would refuse. You go somewhere cold, uncomfortable, and dangerous and stay there long enough to still get bored, for what? Your reward, if you're lucky, is a live fish that you get to kill, gut, then cook yourself."

"And he'd get to spend time with his dad."

"His dad, who thinks there's something wrong with him and probably wants to discuss it at length."

"You never went ice fishing with your dad, Jack?"

"Fred, my dad knew better than to accompany any of his kids out onto anything that remotely resembled an ice floe. No, as near as I can tell, your great story is: 'normal kid's dad is a pain in the ass,' and that's not news. I think we'll just go back to your place, get our car, and be on our way."

Fred said, "I can see that you're hell-bent on going to the university and talking to these scientists you've got lined up. I understand that. I still say you'll regret it, but I understand it. And you're not interested in the Polybius story, for your own personal reasons. Fine. Whatever. But it's a waste of time to go back to my place. I'll drive you to the university. That way, when you see what a bust the stories you have lined up there are, we can move on to the main event."

Jack sagged. "What main event, Fred?"

"I have something special planned for dinner."

"You intend to still be with us at dinnertime?!"

"Yes, and you'll be glad of it! Like I said, I have something lined up."

"What? Homemade Dinner-ables?"

"Why are you so excited about these university guys, anyway? Who are they? What's their deal?"

"They are legitimate, reputable scientists doing exciting, peer-reviewed work. One's a biochemist who—"

"Ugh," Fred moaned. "Biochemists! They're the worst! Their work always sounds so promising, like it's going to change the world, until you ask them actual questions about it. Then they start backpedaling and minimizing until eventually they tell you not to get excited, because their work doesn't really mean anything at all yet. It's something about the university environment. I don't know if it's because they get tenure and then don't feel they need to try anymore, or if they're so hungry to get tenure that they try too hard, but you should just disregard any story that involves a college professor. They're useless, every one of them."

Amber repeated, "Professors are useless?"

"Yes."

"Every one of them?"

Fred nodded emphatically. "Yes."

Amber asked, "Aren't you a professor?"

"Well, I'm not a university professor."

"What kind of professor are you, then?"

"You know, garden variety."

"Are you even a professor at all, Fred?"

Fred smiled sheepishly. "Well, I profess to be."

20

As Jack went over the intro he'd hashed out, attempting to commit it to memory, Amber scanned her inbox. The avalanche of congratulatory emails proved addictive, even though her joy at receiving them was tempered by the knowledge that every person who saw and loved the video brought her closer to the inevitable moment when Jack would discover it, an event the fallout from which might make it impossible for her to make any more videos with him. That said, she found the endorphin rush of reading email headers praising her work too enjoyable to resist.

Of course, the endorphin flow stopped abruptly when she saw a message from Renee Owens, Jack's wife. The message subject line read simply, "Wow!"

Amber tried to ignore the sensation that her stomach and intestines had been replaced with ice and live eels. She actually experienced a moment of tunnel vision as she opened and read the message.

Amber
I just saw the video and I couldn't believe it. It's so FUNNY!
I had to watch it three more times. I kept missing parts because

I was laughing so hard. You're very talented, of course, but I'm really impressed that you got Jack to sign off on it! He's usually so distrusting, and he hates looking foolish. Being okay with this is an enormous step for him. I can't wait to talk to him about it. He hasn't replied to any of my emails yet. No doubt you're both busy working on the next masterpiece.

I had a hunch this project was going to be good for him. Thank you, Amber.

Renee

Amber put her phone away, spent a few seconds with her eyes closed, just breathing and mustering her strength, then said, "Jack?"

"Yeah, no need to rush me," Jack said. "I'm ready to go."

"Jack, I think we should talk."

"Okay. Cool. But can we put a pin in it for now? I'm all ready to shoot the intro, and Dr. Hines has a tight schedule as it is."

"Yeah, sure, Jack. But remember, I want to talk, okay? It's important."

"Sure thing, partner."

Amber gritted her teeth and readied her camera.

Jack stood in an immaculate white laboratory full of large glass-fronted machines holding small vials, dishes, and tubes, all being heated, chilled, isolated from any movement, or gently agitated. He raised one eyebrow and said, "Immortality. Like the famous glass of water that the optimist sees as half full and the pessimist half empty, some view eternal life as a limitless opportunity for enjoyment. Others imagine literally endless suffering. Love the idea of immortality or hate it, every one of us has thought about it, usually around our birthdays. It's always been a fantasy, but that could one day change. I am in the laboratory of Dr. Brendan Hines, professor of biochemistry at Capitol University. His peer-reviewed work, funded by a Fortune 500 company, may well point the way to immortality. Will history remember him as a benefactor who saved us or a monster who cursed us? Thanks to him, we might well all live to find out."

Jack turned to Dr. Hines, a thin man with thin, wire-framed glasses and thinning blond hair.

"Doctor, thank you for taking the time to discuss your work with us. I apologize for the tone of my introduction, but your work raises certain questions."

Dr. Hines said, "No need to apologize, Jack. When you research the field of anti-aging medicine, you get used to being called a monster for trying to prevent deaths."

"Now, Doctor, my understanding is that you've altered the DNA of living organisms to prevent them from growing old and dying."

"That is, essentially, correct."

"So, you have created immortality."

Dr. Hines shook his head and held up his hands, signaling that Jack should slow down. "Well, now, Jack, we can't claim that. The word 'immortal' suggests that the subject won't ever die. We are merely arresting the aging process. Excessive heat, lack of food and water, or physical forces could still easily kill our test subjects."

"Point taken. But if all the subjects' basic biological needs are met, they will never grow old and die. Correct?"

"See, again, Jack, we can't really claim that. First, simply by existing, an object grows older. A solid block of granite doesn't noticeably change over millennia, but it grows older. Our subjects are growing older, but they are not deteriorating with age. Furthermore, while they are not aging or dying right now, we simply cannot claim to know yet whether they will ever age or die."

"When will you know that?"

"Logically, not until a subject ages and dies. At that point, we would know that we've failed. If the subject continues to live and show no signs of aging, all that will prove is that it has not aged or died *yet*. We can't know if the subject will never age until it never does, which, if we've been successful, it never will. In science, you need to be very precise with your language. Sadly, it often makes things more confusing, not less."

Jack said, "Agreed."

"What I can claim, with one hundred percent accuracy, is that using CRISPR methods, we have altered the genetic code of living organisms to seemingly arrest the aging process and dramatically extend their longevity well past their expected lifespan."

"Extended how long?"

"So far, by three hundred percent."

"So, to put it in easily understood terms: if your subjects were humans, they'd be"—Jack paused as he did some quick math—"two hundred and ten years old, roughly?"

"Roughly, but I cannot stress enough that we are not experimenting on humans and have no plan to for a very long time."

"I understand."

A voice from the corner of the room asked, "Who are you experimenting on?"

Amber whip-panned to show Professor Frederick Franks sitting in the corner, arms folded, looking thoroughly unimpressed. "What exactly are your test subjects?"

Jack said, "Fred, Amber and I agreed you could tag along if you didn't interfere."

"I'm not interfering. I'm participating. This is exciting research, and I'm just naturally curious what organisms have benefited from its miraculous results."

Dr. Hines said, "I wouldn't describe my results as miraculous. Encouraging is a more—"

"Yes, of course," Fred interrupted. "Well backpedaled. What are your subjects? Chimps? Rabbits? Mice, perhaps?"

"Bacteria."

"Naturally," Fred said. "Makes sense. Only one cell to keep track of. And you've tripled their life span? How long do the bacteria usually live?"

"One hundred days, depending on conditions."

"And you've extended that to a year!"

"Nearly."

Fred smiled. Well, I can see why you're describing your work as 'finding the key to immortality.' It sounds a lot better than 'prolonging the lives of germs.'"

Jack retook control of the interview. "The point, Doctor, is that your method has reliably arrested the aging of actual living organisms."

"That's right," Dr. Hines said, turning toward Jack and away from Fred. "It's very exciting."

"I'll say. And now that you've proved the concept in bacteria, you move on to more complex organisms?"

"Eventually. First, other labs around the world will try to replicate my work on *E. Coli* bacteria. That's just started. When they complete their experiments and publish their results, if they find our work repeatable, then we go through the same process with other bacteria. If the method proves adaptable, in as soon as ten years we could move on to larger vertebrates."

"Primates?' Jack asked.

"Oh no. I should think brine shrimp or something similar."

"But how long until you can start trying your treatment on people?"

"Oh, Jack, I wouldn't want to speculate."

"Just a ballpark, Doctor. Are we talking about years? Decades?"

"If pressed, I'd say within several score."

"Score?"

"Yes, Jack. A score is twenty years."

"Yes. I know. We all read the Gettysburg Address. So, within twenty to forty years—"

"Several score, Jack. Somewhere over three, if it all pans out. I know that's disappointing, but I don't want to over-promise here."

Professor Fred said, "And you haven't. Essentially, what you're saying is that we shouldn't get too excited, because your work, from a practical point of view, doesn't really mean anything yet."

Hines shrugged. "That's one way to put it, I suppose. But my work is an important early step in the study of immortality."

"Yeah, of course. Um, *E. Coli*, I feel I've heard of that bacteria before. It lives in poop. And now, thanks to you, it can live in poop"—Fred made his voice low and tremulous and waved his hands as he spoke in a spooky version of jazz hands— "Foooreeeeveeeeer!"

"No. I mean, yes, it is found living in poop. We prefer to call it feces. But that's not its habitat. It is excreted with feces, but its preferred environment is in the colons of mammals."

"Ah," Professor Fred said, "So poop isn't its home. The colon is its home. The poop is its furniture. It doesn't live in poop; it lives with poop—foooreeeeveeeer! And doesn't *E. Coli* make people sick?"

Dr. Hines said, "It can, yes. If a person ingests *E. Coli*, it can cause diarrhea and nausea that can lead to death by severe dehydration in rare cases."

Jack blinked at Dr. Hines. "And you've made it immortal?"

"Not immortal, Jack. We don't know that. We've made it very long-lived."

"But is that wise, Doctor?"

"It's only harmful if it gets out into the wild and people ingest it. That's not going to happen, because we're going to keep it locked up safely in this lab."

Professor Fred said, "Foorrrreevvvvvveerrrrr!"

* * *

They left Dr. Hines's lab, stopped to wash their hands thoroughly, then hustled across campus, moving with too much urgency to even check their phones. Amber alternated between feeling happy that Jack had forgotten that she wanted to talk and feeling guilty for being happy.

When they arrived at the lecture hall of their next subject, they had only five minutes for Jack to throw together an intro and Amber to get it committed to video before the class ended and the corridor flooded with college students.

After some rushed scribbling and mumbling, Jack announced he was ready. They set up in front of a window across the hall, and Jack began.

"Often, science is seen as the enemy of religion, because they attempt to answer many of the same questions, and the answers science comes up with have a nasty habit of contradicting the ones religion has been providing for hundreds of years. But science is an iterative process; the answers it provides can change, sometimes drastically. There are even rare occasions where science's new answers change so drastically that they go around the horn and resemble the answer religion gave in the first place. For example, Jarred De Jong, professor of theoretical physics, extols a legitimate scientific theory that offers a surprising answer to one of mankind's most fundamental questions: is there life after death?"

Amber said, "Cut. I'm happy with that. You?"

A bell sounded.

Jack said, "I'd better be."

Almost instantly, students coursed into the hall.

Professor Fred shook his head. "A theoretical physicist! They're the worst!"

Amber said, "You said biochemists were the worst."

"And they are. Biochemists are the absolute worst, except for theoretical physicists, who are even worse. They make these attention-grabbing grandiose statements about what their work proves, and they claim it's all so simple, but when you ask them to explain it, the first thing they ask you to do is imagine something that's completely impossible. Then they just bury you under an avalanche of nonsense until you don't know which way is up.

Then the worst part is that you walk away thinking it all adds up, until you try to explain it to someone else. Then you realize that you're talking crazy and you sound like an idiot."

Once the flow of bodies out the door stopped, Amber, Jack, and Professor Fred walked into the lecture hall. A few straggling students finished gathering their things and vacating as a portly man used a spray bottle and paper towels to clean the dry-erase boards thoroughly enough that only faint traces of red ink showed.

Jack said, "Professor De Jong?"

The man at the dry-erase board turned and saw them. His beard and eyebrows warped in such a way as to suggest a smile. "Mr. Owens! I was afraid you wouldn't make it."

Jack, Amber, and Fred walked down a set of steps that flanked the tiered rows of seats as Professor De Jong ambled to the corner of the room to meet them. After a round of introductions, handshakes, and a strangely steely glare from Fred, De Jong said, "I'm delighted you came, but having seen the video you posted today, I don't know how suitable my theory will be for your show."

Jack blinked at him. "The video's up?"

"Yes, and I enjoyed it very much."

Jack turned to Amber, delighted. She feigned surprise and happiness at this news, managing two lies with one weak smile—which made her feel like a terrible person, but an efficient one.

De Jong continued, "I don't know that my work will really work for your purposes."

Professor Fred said, "Good of you to admit that. So, let's not waste any time. I still have another story lined up. We can be there in—"

"Fred, we aren't going anywhere," Jack cut him off, then turned his attention back to Professor De Jong. "I know that your work is complicated and not terribly visual, but it's more than interesting enough to hold the viewers' attention."

"You're the experts. Well, please, have a seat, and I'll talk you through the theory."

Jack sat in the front row. Amber sat two rows back so she could keep Professor De Jong as he explained and Jack as he listened in the same frame. At first, Professor Fred tried to sit next to Jack, but Jack insisted that he sit far away, out of frame. Amber surreptitiously clamped a sport camera to a chair back and aimed it at Professor Fred.

Professor De Jong said, "My theory is very simple. A child could understand it, as long as you keep a few key concepts in mind. First, please picture a bottomless pit."

Amber glanced at Professor Fred, who smirked back at her.

De Jong said, "It's a big hole, straight down, that never, ever ends." De Jong turned to the dry-erase board and drew two long, parallel vertical lines with a circle at the top denoting the pit's rim, an arrow pointing down, and an infinity symbol at the bottom.

"Now, imagine a pregnant woman falling down the hole." De Jong drew a stick figure falling and added long, streaming hair and a round belly.

Professor Fred asked, "Did she jump in, or was she pushed?"

De Jong said, "Don't know. It's not relevant to the story."

Fred snorted and muttered, "Because either of those stories would be interesting."

Jack glared at Fred. "I'm sorry, Professor De Jong. Please continue."

"So, imagine the woman gives birth while falling down the bottomless pit." De Jong drew a baby. "And that baby lives his entire life, grows old, and dies of old age while falling down the bottomless pit." He drew an arrow leading from the baby to a stick figure wearing a baseball cap, then another to one wearing a tie, and finally to one holding a cane. "For this man's entire life, he has known nothing but falling down a bottomless pit. With me so far?"

Jack said, "I think so."

Fred asked, "What do they eat?"

Jack said, "That's not relevant."

De Jong, though, without missing a beat, said, "They brought food with them," and drew a box falling just above the two figures, marked Soup.

"That'd be a lot of food," Fred said.

"Yeah, but it's not like they have to carry it."

"What about water?"

"The food's all soup, so it does double duty."

"So," Jack said, "moving on—"

Fred cut in. "What about when they go to the bathroom?"

Again without hesitation, De Jong said, "They aim it toward the walls of the shaft, where most of it sticks, and what little doesn't is decelerated by the impact and remains above them, splashing against the walls until it completely disperses."

Jack said, "I'm sorry about this."

De Jong smiled. "Don't worry about it. I've used this example in my classes for years. There's no smart-aleck question he can ask that I haven't heard before."

Fred asked, "What does he do when his mother dies of old age?"

"Same thing as when he goes to the bathroom: shoves her toward the wall, but more solemnly. And he says a few words first. Okay. So, as you know, there are three directions a person can travel in three-dimensional space. Forward-backward, left-right, and up-down. In physics, we call up-down the z-axis. To this man, the man falling down the pit, his experience of the z-axis differs greatly from ours. At any given moment, he is at one unique point on the z-axis. He can speed up or slow down slightly, but he cannot stop, he can't jump ahead to a part much further down, and once he's past a spot, he can't go back. It's gone forever. Make sense?"

Jack said, "So far."

"He experiences the z-axis the way we experience time. To him, height is linear. We like to say that the past is gone and the future hasn't happened yet. To him, the above is gone, and the below hasn't happened yet, but it's only his perception that it's all blinking in and out of existence. We can see that everything above and below him exists at the same time, because we're standing off to the side, stationary. He can't imagine a world in which he isn't falling, because he's never experienced a floor."

Jack furrowed his brow and said, "Huh."

As professors have for generations, De Jong took this sign of confusion as the signal that he had made his point and could move on. "That's the first of the basic concepts you need to keep in mind. We perceive time as flowing, but that doesn't mean that it does, or that ours is the only way of perceiving it. Now the second is a little harder to get your head around."

"Harder?" Jack asked.

"Yes. It's not complicated, but it's kinda weird."

"Weirder than the first one?" Jack asked.

"Imagine a person walking due north at one mile per hour, and a second walks west at one mile per hour." De Jong drew two lines connecting at a right angle and stick figures at the far ends. "Now, imagine a third person, between them, walking to the northwest at one mile per hour. That person moves the same distance as the other two, but does not go as far north or as far west as they did. The speed in either direction has slowed, split with a second direction. See, Jack?"

"Yeah?"

De Jong said, "This effect, where you split your speed between two directions—it also happens with time. Einstein proposed it, and we've proven it many times."

Fred asked, "How?"

"With math. And clocks. And jets. See, if our speeds aren't the same, our times are also not the same. If I walk across the room while you sit still, I move faster through space than you but more slowly through time, and what for me feels like right now is actually a tiny amount forward in your future. What feels like now to you is my past. See?"

Jack sat with his mouth slightly open and said nothing.

De Jong said, "Good. And here's the weird part."

Fred said, "Finally!"

"This effect, this discrepancy in our nows, it magnifies depending on how far apart we are. Since we're both here on the same planet, it's never large enough to measure, but if we were on different planets, across the galaxy from one another, my now could be your one hundred years ago, or it could be your one hundred years from now, and it swings back and forth, through this huge range of your time, depending on what direction I'm moving at any given moment. And if that's true—"

"Is that true?" Jack asked.

"Yes. And that means, logically, that the past can't be gone, and the future isn't yet to be."

Fred said, "Because for someone in the universe, they're both now."

De Jong smiled and pointed at Fred. "Yes! You've got it! Though, technically, what you just said is wrong. Neither the past nor the future is really now. Essentially, there's no such thing as now, and there never will be."

Jack groaned.

Fred said, "So, what you're going to tell us is that nobody is ever truly gone, because somewhere out in the cosmos, there's an alien walking toward us instead of away?"

De Jong said, "No, that's not what I'm saying, although you make a valid point."

"I do? I wasn't trying to."

"I know. Now that we have these two basic concepts in mind, I can get down to business."

Jack muttered, "Basic concepts?"

"Yes. Science has always presumed that there is no consciousness after death, because the brain is the seat of consciousness and as part of the process of death the brain stops functioning and is irrevocably destroyed, so when your time is up, it's up. But science proves that time is just a matter of perception. We perceive time passing, but it doesn't really move. And science also proves that nothing is created or destroyed. It all still exists in space-time. So the brain still exists and functions, and perhaps death simply changes its perception. Perhaps it loses its linearity. Maybe the moment of death is like the man in the bottomless pit finally hitting the floor."

Fred said, "Sudden and painful."

"No doubt, but also a revelation, maybe, because now he can perceive the pit as it really is. He can look back over the entire thing at once."

"And that's what you think happens when we die?" Jack asked.

"I don't know," De Jong said. "I mean, imagine having the ability to perceive your entire life all at once."

Jack said, "Your life flashing before your eyes."

"Perhaps. Or you could conceivably see your existence from a perspective you've never experienced."

Jack said, "An out-of-body experience."

"Could be. Conceivably, you might relive moments from your life, as many times as you want, in whatever order you want."

"That's interesting," Jack said. "I suppose if you lead a good life, that could be very pleasant. And if you know you were a terrible person, it could be awful, not being able to change anything."

"And that brings us to the alternate-universe theory. Are you familiar?"

Jack said, "A bit. I've had people on the show talk about it. The idea is that the universe is infinite, but the number of atoms of the periodic table is finite, as are the kinds of molecules they can combine into and the ways those atoms can interact. So, given an endless amount of space and time, anything that is possible, even if it's unlikely, becomes inevitable. That means there must be other Earths, where other versions of us are having this conversation, only in one we all have hats, in another women have beards instead of men, and so on."

"Idiocy," Fred said.

"But the math bears it out," De Jong said. "Given infinite time and an infinite universe, there will be an infinite number of everybody and everything. But that's not what I was referring to. No, I meant a theory that explains the paradox of the Schrodinger's Cat model, the mind experiment where a cat could be both alive and dead at the same time. It seems, according to the math, that the way it works is that when a quantum event occurs, as it does with Schrodinger's cat, at that instant a second parallel dimension springs into existence, so now there are two, one with a live cat and one with a dead cat."

Jack asked, "How often do quantum events occur?"

"Could be as many as millions every second."

Professor Fred said, "Wait a second. Are you telling me that instead of one infinite universe with an infinite number of me in it, there's an infinite number of universes with an infinite number of me in them?"

De Jong said, "Yeah."

But each of those universes is infinite and holds an infinite number of me?"

"Yes."

"So, you're telling me that there's an infinity of me, times two?!"

"No," De Jong said, laughing. "I understand why you'd think that, but that's not really how it works."

"Good."

"You can't multiply infinity by two. There's only one infinity of you, but two different ways. And who's to say that once it untethered from linear time, our consciousness wouldn't become untethered also from any one dimension, free to explore any of those infinite possibilities . . . well, not all the infinite possibilities. Half of them, though infinity doesn't work like that. The ones formed by quantum events, you might be able to explore those."

"Free to experience all the possible outcomes of every decision, undo every bad break. I really like that idea."

"It is appealing," De Jong said.

"And you can prove it?" Jack asked.

De Jong said, "No."

"No?"

"Absolutely not. Others have proved the parts about how we perceive time and about all times existing at once, and math bears out parallel universes and doppelgangers. That's all established science. The part I've added, the part about consciousness possibly continuing after our perceived death, that's conjecture at this point."

"And what would you need to prove it?" Jack asked.

De Jong stroked his chin and looked at the dry-erase board. "That's a good question. I have no idea. I think it may be unprovable."

Jack sighed. "So all you have is a theory."

Fred said, "It's not even a theory. A theory can be proved or disproved. What he has is a supposition."

De Jong said, "I prefer to call it conjecture. You're right that I can't prove that my conjecture is true, but my point is that nobody can prove that it isn't. And if nobody can prove that it isn't true, people can hope that it is."

"Listen to yourself," Fred said. "You're a scientist. It's not your place to give people hope."

Jack said, "I don't know if that's true or not, but I really don't like hearing it."

De Jong said, "There's nothing wrong with hope. For a long time, the overwhelming consensus has been that the very idea of any sort of consciousness after death has no basis in science. This idea casts that certainty into doubt."

Fred said, "So your contribution to the field is that we know less now than we did when you started. You must be so proud."

"I am!"

21

Professor Fred turned around and walked backward to look at Jack, who trudged down the hall a few steps behind him. Amber followed several feet farther back, recording the two men as she walked.

"I told you that was going to be a waste of time," Professor Fred said.

"Yes," Jack said. "And then you made sure you were right by deliberately wasting everybody's time."

Professor Fred raised his hands to fend off Jack's verbal attack. "Hey, all I did was ask questions."

"Telling him his work is useless isn't a question, Fred."

"Not on its own. That was part of the setup for the question that came after. Remember? When I asked him if he felt guilty for accepting a salary?"

"Yes," Jack said. "I remember."

Perhaps sensing from Jack's demeanor that if his goal was to improve Jack's mood, talking more wouldn't get the job done, Fred turned back around and continued his walk to the exit.

Amber wondered if now might be the perfect time to bring up the video. Jack's anger at Professor Fred took up so much of his attention that his anger at Amber might not even register, as when someone scraped their elbow while breaking their arm. She knew that was wishful thinking, but she figured that at the very least he was already in a terrible mood, so telling him about the video wouldn't make much difference.

She shut off her camera and sped up to walk next to him. "Hey, Jack. I need to tell you—"

"I'm sorry," Jack said. "Please hold that thought. I really need to use this restroom here."

As he disappeared into the men's room, Amber decided he had a good idea, and she went to the ladies' room as well. Of course, men's rooms and ladies' rooms are very different beasts. Jack emerged from the restroom much sooner than Amber, and he put that time to good use.

She came out into the hall to see Jack leaned against the wall, holding his phone sideways and staring at it, his eyes wide, mouth shut tight, and no blood in his face. Fred watched over Jack's shoulder, alternating between stifling a laugh and hiding a full-body cringe.

More than an hour of the most intense silent treatment Amber had ever endured followed, as Fred drove his van through the DC rush-hour traffic back to his house so Amber and Jack could grab their rental car and catch their flights out of town. Amber said many times that she was eager to discuss the situation. Jack said nothing, made no noises, and utterly refused to acknowledge her.

Professor Fred cleared his throat. "I think I know what you're going to say, but since the afternoon was a bust, if you'd like, you might see if there's a flight out in the morning. I still have another story lined up for tonight. After that, you could sleep at my place."

After an uncomfortable silence, Jack asked, "You have guest rooms that aren't full of crap?"

Fred winced. "It isn't crap, Jack. It's evidence. And, no, all my rooms are full, but I can clear some floor space and loan you a couple of sleeping bags."

"You have a lot of people sleep on your floor?" Jack asked.

"No."

"Then why do you keep multiple sleeping bags around?"

"They're evidence. That doesn't mean I can't get some use out of them."

Jack asked, "What? What are they evidence from?"

"A ghost encounter. A really interesting one. The ghost was seen in multiple places, but always in the same tent."

"Haunted camping gear. You wanted us to sleep in haunted camping gear."

"Come on, Jack. Don't be silly. The tent's haunted, not the sleeping bags. If they had found the ghost in the sleeping bag with them, that'd be another thing."

"But Fred, if the tent's haunted, something terrible probably happened in there, and the sleeping bags were probably in the tent when it happened. Right? Am I right?"

Professor Fred said, "I promise you, I wouldn't offer to let you use the sleeping bags without washing them first."

"No, Fred. The answer is no."

"Yeah," Professor Fred said. "I figured that out."

Amber asked, "Professor, do you have the haunted tent? It might make a good segment. A portable haunting."

Fred shook his head. "I know I offered and all, but seeing the general vibe in the car right now, I think it might be best if I just get you both to your rental car and let you be on your way."

Jack turned around and smiled into Amber's camera. "Fred wants to get rid of us, Amber. Just think about that for a minute. *Fred* wants to get rid of *us*."

"What's that supposed to mean?" Fred asked.

"Oh, come on, Fred. Don't pretend you don't know. I've been trying to shake you all day, and I've been wondering why she wasn't cooperating. Now I get it. She wants to shoot as much footage of your antics as she can so that editing it all into a ridiculous spectacle will be easier. Admit it, Amber. He's a gold mine for you."

"That's not fair," Amber said. "You've had him on your show dozens of times. But I suppose you'll say you're laughing with him and I'm laughing at him."

"I didn't laugh at him at all, until after the show. During the show, I just let him talk while I worked on one of my models. All I had to do was raise my head now and then to say 'That's a provocative idea.' Everything seems more plausible over the phone in the middle of the night. But when you broadcast his work in four-K video, he's going to look ridiculous, because that's exactly what he is. Fred, she was only humoring you so that she could mock you on the internet. How does that make you feel?"

Fred thought for a moment, then shrugged. "Eh, any press is good press."

Jack muttered, "Idiot."

Fred said, "Hey, Jack. Don't take it out on me just because you're mad at her."

"I'm not mad at her, Fred. I'm mad at you *and* her. I can multitask like that. It's just goes to show what they say is true: Never meet your heroes."

Amber said, "Fred was never your hero, Jack, and I certainly wasn't."

"No, but I was your hero—both of you! And you two meeting me has been a disaster. A disaster for me!"

Amber said, "That was mean, Jack."

Jack let out a long breath. You're right. It was. I'm sorry. You didn't deserve that, Fred."

Fred said, "You're upset. I get that. Apology accepted."

Amber asked, "You really think meeting me has been a disaster, Jack?"

"Do you think it hasn't? Look, I don't blame you. I'm unhappy with you, but I don't blame you. You're a producer with a talent for making funny videos where people look like jerks. They hired you. You made a funny video where your subject looked like a jerk. I've seen the video now, and I have to admit, it's funny. It's hilarious. And I look like a jerk in it. A huge jerk."

"I didn't mean to send them that video. This is all an accident."

"You didn't mean to send it, but you made it on purpose, didn't you? So it was, at best, half an accident."

"Jack, I never intended for anyone to see that video. I only made it because I was desperate to find a way to keep my job."

"And you have kept your job, only it's changed to making videos specifically to mock me. I guess the question is whether you intend to keep that job?"

Amber took a moment to gather her thoughts. When she spoke again, it was in a calmer, lower, more soothing tone. "It's my hope that you and I can work together to make the videos they want in a way that's acceptable to you."

"So the answer is yes, you plan to keep the job mocking me, and you want me to help you do it. Lovely."

Amber said, "Jack, you trusted me. I betrayed your trust, accidentally, and I'm sorry."

"I agree with the first two things you said, and I only have your word for the third. I've seen what that's worth."

"So you're never going to trust me again," Amber said.

"I might," Jack said. "I've been known to make the same mistake twice."

The Smallcano

22

Amber leaned heavily on the door and pointed her camera out the open window of the rented SUV to frame her shot. Jack, in his tweed jacket and bolo tie uniform, stood in the middle of a freshly tarred road that stretched out behind him. Weed-filled ditches ran along both sides like the gutters of a bowling alley. Beyond them, walls of corn stalks, ready to be harvested at any moment, swayed in the substantial breeze.

Amber said, "Ready when you are."

Jack groaned, "Uh-huh," and took a moment to put on his game face.

"Of all the thousands of stories I have covered on *That's Not Right*, there is one that has generated the most interest. Of course, while we all are drawn to nature, we are also acutely aware that nature is constantly trying to kill us. Maybe we have a natural interest in anything that sounds like a new weapon in nature's arsenal. No matter what the draw is that keeps people fascinated with this story, we're about to get more of it, as we take our first in-person look at the smallcano."

Amber said, "That's great. We can do another if you'd like, though."

Jack answered her question by starting back to the SUV before she finished her sentence. He grimaced and walked with difficulty, pulling his feet upward forcefully with each step. A layer of gooey black gunk stuck to his shoes, leaving ill-defined footprints in the road behind him and pulling up chunks of gravel that stuck to his soles like nuts in a layer of frosting. With each step, an additional layer of tar and gravel adhered to the one before, making his shoes larger, heavier, and more misshapen. Walking required tremendous effort. He extended his arms wide for balance.

He asked, "You getting this?"

Amber said, "Yes."

"Silly of me to ask."

"Be careful. You don't want to fall and get that stuff on your clothes."

"Oh yeah, I'm sure you'd hate that."

"I would, Jack."

Jack stopped walking and stared at her.

Amber said, "I'd film it and use it in the video, but I wouldn't be happy that it happened."

Jack reached the edge of the road and stepped off the tar-gravel mix into a ditch full of assorted weeds growing in loose dirt, all of which stuck to his shoes. He hoisted himself up sideway into the driver's seat with his legs hanging out the open door. After he pulled off one shoe, he held it up so Amber could get a shot of it. The unremarkable Costco-grade black fabric sneaker's sole was coated completely in tar, gravel, and plants. He tilted the shoe around so that the camera could capture it from all angles.

Amber said, "I gotta say, you're handling this pretty well."

Jack reached back to place his shoe on the floor behind the passenger seat. "I know if I throw a fit, it'll end up on the internet. It sort of stops me in my tracks. Congratulations. Renee has been trying to get me to watch my temper since before we got married, and you finally found a way to do it. All it took was publicly shaming me on a global level." Jack bent down to remove the other shoe.

"I wasn't trying to shame you."

"You didn't try to not shame me either. You were trying to get laughs. Shame is a byproduct."

Amber winced, as if she were about to pull a Band-Aid off a particularly painful spot. "How's the radio show doing? Are the listener numbers down since the Battery Boy video dropped?"

"I think you know they're way up. But how long do you think those new listeners will stick around? I'm going to have to figure some way to change the show and give them what they want, but it's radio. They can't see me get humiliated. I'll have to come up with things I can do that would cause me to make amusing noises. That doesn't sound like a fun way to make a living."

"I don't think you need to change your show, Jack."

"You already did. You can see it in my callers."

"Fewer callers?"

"No, they're up too. All asking questions about the Battery Boy, or what it was like to wear the Normalizer. A bunch called in to talk about winning strategies for the board games I lost."

"That doesn't sound so bad."

"It is when you're doing a show about the yeti. It's difficult to make that segue. Asking your guest if he thinks the abominable snowman would be good at Monopoly is funny maybe twice."

Amber shrugged. "So maybe you just adapt a little. You could have an expert in game strategy on."

Jack shook his head. "Amber, it's tedious to play Monopoly. Do you think it's going to be more fun to talk about playing it? At least now that there'll be a new video, the callers might ask about a different topic that isn't related to the show I'm doing. What video drops this weekend?"

"The Eel-Man. I re-edited it to make it, you know, fit the new format."

"Uh-huh. Was it difficult making me look like a buffoon?"

For a long moment, Amber chose not to respond, but the silence grew more and more uncomfortable until she finally said, "I had a lot of shots where it was obvious you were wearing shorts under your suit jacket."

"Yeah, I expect you did."

He placed his second tar-coated shoe behind her seat, closed the door, and started the engine. "Now let's go see the smallcano, which I figure is probably a pile of loose dirt with a Roman candle sticking out of the top."

They pulled up to their destination: a classic two-story farmhouse that looked a little like an Arts and Crafts home, but with no hint of artistry or craftsmanship. It was a house built long ago by a farmer who needed a place for himself and his family to bathe, eat, and sleep after a hard day's work. Exterior ornamentation would not help with those tasks, and had been omitted. The house sat in a perfect rectangle of lawn, driveways, and outbuildings carved into the vast expanse of corn fields.

Tall trees stood in a straight line, acting as a windbreak along a gravel driveway stretched down one side of the property. Jack drove the SUV into the driveway and stopped before they drew next to the house, shifting into park and killing the engine with the car flanking the lawn.

Jack reached behind Amber's seat and hauled up his encrusted shoes, wincing when he saw a discarded straw wrapper from the footwell stuck to one of them. Amber rushed around the back of the car with her camera in time to get decent footage of Jack pulling on his mutated footwear. He muttered irritably as he tied the laces of the two clumps of tar and plant matter, then stepped down into the gravel, some of which inevitably became one with his foot-clumps.

They walked across the yard, stepped up onto the concrete porch, and rang the doorbell. The door opened immediately to reveal a woman with a full face of makeup and carefully styled hair, wearing a garment that was either a robe-like dress or a dress-like robe. Her eyes flashed with feigned surprise as she said, "Mr. Owens! It's so good to finally meet you." She extended a limp hand for Jack to shake.

Jack shook her hand. "Mrs. Larson. It's nice to meet you in person."

"Please, call me Joan."

"And please call me Jack. This is my field producer, Amber."

Joan almost imperceptibly smiled and nodded a greeting at Amber, then craned her neck to follow a car driving past. Returning her undivided attention back to Jack, Joan asked, "Um, could you move your car around back? If you could do that now, I'd appreciate it. You're sort of blocking the driveway is all."

"Sure," Jack said. "No problem. Oh, say, I stepped on the road."

She looked down at his shoes. "Yes, you did, didn't you? Sorry about that. They just re-tarred it. Come back in a couple of weeks and it won't be sticky at all. The only way to get it off your shoes is to pick it off with a stout stick and elbow grease. Now, if you'll just move your car, I'll meet you around back."

Jack turned to Amber. "I don't want to take my shoes off and put them on again."

"I'll move the car."

Amber hopped in the SUV and pulled behind the house, where she found a gravel area large enough to accommodate four vehicles, with room for them to turn around and drive out. She parked the SUV next to two pickups; one was champagne-colored and immaculately clean with a four-door cab and a decal on the window that read Hers in a font so loaded with decorative loops and swashes that it became almost impossible to read. The other was a larger red two-door that was much dustier, with many scratches and nicks in its bed liner.

Between the house and the parking lot, Amber saw a swimming pool, a wooden deck with a stainless-steel barbeque grill, and a putting green carpeted with sun-faded AstroTurf and set into a concrete slab. She had no time to take establishing shots or B-roll. She leapt from the driver's seat, camera in hand, and ran back around to the driveway to film Jack walking to the rear of the house on clumpy, misshapen shoes. He stopped gathering new gravel after several steps, but the soles of his shoes were no longer flat, so balancing was difficult, and with every step, tiny rocks flew in every direction.

Amber recorded his trek to the backyard and his hunt for a good stout stick. He sat down at a wooden picnic table, threw his left leg over his right knee, and pressed the tip of the stick into the mass of detritus stuck to his shoe. The stick sank in slowly and broke, one end staying in his hand, the other protruding from the tar clump.

Jack shook his fists and let out a staccato series of single syllables, all of which were recognizable as the first few letters of incomplete curse words, but he finished none of them. Instead, he glared into the camera and got a hold of himself. With a look of utter calm, he moved his hand further down the stick and used the now-sharper broken end to push tar off his shoe.

The new tip of the stick broke.

Jack did not react, which was just as well. The footage would not have been usable, as Amber's poorly suppressed giggling shook the camera.

Despite himself, Jack cracked a smile, avoiding looking at Amber or her camera as he did so. Having given up on removing the tar, he pulled the shoe off and scraped its sole against the leg of the picnic table, at least creating a semi-flat walking surface.

Amber asked, "So, first impressions. What do you think?"

"I think Joan is lonely and likes attention."

"Agreed, but that's not what I meant. What do you think of the place? Think we'll find a smallcano here?"

"I haven't seen one yet, but if it really is small, we might not have noticed it." Jack looked around as he put one shoe on and took the other off.

Amber said, "With the wall of trees and all the corn and this place being so remote, this would be a pretty good place to hide something. It won't be easy for Agent Carmichael to spy on us here."

Jack said, "Agent Carmichael helped you save my bacon with the Battery Boy."

"Yeah, but that doesn't mean I want him watching me all the time. And even if there is a small volcano here, I doubt it will try to kidnap you, Jack. You know, just a hunch."

As Jack finished hastily scraping his other shoe, the back door of the house opened and Joan stepped out, wearing the same robe-like-dress, now accessorized with slip-on rubber boots and a straw hat with a floppy oversized brim. "I'm sorry to make you wait," she said. "I had a terrible time finding my good sun hat."

Amber said, "No problem. That one's fine."

Joan said, "This is my good one. I found it."

"Of course," Jack said, "and it looks smashing."

Joan smiled at Jack, touching the brim of her hat with one hand and the collar around the plunging neckline of her robe with the other. "Oh! Thank you, Jack! A girl does her best. Now let me show you the smallcano."

She took Jack by the arm and led him into an old wood-frame-and-metal-sheeting barn, giving no indication that she was even aware of Amber's presence. They entered through a large sliding door, which stood open. The central bay of the barn was empty at the moment, with the sliding door at the far end closed, but tire tracks on the floor showed that the barn functioned primarily as a parking and maintenance structure for a medium-sized tractor. The air inside smelled of hay, sawdust, and motor oil. Various tools for working with wood or working on tractors lined the bay to one side, while large implements that all looked tractor-towable and capable of thoroughly killing a person sat parked along the other side.

Joan said, "My husband, Bruce, and I bought this land from my uncle right after we got married. My parents helped as a wedding gift. We had just graduated from high school, and there's no way we could have scraped together the money otherwise, what with Bruce's blown-out knee scaring all the college scouts away. We noticed the volcano forming in the ground about ten years ago, and it's slowly gotten bigger ever since. But it's like any other slow-growing lump. First you think you're imagining it, then you think it's no big deal, then you hope it'll go away on its own, and by the time you realize it won't, you're too embarrassed to mention it to anyone—or at least Bruce is. I think it's a hoot. Jack, would you please be a dear and open the back door?"

Jack disentangled his arm from Joan's and opened the back barn door, leaning heavily as he pulled against the door's weight and the resistance of its rusty runners.

The camera had adjusted to the lower light level inside the barn. As the rear door slid open, light flooded in, and for a moment the camera was effectively blind. Amber heard Jack mutter "Holy crap" as the autofocus got a hold of the situation and the image resolved.

The area behind the barn was basically a courtyard, walled in by tall green trees on one side, a metal-roofed shed and some apparently disused wooden chicken coops on the other, and the ever-present wall of corn stalks straight ahead. In the middle stood a cone-shaped mound of black dirt about as tall as an adult, with a hole in the top piping out a thin stream of nasty-looking sooty steam.

Jack stepped out into the courtyard, slowly approaching the smallcano as if he were amazed at what he was seeing and afraid it might explode at any moment—both of which, Amber supposed, were probably true.

"There it is," Joan said.

"Yes," Jack said. "I see."

Joan asked, "It's weird, right?"

"Yes!" Jack said. "Very!"

23

Jack edged closer to the smallcano, then asked, "Is it dangerous? Is there a chance it'll erupt?"

Joan said, "Yeah, there's a chance, but usually the ground shakes first, so that gives you some warning."

"Seriously?! There are tremors?"

"Sure. Nothing huge. The big ones might knock stuff off the shelves in the house. It's a pain in the butt."

Jack crept forward. Behind him, Amber followed suit, matching his pace and keeping him and the smallcano in frame.

Amber saw no obvious signs that the smallcano was false or man-made: no shovel marks, no signs that anyone had brought large amounts of dirt onto the site. She didn't sense that strange, overly perfect look of a simulation made a little too artistically that is familiar to anyone who has ever visited a Disney theme park. If anything, the smallcano was ugly, and it set off an instinctive fear response deep in Amber's psyche, albeit a small one.

The uneven rim at the top of the cone gave the impression of a crookedly sharpened pencil. As they watched, a small chunk of singed rubble broke loose from the lip and rolled down the side, trailing a streamer of wispy smoke behind it. A line of harder, darker rock extended from the rim's lowest edge down the side of the mound, long and smooth at the top but widening as it descended and pooling into a broad, flat expanse of spongy black rock about the size of a tennis court.

Jack pointed at the wrinkled mass and asked, "Is that . . ."

Joan said, "Yeah, lava. It doesn't spit it out often, but when it does, it's a pretty good light show, as long as it doesn't set the barn on fire."

Amber asked, "And you've never had a geologist come out here to look at this?"

"No. Bruce wouldn't like that. And I'd have no idea where to find one, anyway."

"I'm pretty sure I could, if you can talk your husband into it."

"Sure," Joan said. "You take the easy job."

Glancing around at the actual environment instead of her camera's viewscreen, Amber could see small black blobs of cooled magma littering the area, and more than a few scorched dents on the metal wall of the barn. It was while she was looking around that Amber first heard the rumbling sound. She looked to Joan and saw sudden shock and panic in her eyes.

Joan said, "Uh-oh. Um, you two should clear out."

Jack trotted away from the smallcano, his head darting back and forth between the path ahead of him, to keep from tripping or running into anything, and the smallcano, so that if it exploded he would at least see what killed him. He and Amber both moved well back into the barn, but stopped when they noted that Joan herself had not moved.

"Joan, what are you doing?" Jack asked, as the rumble grew louder.

She turned around and said, "Get out of here!"

Jack asked, "How big of an eruption—"

"It isn't an eruption," Joan snapped. "We've got a real problem."

Amber listened, and realized that the rumble was too steady and too distant to be the smallcano, though it grew closer every second. A dull-red tractor emerged from the corn, driven by a man with a bright red face. He killed the engine, whipped a leg around, dropped to the ground, and took three strides toward Jack before the tractor stopped running.

"Who the hell are you? Get off my land! You have no right to be here!"

Jack put his hands up and took several steps backward. "Sir, my name's Jack Owens."

"I don't give one half of a fancy metric shit who you are!"

"You asked."

Joan said, "You're back early, Bruce."

"Yeah, old man McMenemy called and said some strangers in an SUV were messing around out in front of my place, so I figured I'd come see who's invading my home."

Jack said, "We were invited here."

"I didn't invite anyone here, especially not some shit-heel like you."

Jack looked down at his shoes. "That's tar."

The man stopped and scrunched his face. "What?"

Jack lifted his right foot and pointed at the clumpy mass on the sole of the shoe. "It's tar. From the road. I walked on the road . . . and . . . the tar stuck."

The man said, "Oh. Okay. I understand. You're an idiot. I'm going into the house to get one of my guns. It may take me a while to decide which one I want to shoot you with. If you wanna see what I pick, be here when I get back out."

Joan said, "Oh calm down, Bruce. I asked them to come."

"What?" Bruce sputtered. "Why? Wait, them?"

He tore his attention away from Jack and Joan and for the first time noticed Amber standing in the shadows of the barn, capturing everything with her camera.

"Stop that!" Bruce bellowed. He advanced on Amber, jabbing a finger forward her, but stopped when Jack lunged to the side, putting himself between Bruce and Amber. Jack kept his hands up, and shouted, "Amber, stop recording, okay?"

"Done," Amber said, as she dropped the camera to her side—but absolutely kept it recording.

Bruce looked at Jack and Amber, then turned and looked at the smallcano before turning to Joan, his shoulders sagging, and whining, "Why? Why, Joan? Why would you invite them here? Now they've seen the secret."

"I invited them here to show them the secret, Bruce."

"Why would you do that? I mean, I call it *the secret*. Doesn't that make my wishes clear enough?"

"What about my wishes, Bruce?"

"You want what I want, Joan: to keep our land. I've told you, if the government finds out about the secret"—he gestured toward the smallcano, still puffing away, oblivious to the human drama going on around and about it—"the first thing they'll do is tell us we can't farm this land anymore because they need to study it. If we're lucky, they'll use eminent domain to force us to sell it to them at pennies on the dollar. More likely they'll just declare the land dangerous, make it unsellable, tell us we can't live or work on it, but let us keep paying taxes on it. All because the Earth has a zit and you want to point at it and shout 'lookie!'"

Jack asked, "Would it help if I point out that we aren't with the government?"

"Who are you, then?"

"I host a radio show."

"You're the media. That's the only thing that's worse."

Joan said, "Come on, Bruce. I told you I called a radio show."

"Yes, and I told you I didn't like it. But at least you called that late-night nutjob, so probably nobody would take it seriously."

Jack said, "That's my show you're talking about."

Bruce said, "Figures."

"You know, you could apologize for insulting me just then."

"But I'm not going to. Now both of you, get off my land."

Joan said, "It's my land."

"Okay, it's our land. Now both of you, get off our land."

Joan said, "It's my land. We got it from my uncle, with my parents' money, and my name's on the deed."

"But my name's on you," Bruce said.

Jack said, "Okay, okay. We don't want to fight either of you, and we don't want to be the reason you fight each other."

Bruce said, "A little late to worry about that."

Joan shouted, "And you're not the only reason!"

Jack said, "We're going. We're going. Amber, come on."

They walked to the rented SUV in silence, Amber making sure to dangle the camera in such a way that the lens stayed pointed at Bruce so she could get some usable footage, or at least document any attack.

Amber climbed into the driver's seat. As Jack got into the passenger seat, he pulled off his shoes, looked up at Bruce, and asked, "You don't know how to remove . . . ? Never mind."

Bruce and Joan watched in silence as they drove away. Bruce looked angry. Joan looked embarrassed.

Amber said, "I kept recording when you told me to stop."

"Of course. I knew you would."

Amber smiled. "You trusted me."

"Yes. I trusted you to do the opposite of what I told you to do."

* * *

Amber leaned against a rack of sneakers, looking at her phone as Jack sat on a vinyl-padded stool with an angled mirror built into its base, trying to decide between two prospective pairs of shoes, both in shoeboxes on the floor in front of him. One pair of two-tone black-and-white leather sneakers and one of plain athletic shoes like a hospital orderly might wear, only in dull black cloth instead of white.

Amber said, "Just got a message from Joan. She says it's her land and she wants us to come back—when Bruce isn't around, naturally."

"Do we want to?" Jack placed one of the two-tone shoes on his right foot and began tying the laces.

Amber said, "I didn't really get much footage of the smallcano."

"How much do you need? It's a smoking cone. It's going to look pretty much the same from every angle."

"I don't like the idea of another shouting match, but if I try to edit together a story with what we have, it's going to be thirty seconds of smallcano and five minutes of you walking in tar-shoes."

"We don't want that." Jack pulled one of the plain cloth shoes onto his left foot. "Well, *I* don't want that. You're probably fine with it."

Jack stood up and peered down at the mirror, thrusting one shoe forward, then the other.

Amber said, "The black-and-white ones are much cooler."

"Yeah," Jack said, "but that doesn't mean they're the right choice. I'm running around in a tweed jacket and a bolo tie. I'm not sure cool shoes will make for a cohesive look."

"We need to go back to the farm, Jack. You know it as well as I do."

"But what's the point? We went out once, saw something that looks like a small volcano, and got chased off by an angry farmer. So we go back now and, what, verify that it's still there, that it still looks like a volcano? That it's still small? That the farmer's still pissed off? I see what you mean that the video needs more material, but I don't see a point in going back out unless we can somehow add new information. Something other than me looking like a jackass."

Amber said, "Maybe I can find a geologist or something to come with us. Get their expert opinion. Have them verify that it's a real volcano, and that it's smaller than usual."

"Great. Make sure they bring a tape measure." Jack looked down at the two-tone sneaker, moving his foot around to admire it from every angle, then shifted his weight and peered without enthusiasm at the black cloth shoe on his other foot.

"You clearly like the leather ones," Amber said. "Get them."

"I'm afraid the all-blacks suit the outfit better. Neither pair is really appropriate, but the black shoes kind of disappear. The others draw attention to themselves."

"But the black-and-white ones are cool, and they sort of read like a modern version of those black-and-white dress shoes. What do you call them? Wingtips?"

"You really think I should get the black-and-white ones?"

"Yes."

"You think they'd work for the show?"

"Yes."

"Then I'm definitely getting the black ones. I know what kind of show you're trying to make, and it's not necessarily in your interest to help me look good."

"I'm not deliberately creating situations to make anyone look or feel foolish, Jack. When we're shooting footage, all I'm doing is documenting what happens, no matter what that is."

"Really?"

"Yes. It's when I'm editing that I look for anything funny that happened so that I can show it to the viewer."

"That's good to know, which specific part of your job is making me look like a jerk. All I have to do, from here on in, is try to keep anything ridiculous from happening. Now, who can we get to come look at the smallcano?"

24

Amber and Jack dawdled over their lunch at a local diner while Amber worked the phone, trying with no success to find a volcanologist who lived within convenient driving distance of the-middle-of-nowhere Iowa. She gave up on that and moved on to trying to find one who was in inconvenient driving distance and would take their request seriously. She progressively lowered her standards until she found someone who could think of a way to help them.

They called Joan to make sure Bruce was not there and drove two blocks out of their way to approach the farm from the opposite direction and avoid the watchful eye of old man McMenemy. This was more inconvenient than it might sound, as farm-country blocks can be well over a mile wide. They parked behind the house, noting the tractor in the barn and the empty space where Bruce's truck had been parked earlier. Joan met them as they got out of their SUV. Amber held her camera. Jack clutched a plastic shopping bag in one hand and with the other held up an open laptop, much the way a restaurant server carries a tray of drinks. The laptop's screen displayed an image of a woman in conservative attire sitting in front of shelves full of books about volcanoes and Pacific islands.

Jack said, "Joan, thanks for having us back out. Please allow me to introduce Dr. Mylie Manu. She's a respected volcanologist out of the University of Hawai'i. She has agreed to consult with us via the internet. She's going to help us verify that the smallcano is genuine, for my viewers, because they are going to ask."

Joan said, "Hello."

Dr. Manu said, "Hello," but it took a moment for her greeting to filter through a cellular internet connection and the laptop's tiny built-in speakers.

Joan said, "Well, right this way, Doctor."

Joan led them through the barn, around the tractor, and out the back, where she again revealed the smallcano.

Dr. Manu leaned in close to her web camera, her face filling the screen. "Huh! I must admit, that looks like a cinder-cone volcano all right. And it is, as you said, small."

"Agreed," Jack said. "So, Doctor, can you help us authenticate it?"

"Verifying that it's small is no problem. As to whether it's a naturally occurring volcano, that's trickier, but there are things we can check. Did you get the items I requested?"

"Yeah. Just let me unpack." Jack handed the laptop to Joan, who held it awkwardly, as if it were a living thing. Jack knelt down and started pulling small cardboard boxes and clear plastic blister packs from the shopping bag.

Dr. Manu said, "Were those streaks of cooled lava I saw?"

"Yes. There's a big glob of it down at the base. Bruce says if we wait long enough, it'll pave the whole lot for us."

"Does it eject lava often?"

"No. It spits some out every few weeks, but most of the time, all we get is smoke."

"All you see is smoke. The mound of a cinder-cone volcano is made up of burnt material that is ejected from the vent. Then again, if this is something we've never seen before, then who knows what's going on. These occasional effusive eruptions, the ones with the lava, are they very violent?"

Joan said, "It threw lava around enough that we had to stop keeping chickens."

"It injured them?"

"They got spooked and stopped producing."

"Interesting. How far did the lava fly?"

"Far enough to hit the barn."

Jack stood up, holding a brand-new carpentry tape measure. "Want me to measure the distance to the barn?"

"Eventually," Dr. Manu said. "First things first. Please measure the mound itself."

Jack pulled on a black-and-yellow painter's-grade respirator and walked toward the smallcano. He reached the base of the cone but stood leaning away from it, instinctively avoiding the heat. He spooled out a length of the tape measure, stepped on the free end, then pulled the spring-loaded case up, playing out tape. Closing one eye, he peered at the marks on the tape and the rim of the smallcano, then jogged back to the others, letting the tape measure retract on its own as he ran.

"About four feet, eight inches," he said as he reached Amber, Joan, and the laptop, ripping off his respirator. "And it is hot!"

Dr. Manu leaned back, her image growing smaller on the laptop screen. "Those findings are consistent with a small volcano. So far, the story checks out. We need a closer look and some more specific data."

Five minutes later, Jack stood with aluminum foil wrapped around his right arm, right shoulder, and the parts of his head not covered by his respirator and clear protective goggles. Poking out of his jacket's breast pocket he had a digital probe thermometer with a long, metal-shielded cord, meant to stretch into backyard barbecues. In his left hand he held a cheap webcam attached to a large coil of USB extension cable looped on the ground and connected to the laptop. In the other hand, he held a very long mechanical grabber, designed to help senior citizens retrieve items from tall shelves. This he had also wrapped in aluminum foil.

Amber kept her face behind her camera, trying in vain to hide her delight as Jack glared at her through his goggles and shook his head.

Jack said, "This is ridiculous. We couldn't come up with anything better for protective gear?"

Amber said, "On short notice, at a Walmart? No, we couldn't. I don't remember you having any better ideas."

"No," Jack muttered. "Unless you count not doing this at all, which I do."

On the laptop, still held dutifully by Joan, Dr. Manu said, "Now you approach the smallcano."

Jack looked at his foil-covered arm and sputtered, "Well, I mean, obviously."

He walked out to the smallcano, holding the webcam at his eye level with his left hand. He got as close as he could without discomfort, and stopped.

Dr. Manu said, "Now put the thermometer probe into the crater."

Her voice came from the laptop's speakers, which weren't large or loud and were now over twenty feet away. Joan cranked up the volume to maximum and shouted, "She wants you to put the probe in the hole!"

Jack draped the webcam over his shoulder, removed the thermometer probe and cable from his pocket, and grasped the probe in the grabber's claw. Extending the grabber and his foil-covered arm to their full reach, he maneuvered the thermometer probe over the smoking hole at the peak of the volcano and dropped it in.

He took a quick step back, pulling the metal-shielded thermometer cable tight. He took its head unit from his jacket's breast pocket and looked down at the readout.

"It says five hundred and fifty degrees, but I think that's as high as it goes. It just went blank." He moved the screen down to show it to the webcam, still draped over his shoulder.

Dr. Manu said, "Pull the probe out."

Joan shouted, "She says pull the probe out!"

Jack pulled on the cord. It flew out of the crater with practically no resistance; the probe was missing. The cord ended abruptly at a black, melted stump, a small greasy flame sputtering briefly from the end.

"It's gone," Jack yelled, holding up the limp, scorched wire. "The probe's gone!"

Dr. Manu again leaned forward, filling the laptop's screen inadvertently while getting closer to her own, and said, "Yes. That's as expected. No cooking thermometer could handle the temperature of a volcano. If it had, we'd have known it was fake."

Joan shouted, "She said she expected—"

"Yeah," Jack interrupted, waving her off. "I heard her that time. I wish she'd mentioned that before, and maybe not told me to buy the nicest thermometer they had."

"Yes," Dr. Manu said. "But if the smallcano had been fake, then you'd have had a very nice thermometer as a consolation prize."

"Right," Jack said. "So, what next?"

Now you're going to get me a good look into the crater. I want you to point that web camera right down the thing's gullet. You'll want to keep it a foot or so above so the camera doesn't melt right away."

"What are you looking for?"

"Anything that doesn't belong in a naturally occurring volcano. Gas pipes. Fireworks. Satan."

Joan said, "Wow. You people really think I went to a lot of trouble to lie to you."

Dr. Manu said, "Please understand, it's nothing personal. They asked me to prove your smallcano is authentic. The way I do that is by looking for signs that it's fake. If I don't find any, we're in business."

Jack pulled on the USB extension cord to make sure he had enough slack, then clutched the cheap webcam in the grabber's claw.

Dr. Manu said, "Please hold the camera steady and get as much height above the vent as you can. We're trying to find evidence of a volcanic plug, or maybe a small lava dome. Volcanoes get a blockage, build pressure, then release it. If it's a small release, you get steam, or spurting lava. A large release, you get Mount St. Helens. The heat will melt the camera. We want to slow that down and make sure what images we get are worthwhile, not a black-and-red blur."

Jack pressed down his aluminum-foil sleeve to make sure it was secure. He got as close as he dared to the smallcano and extended the grabber upward. He slowly extended forward, inch by inch.

Dr. Manu said, "A little more. A little more. Almost there."

Jack suffered a whole-body jolt as an angry male voice shouted, "What the hell are you doing?!"

Jack turned to see Bruce standing in the barn's back doorway, his face livid and the rest of him covered in a silver protective Nomex suit. One of his thickly mittened hands held a small backpack by one strap.

Bruce looked at Jack, then at Amber, her camera now pointed back at him. Then he looked at Joan, who turned to face him, holding a laptop displaying a woman he'd never seen leaning in close to her webcam.

"What the hell are you doing?" Bruce asked again, this time sounding more curious than angry.

Dr. Manu asked, "Who said that? What's going on?"

Jack swung the grabber around so that the webcam pointed in Bruce's direction.

Dr. Manu said, "Whoa! Cool it with the fast camera movements, okay? You're making me queasy. Who's that?"

Bruce said, "I'm the owner of this farm, and I told you two to go away."

Joan said, "I'm the owner, and I asked them to come back."

Jack asked, "I, uh, I don't suppose I could borrow that suit, could I?"

Bruce shouted, "No!" He reached over his shoulder and pulled a cylindrical hood with a reflective visor down over his head. He walked toward the smallcano.

Jack took several steps back and to the side, putting distance between himself and the smallcano, and also Bruce.

"Where'd you get the suit?" Jack asked.

In a muffled but still angry voice, Bruce said, "Army surplus store."

Jack looked at Amber. "Of course! Army surplus store!"

Amber said, "We'll remember that for next time."

"Next time what?" Jack asked. "Next time there's a smallcano? I don't see us stumbling across another one anytime soon."

"You'd better hope you do," Bruce said, approaching the smallcano and reaching into the backpack. "This one's about to go bye-bye."

Bruce pulled out a one-foot length of galvanized pipe with caps screwed to each end and a small circuit board affixed to the side: the perfect image of a garden-variety pipe bomb.

Jack said, "Hey, wait a second! Hold on. Let's talk about this."

"No." Bruce knelt down and pressed the pipe bomb into the base of the smallcano, then stood up and started walking briskly back the way he'd came. "Everybody, get in the barn! Or don't! I don't care!"

Jack followed Bruce, shouting at his back. "You can't blow up a volcano with a pipe bomb!"

"Watch me."

"It won't work!"

"Sure it will. I don't want people to take an interest in my property, so I'm destroying the thing they find interesting."

"Yeah, okay, that idea is sound, but trying to blow it up with a pipe bomb won't work."

"A pipe bomb's the simplest bomb there is. It'll go off."

"I'm sure the bomb will go boom, but you can't blow up a volcano. It's like trying to burn the sun or drown a lake. Think about it. Volcanoes make heat and smoke and fire. Bombs don't reduce any of those things!"

Bruce pulled off his protective hood as he stepped into the barn. "A volcano is a hole in the earth. So is a mine, and they use explosives in mining all the time."

The others followed Bruce into the barn, including Jack, who brought the argument with him. "They use explosives to make holes bigger!"

"They use them to collapse mines too . . . I think."

"Even if they do," Jack said, "This isn't a mine. It's a volcano. The whole reason it's a problem is that it's hot enough to melt and push through rock, and you're going to try to get rid of it by dropping more rocks on it. You might as well try to stop Garfield by throwing lasagna at him. Doctor, back me up on this."

Dr. Manu sat perched on the front of her chair, gripping the edge of her desk. "I'm not that familiar with Garfield, but I must agree that the bomb is a terrible idea. Sir, my school's engineering department works very hard to make instruments for us that can handle the heat. I doubt that something you made in an afternoon will operate reliably."

Bruce shrugged. "If it goes off early, so what? I plan to set it off in about a minute here, anyway. If it doesn't go off, I'll just run into the house, grab one of my hunting rifles, and shoot it until it explodes. Then I'll use the gun to chase you all off my land, old-school style. I might even shout 'Git!'"

"But my real concern," Dr. Manu said, "is that you planted the bomb at the base of the volcano."

"Yeah, further from the heat, so it should be fine."

"But if you set it off, it could release all the pressure the volcano has built up."

Bruce said, "And destroy the volcano. Good."

"No! It could cause an eruption!"

"A bigger explosion! Good! I'm using the volcano to blow itself out."

Bruce reached into his bag and pulled out a radio control—a pistol grip with a trigger and a steering wheel affixed to one side, designed to operate toy cars. Jack, Amber, and Joan stood around him in the barn shouting at him to stop, and Dr. Manu sat in her office in Hawai'i, also shouting at him to stop. Bruce smiled and winked at Joan. Everyone in the barn pressed their backs against the wall and covered their ears. Dr. Manu involuntarily cringed and drew away from her screen.

Bruce pulled the trigger.

25

A popping noise jabbed itself violently into Amber's ears, then subsided into a low rumble. Chunks of debris thudded heavily on the ground outside the barn and clanged heavily on the metal wall and roof.

They all waited for the noise and falling objects to trail off.

They continued waiting.

After thirty seconds that felt like an eternity, Amber asked, "Why isn't the explosion stopping?"

Dr Manu said, "Stay under cover. Jack, would you mind pointing the webcam out the door?"

Jack grasped the webcam with the partially melted grabber, swung it out into the open, and pointed it toward the smallcano.

On the screen, Dr. Manu nodded. "Uh-huh. It's as I feared."

"What?" Jack asked.

Dr. Manu said, "It's still erupting."

Jack said, "Really?"

"Yes. The bomb blew the whole cone off, and now it's just unloading."

Amber asked, "But shouldn't the pressure run out pretty fast, coming through a larger hole like that?"

Dr. Manu said, "You'd think, but it's a fun-sized volcano in the middle of Iowa. It shouldn't exist at all. Seriously, all bets are off."

Amber stood up and pointed her own camera around the edge of the door. She looked at the viewscreen, blinked, then couldn't stop herself from leaning around to see it with her own eyes.

Where the smallcano had been, she saw a fountain of fire. Not a steady stream, but a sputtering torrent of glowing lava and smoldering black gravel that occasionally let out more powerful coughs, ejecting viscous spurts of liquid rock high into the air, along with black boulders that shot upward in every direction, leaving contrails of smoke behind them. Flames spouted from the pens and sheds around the perimeter of the lot. Smoke rose from countless hot spots somewhere out beyond the wall of corn that surrounded the property. Red light emanated from between the stalks, and Amber realized that part of the roar they heard came from the corn, not the crater.

A thick stream of lava poured down the side of what remained of the mound, moving slowly toward the barn, but far more concerning were the smoking lumps of rock littering much of the ground between the crater and the barn, with more falling from the sky every second. Some inevitably made their way into the barn, rolling and bouncing to parts unknown in the dark interior. She looked to the roof, now dented and mangled by the continued impacts. In many spots, the metal glowed cherry red. She looked around at the contents of the barn. Suddenly, she noticed how flammable everything looked. The air seemed thicker and harder to see through than usual, but she was unsure if that was smoke from the smallcano, dust kicked up from the explosion, or the beginnings of a fire smoldering somewhere inside the barn. As she pondered all of this, a smoking rock melted through the roof and fell to the floor in front of her.

She and Jack simultaneously shouted, "We have to get out of here!"

More hot rocks fell through the roof as the four of them made their way around the tractor. They moved as quickly as they could while keeping an eye on the ground to avoid kicking or tripping over a piece of searing-hot pumice. Now getting a better look at the barn's interior, Amber saw small fires in all over the barn floor, many perilously close to the raw wooden timbers that held the barn upright. She rushed to get out of this deathtrap of a building until she reached the barn's front door and got a look at what was going on outside.

What the smallcano lacked in size, it made up for in range. Amber immediately grasped that only a very few of the smallest, weakest projectiles were landing in front of or on the barn. Softball-sized chunks of black rock arched overhead, streaming smoke behind them. Some came down well beyond the house, but most hadn't made it quite that far. Many smoking holes perforated the house's roof, with more appearing every second.

The wind-breaking row of trees along the side of the house was burning and would soon be fully engulfed, making leaving via the driveway a perilous proposition. Not that driving was an option. The rented SUV and the two pickups were all parked together in a row. The middle truck was a roaring inferno. The SUV and truck on either side of it showed definite signs of melting. Amber didn't like the idea of climbing into either vehicle and trying to drive it away. As if to punctuate the point, the SUV's tires on the side next to the burning truck both popped. While parts of the cornfields that flanked the property seemed untouched by the fire so far, other areas were fully engulfed, the stalks taking up the flames like a dry sponge soaking up water and literally roaring as they burned.

Amber said, "Maybe we're safer in the barn."

Somewhere behind them, a plastic jug full of something flammable popped, splashed, and hissed. The timbers supporting the barn groaned.

Amber yelled, "Everybody out!"

They ran out into the gravel parking lot, veering to the right to keep their distance from the burning vehicles. They could see from the pattern of broken pumice on the ground that the barn was acting as a sort of shield, keeping any of the flying rocks from landing in its shadow. The rumble from the smallcano remained ever present and showed no signs of diminishing. Rocks continued to fly over the barn and land on the house and in the backyard, and some landed in the pool, creating large splashes and clouds of steam.

Jack muttered, "And on top of everything else, now it's humid."

Bruce looked at the laptop in Joan's hands. "How long is this going to keep up?!"

Dr. Manu said, "There's no way to know."

"I thought you were supposed to be some kind of expert."

"Typical," Dr Manu said. "When I'm trying to talk you out of blowing up a volcano with a homemade pipe bomb, you don't want to hear what I have to say. Now that the damage is done, you insult me for not being able to predict, over Zoom, exactly when your human-induced eruption will end."

Amber said, "There'll be time to yell at each other later, and we all know we will. Right now, we need to get out of here. We aren't driving out. The driveway's impassable anyway. How about the other side of the house?"

Joan said, "There's only a few feet between the house and the cornfield. Maybe we can go through the house and get to the front yard."

Amber said, "The house is on fire."

"Maybe it's less on fire than the corn."

"Then what?" Jack asked. "We run down the road? It's all fresh tar! Does tar burn?"

Bruce said, "Yeah probably, but not right away. It gets all soupy and sticky first."

"Great," Jack said. "So it'll hold us there like flypaper until it bursts into flames around us!"

Bruce said, "Look, it's not going to be fun, but as long as we stay where we are, here in the barn's shadow, we should be—"

A deep, plaintive groan came from inside the barn as the front wall tilted several degrees, moving toward them like a junior high school marching band: slowly, while making a lot of unpleasant noises. Smoke poured out of the single window and open barn door. Orange light filled the barn's interior.

Nobody shouted *run*; they were all too busy running. Of course, it was impossible to move away from the flaming barn without running toward a flaming something else, but the flaming house was the most distant flaming object, so they all charted a course for the empty space between themselves and it, as that held the one bit of cover that was not on fire: the picnic table.

They only made it three or four steps before Jack and Joan both stopped abruptly, shouting in surprise and alarm. Amber turned around to see what was wrong. Jack still carried the USB webcam. The cord stretched out behind Jack, hooked over part of the barn door's latching mechanism, then reached back, almost to where Joan stood, her hands empty.

Ten feet behind Joan, the laptop sat upright in the gravel, the USB cord yanked out of its socket, the screen tilted at an obtuse angle and displaying Dr. Manu blinking her eyes and cocking her head to one side.

Joan, without thinking, took a step toward the laptop, bending down to scoop it up.

Dr. Manu shouted, "No! Don't come back for me! Go! Save yourselves!"

Jack threw the webcam to the ground and grabbed Joan by the arm. "She's right! Come on!"

Jack and Joan sprinted, getting clear just before the barn wall crashed down on the gravel and the laptop, cutting off the image of Dr. Manu shouting, "Go! Go!"

They all packed in beneath the picnic table, scalding hot rocks still landing all around them, and looked back at the flaming wreckage of the barn.

Bruce said, "That volcano lady was brave. I'll give her that."

Amber pried her gaze off her camera's screen to look at him, amazed.

Jack said, "She wasn't really here. You get that, right?"

Amber said, "Leave it."

"She's in her office in Honolulu," Jack said. "Right now, she's probably on her way to the break room to get a soda!"

"Now's not the time, Jack," Amber said. "Once we get out of this mess he caused, we'll have plenty of time to berate him."

Bruce said, "I told you to stay off my land."

Joan said, "*My* land."

Jack said, "Yeah, and I wish we had."

Bruce said, "Apology accepted."

Joan said, "The house! It's all burning, Bruce."

"It's all just things. We can buy new things."

"Not if we're dead!" Joan shouted. "We can't get out through the house because it's burning. We can't go around the house because the cornfields and the trees are burning. We can't go back the way we came because the burning barn and the smallcano are in the way. What are we going to do?"

Bruce said, "The answer's obvious: we wait it out. We have a buffer zone. We're on a concrete pad next to the swimming pool. They won't burn. I mean, there's the putting green. The flag might melt, but the AstroTurf is flame retardant."

"What about the picnic table?" Jack asked, knocking on a wooden leg of the wooden structure under which they were hiding.

Bruce shrugged. "I dunno."

Amber looked around. "There has to be something we're missing. A way out, or something else we can use."

"See anything?" Bruce asked.

"A croquet set and a barbeque," Amber said. "And the croquet set's on fire."

Jack said, "And when the fire reaches the barbecue's propane tank, that won't be good news."

"Propane?" Bruce said. "Do I look like someone who'd grill with propane?!"

"If we don't come up with something, you're going to look like someone who's been grilled with propane."

"Well, it's a charcoal grill. When the fire gets to it you don't have to worry about it exploding."

"No," Jack said. "It'll be a more even heat with flavorful smoke. Much better."

Joan said, "And there's a bottle of lighter fluid."

"Yeah," Bruce said. "That will probably explode."

Amber said, "Stop bickering and think! There has to be a way out of this!"

They all sat there, hunched uncomfortably under the picnic table, listening to fires roaring and hot chunks of rock falling all around them. After a long moment of total concentration, Amber asked, "Anybody got anything?"

Nobody answered.

"Okay," Amber said. "I guess you might as well start bickering again."

Jack turned, one finger extended as if to stick it in Bruce's face, but paused, looked off into the distance, and pointed at the cornfield. Amber looked at one of the few flame-free expanses of corn left and saw some sort of dark shape moving, mostly obscured by the stalks. A piece of falling rock fell in the general vicinity of the shape and made a hollow metallic sound.

After a second more of rustling, the stalks parted violently to reveal an old Toyota van driving out of the flaming field and onto the burning lawn.

Two large metal plates protruded from the van's nose, looking like the bow of a ship or the cow-catcher on the front of an old steam train turned upside down. The van rode on a lifted suspension and oversized off-road tires, which looked incongruous protruding out from under its small, boxy frame. A camouflage pattern, heavy on vertical lines and colored in greens and yellows, covered the van's painted surfaces. Hundreds of fake corn stalks sprouted out of the roof, jutting straight up as if the van had hair, and was frightened.

The van moved quickly, barely threading the needle between the steaming swimming pool and a melting pickup. It skidded to a stop on the putting green. Behind the wheel, Agent Carmichael shouted, "Get in!"

He didn't have to say it twice. The four of them clambered out from under the picnic table and piled in through the van's sliding side door, rolling around on a rubber-matted cargo bay floor as the van peeled out and sped across the driveway, directly into a non-burning wall of corn. The metal plates on the van's nose parted the stalks and bent them out of the way in a tidy V shape, but Carmichael could still only really see about four feet in front of the windshield as he drove. Their speed slowed drastically as they pushed their way through the dense, stubborn plants.

Jack asked, "What's with this van?"

Carmichael said, "It was just sitting in the motor pool waiting to be used. This isn't the first time we've needed to keep a farmer under surveillance. Somebody get on the scope and guide me around the fire!"

He jerked a thumb back at a metal shaft that hung down from the ceiling, ending with two handle grips and an LCD screen. Jack grabbed the handle and looked at the screen. Amber briefly pointed her camera at the periscope's display and saw the front edge of the van's roof, a seemingly endless flat plane made up of the tips of corn stalks, and pillars of smoke rising all around them.

"What is this?" Jack asked.

"One of the fake corn stalks up top is a periscope."

"Veer left," Jack said. "Uh, eleven o'clock!"

Carmichael steered to the left. "There's no smoke there?"

Jack said, "Less smoke."

"That'll do."

Bruce asked, "Hey, who is this guy? Who are you?"

"The guy who saved your ass," Carmichael said through gritted teeth, exerting great effort to steer the van straight as it plowed through the rows of cornstalks at an angle.

Amber said, "Joan and Bruce Larson, meet Agent Carmichael."

Jack shouted, "Now right, two o'clock."

"Two o'clock," Carmichael repeated, twisting the wheel to the right.

Bruce said, "Agent! See that, Joan, I knew it! I knew the feds had their eyes on us."

Jack said, "No, he was here spying on us."

Carmichael shouted back, "And I'd have left you in peace if you hadn't gone and tried to blow up a volcano with a pipe bomb, the possession of which is a felony, by the way."

"Good thing I don't have one anymore."

Jack shouted, "Hard left. There'll be a little fire, then the road!"

Carmichael turned the wheel and floored the accelerator. For a moment, the rushing wall of corn stalks out the windows remained the same blur it had been, then it went black with bits of glowing red. Then, just as suddenly, the corn stalks disappeared, replaced by open air and a country road. Of course, between the cornfield and the road there was a three-foot-wide ditch, and attempting to drive over it at thirty-five miles per hour felt as if the van had been T-boned by a truck, but from directly beneath.

As the van flew across the road, the four people riding untethered in the back briefly experienced weightlessness.

When the van landed, its front bumper plowed into the three-foot-wide ditch on the other side of the road, stood on its nose at a forty-five degree angle for a few seconds, then fell back down on its tires. The four people riding loose in the back briefly experienced far more weight than they ever had before, both their own and each other's.

They all lay there groaning while Carmichael backed out of the ditch and onto the road with great difficulty and drove the van away from the fire. The front wheels wobbled alarmingly and made a terrible rubbing sound.

Jack said, "Van's not sounding good."

Carmichael said, "After what just happened, what do you expect? This is not *Knight Rider*."

Amber pointed the camera out the van's back window. All she could see was corn, the road, a sky full of black smoke, and a seemingly never-ending supply of glowing rocks flung into the sky in great lazy arcs.

Jack sagged against the van's wall. "Well, Mr. Larson, the Earth put a smallcano on your land—"

Joan said, "My land."

"Yes," Jack said. "Sorry. Your wife's land. My point is, you didn't want the smallcano there, so you tried to erase it, and you made it much worse. I hope you've learned a lesson. No good comes from trying to impose your will on nature."

Bruce said, "I'm a farmer. I make my living and put food on your table by imposing my will on nature."

Jack said, "That is a good point. That is a very good point. So, I guess the lesson is that you shouldn't try to impose you will on nature when it comes to volcanoes."

Amber said, "That's not great."

"No, but I'll keep working on it."

26

Amber struggled to find an exposure setting on her camera that would work. She found she could get a clear, detailed shot of either the brilliant blue sky full of puffy white clouds above or the blackened wasteland of ash and soot below, but not both. If the clouds were visible, the ground was an inky black mass, but if the ground had any definition at all, the sky was a blazing inferno of light.

After a great deal of tinkering, she decided to shoot Jack's outro standing among the ashes with the camera stationary, locked off on a tripod, exposed to capture him well. Later, she'd shoot both the ground and the sky from the same vantage point and see if she could combine them in post, somehow.

Thanks to a series of frantic long-distance calls from Dr. Manu, the fire department had arrived only a few minutes after Agent Carmichael drove them all out of harm's way. In time, trucks from three neighboring towns arrived to help, but they didn't so much fight the fire as establish a détente with it. They allowed it to burn where it already was but fought like the devil to keep it from spreading. As a result, none of the neighboring farmhouses and little of the other farmers' crops was damaged, but on Joan and Bruce Larson's farm, the fire continued until the smallcano stopped spitting hot rocks and the flames consumed the fuel available.

Within a perimeter dozens of acres across, everything flammable had burned. Everything not flammable had either melted away or was scorched beyond recognition. The house looked like pick-up sticks painted black and propped on blackened lumps that Amber suspected were the refrigerator and the hot water heater. The few recognizable bits of the barn's structure had the same appearance as the house, but with charred sheets of tin draped over the carbonized remains of the tractor and the table saw. What remained of the trucks and the SUV sat collapsed on the ground, tires and plastic body panels gone, along with all hoses, belts, padding, and upholstery, their middles sagging and front and rear bumpers pointed upward as if the vehicles' backs were broken.

Instead of water that sparkled in the sun and reeked of chlorine, the pool held a thick black mud, made of water, soot, ash, and debris, that reeked of chlorine. Though the patio and putting green had not burned, they were utterly ruined, pocked with lumps of magma the smallcano had spat out, which either melted through the fake grass or fused themselves to the cement. A rectangular scorch pattern marked the spot where they had used the picnic table as a shelter and showed how that plan would have worked out for them long-term.

At the back of the property, still emitting a steady stream of smoke, there remained the smallcano: shorter now, but already rebuilding its cinder cone and surrounded by a smooth field of cooled lava easily three times larger than it had been before.

Amber set up a shot with a place for Jack to stand in front of the smallcano, puffing away, and the largest possible expanse of burnt cornfield in the background. Jack read over his notes while standing nearby, as there was nothing to sit, or even lean, on.

Amber said, "Ready when you are. Do you have anything?"

Jack let out a long breath. "Yeah, I've got something. It was a grind this time. I had trouble focusing on a new idea because I was so frustrated that the 'imposing man's will on nature' thing turned out to be a dead end. You ready to do this?"

Amber lifted her camera. "When you are."

Jack stepped into the frame and looked straight down the lens. "So, what started out as a simple exploration of a strange natural phenomenon, in the end, is a cautionary tale. A story about two people who shared the same resources but had very different goals. She had land, a home, a dedicated farmer for a husband, a desire for attention, and a smallcano. He had a home, a wife who owned land on which he could farm, a desire for privacy, and a smallcano. They couldn't both have what they wanted. Neither was willing to compromise. They fought, and their prize is that they both have no home, no farm, no privacy, too much excitement, and a slightly smaller-cano."

Jack took a moment to look around at the charred devastation, then continued, in a quieter, more thoughtful tone. "Life can be described as things happening and you reacting. Weather happens. Disasters happen. Other people's plans happen. You can't control any of those things, but you can control how you react. You will probably be tempted to struggle, to fight, to insist that you get your way, that things stay the way they are; but if you do, remember where that ends. Remember this blackened wasteland that used to be a pleasant farm, and say to yourself, 'That's not right.'"

"Very nice," Amber said. "Poignant. I was worried you might start trying to make your intros and outros funny."

"Nah," Jack said. "You ever watch *The Simpsons*?"

"Is there a choice?"

"Not really. Krusty once gave a pretty good piece of advice for my situation. 'A pie gag's only funny if the sap's got dignity.' I figure my job is to do what I do, and your job is to do what you do: make what I do look ridiculous."

"You have to admit, it's fairly easy work. Now that we're at the very end, I'm glad that you're on board."

"Like a bug is onboard a windshield. And I assume it's only the end of season one."

Amber said, "There'll probably be a season two, but I don't think I'll be involved. I've created a format this season. If a new producer and editor comes in, you'll get to help choose them, and you'll have more say in the final product. You can follow my lead if you want, or make the show what you wanted to begin with."

"But what will you do?"

"The last day or so has made me think. I created a show with Brian, and we fought over what it should be. I created a show based on your show and, in the process, warped and twisted it into something you never wanted it to be. I think now, while I have a good bargaining position, it's time to make a show for me. Something I can control."

Jack said, "I look forward to watching it. I wonder which of us Agent Carmichael will follow."

Agent Carmichael groaned and stood up out of the charred wreckage of the barn, wearing a head-to-toe suit and hood made of matching charcoal-black material streaked with irregular stripes of a lighter ash gray and covered with small bits of burnt wood hanging off him like fringe.

Jack said, "A fire-wreckage ghillie suit?"

"Yeah, it's mostly used for investigating insurance fraud." Carmichael carefully climbed out from among the burnt timbers and approached Amber and Jack. With each step, the bits of wood hanging from his limbs banged together and made sounds almost like wind chimes. Carmichael said, "It's, uh, it's better for sitting still than moving around." He pulled off his hood to reveal his face, his hair matted to his head and black makeup around his eyes.

"So, how about it?" Jack asked. "Who gets you in the divorce?"

Carmichael said, "You do. Whether you just stick to the radio or do more videos, you'll still be covering the same subjects, so you'll still need someone to keep an eye on you. Miss Cardoza's new show won't be related to any of this stuff."

Amber said, "You don't know that."

"Yes, I do. I've read your notes."

Amber gasped. "My notebook app is supposed to be the most secure on the market."

"Yes, it's supposed to be, "Carmichael said. "And we regularly report them for making false claims."

EPILOGUE

Amber took a moment before she opened the door of her rental car and stepped out into the cold winter night. There was no snow in Yakima but plenty of ice, and the loose dirt that the autumn rain had turned to mud now felt like concrete. Renee Owens smiled and waved from the partially open front door. Amber forced herself to return the gesture, reminding herself that the situation was not this woman's fault.

As Amber approached to enter the Owens home and studio, Renee welcomed her inside with a genuine-looking smile. "Amber, it's so good to see you again."

"I'm sorry I'm so late. My connection in Seattle was delayed."

"Yes, the office called and told us what was going on. It isn't a problem. That's one advantage of Jack's work—you know we're going to be up late. I'm surprised you came out here instead of just heading to your hotel and getting some sleep."

"Yeah, well, I figured we'd all sleep better if we touched base tonight. Make sure we're on the same page."

Renee said, "Good luck with that. I'm just finishing up packing for him. Spokane is going to be cold, but it's not a bad drive from here. What's the story, anyway?"

Amber said, "A guy there claims he found a portal to hell."

Renee shook her head. "I don't know why Washingtonians are so snotty about Idaho. Jack's in the studio, finishing up the show. He said to send you back. You remember the way?"

"I think so." Amber looked around the living room. She couldn't put her finger on it at first, but something seemed different. She asked, "Did you get rid of the cats?"

Renee cringed. "Never! They're my babies! No, they're here. You'll see them."

Amber walked out of the living room and down the hall toward the tunnel that led to the studio. From a distance, she thought there was a pile of laundry or old blankets heaped against the door. Then she saw movement and realized all four of Renee's gigantic Maine coon cats were lying there, waiting for Jack to emerge. Their chew-marked and slobber-logged toys lay on the hallway floor all around them. As Amber approached, the cats lifted their heads to look at her but didn't show any intention of moving.

Amber said, "Uh, Renee, I found the cats. They're between me and the door."

Renee called out from the other room, "Just shove them out of the way with your foot. They'll move."

Amber used the side of her shoe to nudge the heavy masses of fur aside. The cats didn't budge, instead purring as if they thought she was trying to pet them with her foot. She turned the doorknob and pulled with all her might, pushing the door against the cats with not even close to enough force to move them but enough to irritate them into getting up. As soon as the cats got to their feet, they all tried to force their noses into the crack where the door was open. Amber slid sideways through the gap. As she closed the door behind her, she felt the cats pushing against it and heard them scratching to be let through as she walked down the tunnel to the studio.

The red light at the far end of the hallway glowed, signifying that, beyond the door, Jack was on the air. She crept down the hall and peered in through the window. Jack wore a different shirt than he had on her last visit, and a different model airplane waited, half finished, now sitting on the pool table well away from where Jack did the show instead of on the counter in front of his broadcasting console.

Jack must have caught some motion out of the corner of his eye, because his head shot around until he was looking straight at Amber. He looked delighted to see her and waved her in, all while maintaining his conversation on the radio.

As she opened the door to enter, she could hear what he was saying.

"But what, specifically, is your problem with the project?" Jack asked. "Is there something about that particular stretch of desert that makes it unsuitable for a solar array?"

As Jack spoke, Amber thought she heard tapping and snuffling sounds from beneath his control panel.

The caller said, "It's not the location of the array, Jack. I don't think they should be allowed to build solar power plants anywhere. That sunlight belongs to everybody. Why should they get to convert it into electricity and sell it?"

Jack said, "They're in the electricity business."

The caller said, "That's exactly why they shouldn't be allowed. Electric utilities are the last people we should let build solar panels."

The tapping and sniffing moved along the length of the console, and when it reached the end, a beagle emerged. It wagged its tail as it trotted over to Amber, its nails clicking on the floor.

Amber recognized the dog instantly but couldn't believe her eyes. She bent down to pet him, read his tag, and looked up at Jack, mouthing the name. *Dad?*

Jack smiled and nodded at Amber while talking to the caller. "So, you object to them taking this energy that is provided for free by the sun and selling it to us. What would you say to those who claim solar energy is being wasted right now, just falling on the ground in the middle of the desert?"

"I'd tell them they're wrong, Jack. That energy isn't being wasted. It's warming up the ground. If that sunlight hits a solar panel instead of the ground, the ground gets colder."

"Perhaps, out in the middle of the desert."

"But it's the ground, Jack. *The* ground. There's only one ground. Let me ask you a question. What is your house built on?"

Jack said, "The ground."

"Right, and because of this solar array they're building, that ground is going to be colder, so your house is going to be colder, so you'll have to heat it up, using what?"

"I suppose electricity."

"That's right! Electricity! Electricity they generated with the free sunlight they prevented from hitting the ground beneath your house."

Jack looked as if he was on the verge of laughter. "That's certainly an objection I've not heard before. Of course, the difference the lack of sun on a patch of desert miles away would make to the temperature of your home would be barely noticeable."

"Maybe, but if your house is colder by a barely noticeable amount, then you have to run the heat a barely noticeable amount longer. Then the utilities sell you a barely noticeable amount more power and add a barely noticeable amount to your bill."

Jack arched an eyebrow. "Making a barely noticeable extra profit."

"Barely noticeable, until you multiply it by the number of buildings that touch the ground—all of them—then it becomes pretty damn noticeable."

Jack smiled and shook his head, looking up at the oversized digital clock above his console. "A provocative idea. Thank you for calling in."

Jack pressed a button at precisely two fifty-nine and fifteen seconds. As he continued speaking, his show's theme music slowly grew louder beneath his voice. "Think of it, friends, an entire industry sold to us on the promise of helping the environment when, in fact, they are stealing energy we were already getting for free and selling it back to us at a profit. I think we can all agree"—he pressed the button that added reverb to his voice—"that's not right."

Jack flipped a switch. The red light above his console went dark, signifying that his microphone was no longer live. As the prerecorded outro played, Jack leaned back in his seat and said, "Drivel. Absolute drivel."

Amber had things she wanted to say to Jack, but they all paled in comparison to her curiosity. "What is Dad doing here?"

Jack said, "I told the cops to let his owner know to call me if he ever needed to find another home for Dad. Well, when the cops told him, he started seeing dollar signs. He offered to sell me Dad for five grand. I wasn't going to pay that, but I also didn't feel right about leaving Dad with that guy. Let alone in the domain of Stretch, the Talligator. I talked him down to one grand, which is still crazy, but Dad's worth it. Renee and I flew out to Florida, made a long weekend of it, went to some theme parks, and picked him up. I'm happy to see you, Amber."

Amber said, "It's good to see you, Jack, despite the circumstances."

Jack stood up and walked around the console to stand next to Amber. "You're not happy to be working together on season two?"

"You are?"

"Heck yeah." Jack bent down and picked up Dad, who squirmed slightly, then settled into Jack's embrace as he started walking toward the door. "It turns out the web series was great for the show. My numbers are way up. Who knew?"

"I did. And I told you. Many times."

Jack led Amber back through the tunnel to the main house. "I was worried that kooks wouldn't want to come on the show anymore, and if they did, the new audience would want me to mock them. I thought I'd have to completely retool the show or shut it down. Turns out I didn't have to change anything. Everybody just assumes I'm on their side. The new listeners think I'm deliberately stringing the kooks along to keep them talking, and the kooks all seem to think either I'm with them or they're going to win me over with their evidence and logic. I guess if you're already delusional, there's no harm in throwing one more wrong idea on the pile. It's been two months, and my numbers have just gone up and up. There's a long line of people who want to come on the show to spout their gibberish."

They reached the end of the tunnel. Jack opened the door a sliver and slid through sideways. As Amber followed suit, Jack stepped forward as best he could with the four gigantic cats furiously rubbing against his ankles and leaning up on his legs with their front paws. Dad squirmed as Jack dropped him with a bit of a gentle toss forward.

Dad hit the floor running, becoming a beige streak sprinting down the hall into the living room. All four of the cats followed in hot pursuit.

Jack motioned toward the living room. "So, what have you been up to?"

Amber said, "I've been doing a series I developed for one of the company's music channels, Fifty Years of Favorites. Basically, it's Top Forty music from the eighties on. The series is called *Great Songs Played Wrong*. We have a really good band and singer perform some song everyone knows, but the instruments are off-key or half a beat out of step and the singer screws up the lyrics."

"Sounds painful."

"It is. Painful, but popular."

"As popular as our show?"

Amber didn't intend to answer, and her silence went unnoticed, upstaged by Dad and the cats streaking out of the living room, back down the hall, past her and Jack's feet, and into one of the bedrooms. They ran laps of the bed for a moment, then exited, crossed the hall, and entered another bedroom. Renee darted out the door they had just gone in, fleeing as the sound of hundreds of tiny footfalls echoed through the hall.

Jack said, "Please, sit."

Amber sat in one of the recliners. Jack sat in the other. Renee took the couch.

Amber said, "Look, Jack, I should tell you, I didn't want to come back for the second season of your web series."

Jack said, "I know."

Amber shrugged. "Doesn't surprise me that you suspected."

"I didn't suspect," Jack said. "I knew. They told me you didn't want to come back when they approached me about season two. That's why I told them I wouldn't do it unless they could get you back."

Amber leaned forward. "But . . . you said I screwed up your show."

"And I was wrong. I admit that."

"I went off and made my own show." Amber's voice grew higher and louder.

Jack said, "And well done."

"They yanked me from my show, against my will, and made me come back to yours."

Jack looked slightly perplexed. "I know. I told them to. We've been over this."

Amber slid forward in her seat, still hunched over, as if having her face slightly closer to Jack would make her point more forcefully. "They assigned my show I created to someone else while I'm here with you!"

"Yeah," Jack said. "If they can do that, it raises the question of whose show it is. Something to think about next time you negotiate a contract."

Amber stood up to make her point more forcefully. "It's mine! I created it! And now some other jerk is going to screw it up while I work on your show you didn't want to do to begin with!"

"I figured I was doing you a favor."

"What?! How?"

"I thought they'd offer you more money."

"They did!"

"Good," Jack said. "You're welcome."

"I turned it down!"

Jack frowned. "That's on you."

"They reassigned me and forced me to take it anyway."

"Ah, so my 'You're welcome' still stands, both for the pay raise and the chance to make more great content for my show."

"For your show! That helps you, at my expense! You say you're helping me! This is exactly what you accused me of . . . What the hell is with these cats?"

All four of the huge Maine coon cats swirled around Amber's feet, rubbing against her shins and purring.

Renee said, "That's really interesting. Amber, try sitting down."

Amber flopped back in the recliner. The cats immediately leapt into the chair with her, covering her lap and filling any empty space she left in the seat.

Jack said, "Maybe they just like yelling."

"Or," Renee said, "they might think angry shouting is the signal that it's time for chair snuggles."

Amber let out a long sigh. "They just radiate heat like furry little furnaces. Where's Dad?"

Jack said, "If he's smart, hiding while they're distracted."

"Here, let me try something." Renee stood up from the couch, shook her clenched fists, stomped her feet and shouted, "Blah blah blah! Harg farging! Gargle bargle garg!"

The cats left Amber's chair and clustered around Renee's feet, looking up at her, confused.

"Grumble! Mumble! Apple fapple!" She sat back down, and the cats leapt into her lap. She smiled, pet them, and in a mock-angry voice said, "There, you two can continue your conversation, but keep the tone civil or the cats will attack!"

Jack said, "Look, I'll admit that at times my attitude was less than stellar, but at first I was afraid you'd make me look stupid; then I was angry that you had, in fact, made me look stupid. In the end, the audience was laughing with me, not at me, so all's well that ends well."

Amber said, "I still think an apology is in order."

"You want to make one?"

"No, to receive one!"

"From whom?" Jack asked.

"From you."

"What for?"

"What do you mean, what for?"

Jack said, "I'm not saying you're wrong. I'm just looking for specifics. I don't want to apologize for something you don't think I owe an apology for."

"Like that would be so terrible?"

Jack said, "Apologizing for something somebody's already forgotten just makes them mad again. What would you like an apology for?"

"For doing to me exactly what you said I'd done to you. For screwing up my show and dragging me into a situation I didn't want, entirely for your benefit, while claiming you were doing me a favor."

Jack said, "Oh. Yeah. That. Okay."

Amber squinted. "*Okay* what?"

"Okay, fine. You say I owe you an apology. I'm agreeing to that, so there you go."

"That's—" Amber began to shout, then stopped as the four cats on Renee's lap looked in her direction. "That's not an apology."

Jack said, "Now you're just arguing semantics."

Renee said, "He isn't great at apologizing. He doesn't get a lot of practice."

Jack said, "I seldom need to apologize."

Renee smiled indulgently. "That's true."

Jack smiled.

Renee added, "Because I don't make you."

Jack's smile faded. "Okay, look. Amber, it takes a big man to admit that he's wrong. And never let it be said that I am not big enough for that."

After a long pause, Amber asked, "For what?"

"What we were just discussing."

"Just admit you were wrong, Jack."

"I kinda did."

"So you've kinda apologized?"

"Yeah. And by admitting it, you've kinda accepted. Look, you said yourself that you contractually have to work with me again. Actions speak louder than words. My actions over the next few weekends while we work on stories will show whether or not I'm sorry. Either I've learned or not. Isn't that the best kind of apology?"

"No."

Renee said, "Yes it is, because it's the kind you're going to get."

Movement outside the window caught Amber's eye. She looked and saw a man in a camouflage parka, the furry edge of the hood hiding his face, standing just outside the window. His left hand held a metal disk to the glass. With his right, he pulled down his hood. It was Agent Carmichael. The metal disk was the business end of a stethoscope, the other ends of which dangled from his ears.

He said, in a voice loud enough to be heard through the window, "She's right. Now would you just accept it and go back to your hotel for the night? It's freezing out here."

Jack stood, walked to the door, and opened it. "Just come on in and act angry. The cats will warm you right up."

ACKNOWLEDGEMENTS

As always, my heartfelt thanks go to my wife Missy, both for her help in creating this book, and for just generally putting up with me. I also want to thank my friend Rodney for his assistance with the book, his friendship, and the inspiration he has provided over the years. I don't know that he has ever understood how much he is a mechanical rabbit being chased by the greyhound that is me.

And I need to thank my friend Ric, whom I have systematically tormented and reviled for decades. I hope to continue for decades more.

And finally, I want to thank Art Bell, who kept me company on many long, late-night drives, even though he never had any idea I existed.

ABOUT THE AUTHOR

After an unsuccessful career in radio, and a mediocre career in stand-up comedy, Scott Meyer found himself middle-aged, working as a ride operator at Walt Disney World.

In his spare time, he produced the successful web comic *Basic Instructions*. He slowly built a following of fans all over the world, whom he begged to purchase his first self-published novel, *Off to Be the Wizard*. The book's success brought him a publishing deal.

Scott Meyer now makes his living as a novelist and a web cartoonist. He lives with his wife and two cats, all of whom try their best to keep him in line.

www.ingramcontent.com/pod-product-compliance
Lightning Source LLC
Chambersburg PA
CBHW052025240626
47153CB00006B/1951